ORHAN KEM

Orhan Kemal – the pen name of Mehmet Raşit Öğütçü – is one of Turkey's best-loved writers. He was born in Adana in 1914. His father became a Member of Parliament in the first session of the Turkish National Assembly and founded the Popular Party in 1930. The consequences of his political activities led the family to emigrate to Syria and Lebanon, leaving their son unable to complete his secondary education. These events are covered in Orhan Kemal's semi-autobiographical novel *My Father's House* (1949), which he referred to as the 'diaries of a nobody'. He was later to return to the town of his birth and worked in a variety of jobs in cotton factories and as a clerk at the Foundation for the Eradication of Tuberculosis. This period of his life, including his marriage to the daughter of a Yugoslav immigrant in 1937, was to become the subject of four future novels.

During his military service in 1939 he was sentenced to five years' imprisonment for his political views. Time spent with the celebrated writer Nazım Hikmet in the Bursa State Prison had an important influence on Kemal's socialist political stance, and these are described in his memoirs of this period.

He moved to Istanbul in 1951, where he started to write full time. His works often centre on ordinary people struggling to make a living. Inspired initially by his own experiences in the 1920s and 1930s, he went on to explore such themes as the problems of farm and factory workers, the alienation of migrant workers in big cities, the lives of prison inmates, blind devotion to duty, child poverty and the repression and exploitation of women.

He was the author of thirty-eight works of fiction, comprising twenty-eight novels and ten collections of stories, several of which have been filmed or turned into plays. He died in Sofia, Bulgaria, in 1970 and is buried in Istanbul.

Orhan Kemal in Beirut, 1932

ORHAN KEMAL

THE IDLE YEARS

My Father's House

and

The Idle Years

Translated from the Turkish by Cengiz Lugal

Peter Owen Publishers
London and Chester Springs, PA, USA

PETER OWEN PUBLISHERS
73 Kenway Road, London SW5 0RE

Peter Owen books are distributed in the USA by
Dufour Editions Inc., Chester Springs, PA 19425-0007

Translated from the Turkish *Baba Evi* and *Avare Yıllar*

First published in Great Britain 2008 by
Peter Owen Publishers

ISBN 978-0-7206-1310-0

Printed and bound in Great Britain by
Windsor Print Production Ltd, Tonbridge

Published with the assistance of the Orhan Kemal Culture Centre
www.orhankemal.org

This book is published with the support of Ministry of Culture and Tourism of the Turkish Republic in the framework of TEDA Project.

FOREWORD

A rather strange fact, observable in the world of literature, is that writers of an optimistic nature come less frequently from prosperous, comfortable and materially secure backgrounds than from ones where they had to struggle against hardship and deprivation. This is a rare brand of optimism that defies our usual understanding of the word. This is why I value it more highly. We can see many examples of this hard-won wisdom in the early fiction of Orhan Kemal.

As I read his books again I detect Orhan Kemal's keenly observing eyes flitting back and forth between two modes. He describes the struggle to make ends meet, a theme that would easily induce pessimism in a reader even if it were not being expressed by a naturalist writer. The novels depict troubled lives where fighting to survive is central, in a poor and underdeveloped country in which capitalism is slowly making inroads alongside arduous working and living conditions. The author offers reflections on poverty, disease and unemployment in the provincial city of Adana with its bosses and petty bureaucrats and its workers newly arrived from the countryside. But at the heart of Orhan Kemal's fiction is another world, a world not full of anxiety about getting enough to eat – one he seems to enjoy telling us more about. Here we find close friendships, the intimacy of family life, brotherhood and solidarity, meals shared, innocent neighbourhood romances and the pleasures of simply whiling away time.

Suffused though they are with the dark realities of poverty, Orhan Kemal's novels are celebrations of this other world. The optimism I find in them comes not from literature but from life itself.

Orhan Pamuk, Nobel Prize winner
and recipient of the Orhan Kemal Literary Prize

PREFACE

I met this 'nobody' by chance in one of Adana's cafés. He was deep in thought, his bearded face resting in his cupped hands. He had pale blue eyes and a head covered in blond curls. After we stared at each other for some time he stood up and approached me. He started to apologize, telling me he had mistaken me for someone else. I realized that he was just trying to start a conversation.

We immediately became friends. He told me his life story much later, as I had been asking him to do for some time. When I told him he should write it all down, he laughed. 'You can if you want to!' I kept extensive notes while he enthusiastically told me his whole life story. So after this volume there may be a second, a third, perhaps even a fourth . . .

You want to know what he's doing now? Who knows? Just plodding through the dreary life of a 'nobody', I suppose, perhaps in Izmir or in Istanbul, or even in Van . . .

Orhan Kemal

CONTENTS

MY FATHER'S HOUSE

1

At the time of my birth my father was a chestnut-moustached lieutenant in the artillery corps, in charge of his battery at Dardanos, near Çanakkale. I am told my grandfather notified him of my arrival with a telegram, ostensibly from my hand: 'I, too, am here now to suffer the material world!'

Apparently when I was five months old my grandfather took me out into the courtyard in my crib. The moon was glowing bright in the evening sky. I stared and stared and uttered a burning sound: 'Tsss . . .'

This caused quite a commotion at home. 'He said "Tsss". Y'know, as if it would burn: "Tsss . . ." He took one look and went "Tsss . . ."'

2

They tell me I was five. I recall our large mansion casting its dark and damp shadows among the leafy trees of the garden. To one side was a drinking fountain which would pour its sparkling water into a basin, and bubbles would froth up as it gushed. I would paddle in the basin and try to drown our ginger cat in it, whereupon my youngest aunt would come and grab it, rescuing the poor half-dead animal from my arms.

My aunt was seven years older than I. She would get to share my chocolates and biscuits yet exaggerate my smallest misdemeanours so that I would get a sound thrashing from my father.

I had a primer bound with green silk. My father would call me before he went to work, bone-hard starched collar pressing against his red neck. He would wet the tip of a pencil, mark out my lesson for the day and command, 'Here!' He would then pass me the book. 'Make sure you have learned it well by this evening.'

I would be locked into the broom cupboard under the stairs which led up to the next floor. If I managed to escape, my aunt would make sure my father got to know about it.

While my youngest aunt gallivanted, the red ribbons of her plaits flying out behind, my older aunt would sneak over and rescue me from my prison. She would spirit me away to her room on the top floor. And what a beautiful room it was! The sun would strike its two adjacent windows, filter through the delicate lace curtains and glow among the greens, purples and yellows of her shaggy carpet while I lay down and rolled in its thick warm pile.

This aunt had long golden-blonde hair which flowed down in ringlets. I found myself growing jealous of her husband. One day I got so frustrated I grabbed a pair of scissors and shredded her bed covers, yet she never complained to my father.

As the evening approached, shortly before he was due back, I would be replaced in my prison. A little while later he would arrive. As I heard his slow footsteps coming closer, making the floorboards squeak and shaking the house, I would shrink in fright. I would wait there, dreading the beating that would inevitably come.

So who was my father? What did he do?

I never knew.

With his silver-topped walking cane, his yellow briefcase, his red fez and his heavy eyebrows constantly set in a stern frown if he was looking in my direction, he was, to me, a large and terrifying being.

He would arrive coughing heavily. 'Where is that boy?' As if he didn't know. 'Has he done his homework? Eh?'

To which my grandmother would usually be the one to reply. 'Of course he has! He's been working hard all day!'

The prison door would open. There I would wait, eyes cast down, standing with my book under my arm, my large fair-haired head sticking out of the top of my long white nightdress, heart pounding.

'So, have you done your homework?' He would lift up my chin, search my eyes. 'Tell me. Have you done it?'

I always knew exactly what mood he was in by his tone of voice.

'Speak up, boy. Have you done your homework?'

'I have.'

'Properly?'

'I . . .'

'Eh? Learned it all properly?'

'Yes, Father.'

'Go on then. Start reading.'

His fat hairy finger would be poised at the beginning of the line he wanted me to start from. Yet for all my reading practice with my eldest aunt my mind would go blank. I'd stare at that hirsute digit on the page and be mesmerized by it.

'Read!'

My back would start to itch. The follicles on his finger would expand, contract, move in and out of focus. They would turn into little mouths or little eyes. If they turned into mouths, they would poke their tongues out at me. If they turned into eyes, they would wink. As for the letters, they were engaged in a wavy, squirmy movement all of their own.

I would suddenly feel a slap and a kick. Then someone, usually my grandmother, would pick me up off the floor and usher me upstairs, out of my father's way, as he stomped around in fury.

'This is what I get! This is what a man like me has for a son!'

As for my mother – brought up as a young lady who would never interfere with a father's discipline – she would stand quietly on the sidelines with tears in her eyes.

One day my father came home in a good mood. He didn't even ask for me. He was laughing and whistling. He changed his clothes, the tune still on his lips. Still in the same good spirits he came and sat down at the dinner table. Then he remembered me. I was let out of my prison, where I had been observing all this from a knot-hole in the wood, and was sat on my high chair at the end of the table, my book under my arm.

My father said, 'Well, then, you little whippersnapper, how's the work going?'

I started shaking.

He ignored it. 'Look, son. Let's make a deal. As you know, everyone on this earth has their own path to follow. Some become grocers, some become cobblers, some are farmers and some are . . . I don't know, dustmen, say. And why? Because Allah has given everyone different abilities. Just as a dustman couldn't do a doctor's job, the doctor couldn't go and haul people's rubbish. Maybe your mind is simply not suited to studying and becoming a gentleman. Perhaps you tell yourself that you don't want to study and become a gentleman. Perhaps you tell yourself that you would rather be a cobbler or a dustman. Hmm? What do you want to be, do you think?'

He wanted to get me to say something.

'Tell me what you think. There's nothing to be afraid of . . . Look at the dustmen . . . No textbooks, no fathers asking them about their homework every evening . . . If you say you really want to be a dustman, that you really don't want to study, I'll stop pestering you about homework . . .'

To cut a long story short, I said I wanted to be a dustman.

How dare I? I got kicked, slapped, punched to the floor; even the chair got knocked over. And after that the lessons got even harder. So did the beatings.

He would often say, 'Oh Lord! Oh God! That my son should be like this!'

It seems he had already learned the whole of the Koran off by heart by the time he was five.

3

Later I was sent to school. When? Where? Which was the first? I went to so many different schools I really don't remember now.

I was first placed in what was an old-fashioned religious school. It had just one class, and our teacher wore a huge turban on his head. We studied in a gloomy little room inside a mosque – or was the whole place one small mosque? Anyway, our teacher had a long beard, a thick, bushy moustache and eyebrows that were forever frowning. He reminded me of my father.

We would file in and kneel down on the floor. Each of us would have a bound section of the Koran in front of us, and the teacher would choose someone at random to start reading. The rest of us would while away the time attempting to stick bits of paper to his backside. Occasionally an indolent fly might buzz in lazy circles and land on a friend's ear or the teacher's turban.

In the days of our war of liberation following the Great War enemy aircraft would bomb the city from time to time, and I was taken out of school. I don't remember how old I was. I don't remember how old my brother Niyazi was either.

Then one day they announced, 'The enemy is coming!' Our house overlooked the street, and we started to spot an ever-increasing number of soldiers on stretchers, groaning, wrapped in bloody bandages. There was blood and dust everywhere and mud and blood on their faces. As members of our household looked anxiously on, my father would draw diagrams of the war's military strategies. Using long arrows of varying thicknesses he would describe enemy attacks and our defences.

The enemy didn't fly over every day. If they did appear, and my brother and I were playing in the garden, I would grab him by the hand and run to safety. Our garden was huge and surrounded by thick, high walls. There was a small cabin in one corner where Uncle Pavli lived. I was never too clear about who he was or what he did. He was just a wrinkled old man to me. The children in the street would run up to him, shout 'Fleabag, fleabag!' and throw stones at the poor man. He would look up, his small bloodshot blue eyes filled with fear, hunch his back and run away from them.

I think I was the only friend Uncle Pavli had. He was never afraid of me. I would go through rubbish for him, picking out buttons, hairpins, cigarette packets or pieces of cloth for him, and carry these to his cabin. It was full of bits and pieces found in piles of garbage.

Uncle Pavli had a terrible laugh. He didn't really laugh; it was more a cry. My grandmother would get cross with me for being friends with him and mutter things like 'Dirty man. Flea-ridden foreigner.'

One cold morning, when we were knee-deep in snow, my grandmother asked me to take Uncle Pavli some leftover lentil soup. I walked over to his cabin, but the door was shut. I pounded on the door, but there was no reply. I pounded on the door again. Still nothing. Niyazi came over. Then, suddenly, enemy aircraft were overhead. We left the bowl in front of the door and ran away. The aircraft took turns to drop a bomb each, then flew off.

One morning she came up to us. 'Oh, boys, boys,' she said, 'poor Uncle Pavli's died!'

I flew out of the room. When I got to his cabin there was a small crowd outside; all the fathers, uncles and aunts of those children who used to call him a fleabag. Everyone telling everyone else what to do. I poked my head through the door of his cabin and immediately was hit by the smell. It was such a stench it made me heave. But I didn't care. I just had to see his body. And I did . . . They had covered it with sackcloth, so I saw only two bare feet; the filthy cracked skin of his heels and two long yellow nails protruding from his toes.

My stomach turned, and I threw up. But I didn't leave until they had loaded his body on to the rubbish cart.

One grey morning soon after, with ashen clouds blanketing the sky, my grandmother, mother, aunts, Niyazi and I set off down the road. My grandmother led the way with her wide hips, brows furrowed, tense and aggressive. Our luggage had already been sent on ahead. We arrived at the station where there was a huge crowd. A mass of people, waiting for trains, all running from the enemy, losing patience and shouting. All sorts of people coming and going, confusion everywhere. Within all this chaos I caught glimpses of children, veiled women, men with drooping moustaches and long beards, and barefoot soldiers. I saw the railway tracks, stretching from one grey horizon to the other.

Everything was covered in snow. Birds huddled together on the telephone wires, heads drawn in between their wings, staring anxiously out at a bleak future. Poor birds.

We could hear cannon fire from a distance. I calculated that the cannon were further than the purple glow of the horizon, although I suppose they may have been closer than that. A nearby officer in a fur cap turned to someone and said the enemy was only an hour away.

The enemy! What sort of thing was the enemy? Why was it coming? Why were we running? And what did a cannon look like?

Everyone turned their heads at the sudden shout of 'The train's coming!' I looked across to see what they were observing and saw a distant line of jet-black puffs of smoke. The birds on the telephone wires shook themselves, poked their heads out and stared at the train.

I heard the cannon fire once more . . .

The train hadn't completely come to a halt, but I lost sight of it in the mass of humanity. People were swarming around it.

My grandmother yanked me sharply by the arm. 'This is not the time to gawp,' she snapped. She was right, but . . . What about the poor birds? I worried that they had no one to spirit them away from the enemy!

Once we were on the train I mulled over recent events. And all along the way there were so many poles chasing each other, so much wire strung between them!

The train was packed. I had been allocated a place on top of the cases, and I was comfortable. But what of the birds? I fell asleep and woke up thinking about them. I fell back to sleep but woke up again, still concerned for them. I'm not sure when I stopped thinking about the birds.

The following day, as we chugged over a mountain plateau through heavy snow, our train got stuck. Everyone got out, and so did we. The weary locomotive hissed gently as a light smoke escaped its funnel. The snow came at us from all directions.

I didn't hear what the engine driver said or what the passengers said to him. But I did overhear someone say the train had run out of fuel.

Later some horse carriages arrived. I have no idea if everyone managed to get on. The sprung carriages were decorated with engravings, embroidery and little bells. They were pulled by large, powerful horses. The bells around their collars echoed across the plateau as we plodded along, the sweaty, steaming horses scrunching their way through the snow.

Darkness descended. Stars came out, only to be frozen in the sky . . . The large, perfect circle of the moon was white and still. No one talked. My head was resting on my grandmother's knee as I stared at the moon, just above the coachman's shoulder. My brother Niyazi was asleep on my mother's lap. My mother, grandmother and my aunts were all in purdah. The night descended further and the stars multiplied, almost jostling one another. The coachman was smoking a cigarette. He slowly leaned sideways, resting his fur cap against the carriage, only to jerk up again, awake once more.

My grandmother questioned him about wolves. He responded without turning around. It seemed that packs of wolves had recently attacked two riders, dragging them off their horses and tearing them apart . . . A protracted attack of coughing on his part ending the discussion. My grandmother muttered some rapid prayers in a shaky voice and turned to my mother. 'Come on, girl,' she said. 'This boy's getting cold. Hand me that blanket.'

I woke suddenly to find my grandmother shaking me. We were in a village. There was no moon, no stars. A large man in a great fur cap was holding a lantern. We were taken to a room in an inn which smelled like a toilet. They brought in a brazier of smoking charcoal and a gas lamp that had glass decorated with fine paper. My grandmother enquired about bandits in the area. Horrible questions about bandits, pillaging army deserters, the enemy and packs of wolves. The man replied briefly in a deep, reassuring voice. Offhand, suspiciously casual replies.

He left, and my grandmother knelt down and prayed. Mysterious whispers drifted around outside. Someone coughed harshly, then spat. My mother and aunts exchanged worried looks.

How could I sleep? Niyazi, though, was already out for the count, unaware of any of this. A horse neighed; a dog barked.

Early the following morning we set off once more. It wasn't snowing, but there was no sun either; just a bitter wind, howling across the white plateau. Toward lunch we started to ascend and eventually reached the mountains. These, with their long, winding, deserted pathways, seemed ominous and frightening. The only signs of life were the occasional tracks left by those who had gone before us.

We passed by the edge of a cliff. There were towering sheer rocks to one side of us and dizzy, craggy depths to the other. 'A horse fell over the side the other day,' said the coachman; 'just down here.'

My grandmother, through trembling lips, uttered one prayer after another. My mother and aunts blanched. I clutched my grandmother tightly as if I was about to be pushed over the edge.

For a long time we continued up and down, through and over, and then . . . Wooden houses, lead domes and tall, dark cypress trees loomed before us. A town. We were saved.

Later my father joined us. He seemed drained and plainly hadn't slept for days. His beard had grown long. He lifted me up and kissed me first. Things were said in the house in which we stayed about joy, relief and hope. Then I awoke one morning, and my father was no longer there. He had quietly disappeared.

I didn't know where he had gone.

I later found out that he had gone to Ankara. Ankara! When I think of this city I always remember its houses of burnt, rotten, rust-stained wood or sun-dried bricks, all crowded together. They overlooked the narrow, uneven streets full of soldiers in their military hats, police in their brimless fur caps and children selling nationalist newspapers. I also recall a cracked old jug of water, frozen solid overnight.

But before we went to Ankara we spent time in Konya.

Our house in Konya was between Alaettin Hill and the Armenian School. It was a tall house owned by Greeks or Armenians. The landlord lived on the ground floor with his children. His wife was almost constantly knitting, her black shawl around her shoulders.

One day, quite unexpectedly, we found ourselves in the middle of an uprising. At least that's how it seemed to me. Peasants in coarse caps were running around, shouting, 'Don't want them! Don't want this government!'

I was told that if anyone asked I was the coalman's son. My grandmother took all the books, papers, photographs, swords and guns belonging to my father – that is, everything belonging to my real father in Ankara – and concealed them in the cotton stuffing of the mattresses or up in the attic.

They said that a bullet fired from Alaettin Hill had gone straight though our top-floor windows and had hit the Armenian School and that a bullet fired from the Armenian School had gone through the windows of our house and hit Alaettin Hill. We would see thick moustachioed heads in the windows of the Armenian School and spend our days and nights huddled together on the stairs near the ground floor.

One day we heard that the rebels had tied up the governor in a barn. Another day news spread that the rebels occupying Alaettin Hill had garrotted a young police officer and had laid his body across his mother's knees.

'We want Shariah! We don't want this foreign government! We don't want these infidels! We want Shariah!' people yelled. We heard the screams of those being dragged away and endless gunfire; doors being broken down, people strangled.

The days went by.

'We don't want it! We don't want them!' echoed down the streets. Then one day, amid all the screams, gunfire and don't-wants, news of the imminent arrival of the National Independence Army spread like wildfire. The Don't-Wants went quiet, the men in the heavy shoes scattered, and the guns fell silent.

One sunny morning, handkerchiefs in hand, my brother and I joined the crowd gathering to meet the army in front of the Prosecutor's house. The military horses approached, frothing at the mouth, the heavy thud of their hooves thundering in our ears. We broke into rapturous applause. Old women, children, young women, girls crying for joy, the entire crowd undulating in shrieks of delight.

The horsemen rode by, those glorious horsemen! Hats and moustaches resplendent under the glorious sunshine. These were followed by the Don't-Wants, the peasants in their caps, hands tied behind their backs, martyrs for the Shariah. Then the wagons, piled full of dead bodies, necks cut, covered in blood . . . That day I shouted so much I grew hoarse and became ill.

Local children started to play with the empty cartridges in front of the Armenian School. The streets were full of cartridges.

4

I remember the farm we moved to from there. It was outside a southern town full of crows, by a river that appeared to be still even when in full flow; a farm surrounded by great mulberry trees.

How old was I around that time? How old was Niyazi? I really don't remember. We would run around in our white nightgowns until we were sweating, then, parched, consume vast amounts of water until we couldn't drink any more and sometimes make ourselves sick. If we were ill my mother, my good mother, would sit by our bedside, look into our eyes but not shed any tears and spend the whole night with us. She would put a thermometer under our arms, take our temperatures, cool our foreheads and place dry towels beneath our backs. She refused to get cross or angry because we didn't want to drink our bitter medicine but instead tried to persuade us with gentle encouragement, to sweet-talk us into taking it.

My father was a brilliant civil servant, distinctive with his bone-hard starched collar against his thick red neck and his smart yellow briefcase. He used to travel to far-away towns. On days he left for such distant places Niyazi and I would race and jump around in the ante-room and kick out at imaginary villains. We would get the son of the handyman to summon the children of the village and run around with them all day, playing in the sunshine. We would teach them our school tricks and city games. They had no manners but were very bright; they were swift to grasp whatever they were told or shown. When I read to them from my copy of *Two Friends Travel the World* they would shiver with excitement. And they had been stunned when I had showed them how to vault with a long pole. I had cleared a string drawn taut above head height, and they had been very impressed. But they quickly grasped what to do. Seeing me bring the string down a few times on an off-day, a bright little boy with short spiky hair came over, took the long rod in his hands and flew over the high string with amazing agility.

But we would soon tire of our games. We would reach a point where, for something to do, we would decide to steal some aubergines. They grew in a big garden next to our farm. The owners kept large sheepdogs, so we would sneak in quietly from the far end of the garden. The branches around us would be laden with varieties of plum and apricot. But their aubergines were truly magnificent. Our handyman's son Haso had eaten some raw ones and, having witnessed this with our own eyes, we ate them raw, too. Occasionally, I suppose because they caught our scent, the dogs would start barking incessantly, and we would scatter in all directions. As we leaped over hedges, running for dear life, the vicious thorns of the barberry would leave our legs covered in blood.

I normally played with my brother Niyazi. We would occupy ourselves for hours with the countless chickens and cockerels at the farm. My brother and I would be the kings of the farm, and the chickens, cockerels, turkeys, dogs and other animals would be our subjects. Sometimes a chicken would break one of our laws. We would immediately issue orders for the arrest of the guilty party and demand that it be taken into custody. We would take one of the huge wheat sieves used by the women farm workers, place it on its edge in a corner of the farmyard, tie a long string to the top, scatter seed in front of it and crouch down in a far corner of the yard so as not to frighten the bird.

When the hen to be arrested 'by order of Their Majesties' walked in front of the sieve we would pull the string. The bird would then be trapped, and no matter how much it clucked and flapped there was no way it could escape. As it had broken the laws of its gracious Kings, our subject would have to be punished.

We would first conduct a short trial. Employing phrases our father used to frighten us we would threaten the animal, staring into its hard, beady little eyes. It would hear us out in an annoyingly uninterested manner. In the end we would hang it from one of the boughs of a mulberry tree and beat it. Each thwack would send it wild. It would squeal in an agonized way and thrash from side to side, and eventually my mother would come running.

'What do you think you're doing? What on earth are you up to now?'

We wouldn't tell her about the laws of 'Their Gracious Majesties'.

'We're training it!' we'd say.

'What do you mean, training?' she'd ask incredulously. 'You can't train a hen! Who ever heard of training chickens? You half-wits!' She'd release the bird and say crossly, 'Do as you would be done by – even if it is only a hen.'

We loved it when my father was away in far-off towns. At these times, particularly in the evening, my mother would call our handyman's wife, Auntie Seher, and the young maid Gülizar. 'Come on,' she'd say. 'Let's get out some food, sit on the floor and have a nice meal together while he's away.'

My father always hated eating on the floor and the fingers of bulgur and fresh vine leaves which people ate by hand. He would get particularly annoyed at my mother being informal and familiar with the servants. Our house was never short of gossiping daughters-in-law, mothers-in-law and sisters-in-law, and my grandmother and aunts would gang up on my mother. 'You low-minded woman, how could you treat the servants like equals? Have you no dignity?'

But my mother . . . Well, she used to be a teacher, and she simply couldn't discriminate. It just wasn't in her. So they'd lay out mats on the floor, cover them with tablecloths, bring out the pickles, crudités and dips and prepare large dishes of bulgur cooked with plenty of onion.

Then my mother would grow uneasy because the handyman's wife and the maid would sit looking ill at ease. 'For goodness' sake,' she'd say, 'don't be bashful. Look, it's just us. Let's have a good time together!'

Then they would relax. As they ate and laughed the handyman's wife would come out with all sorts of stories, and the risqué ones in particular would have us doubled up in laughter.

After we ate, the lady of the house and the servants would clear up together, and we would start on the dried fruit and nuts. The handyman's wife, a dark and lively woman, would then start fiddling with her silver bracelet which was too small for her wrist and tell us fairy-tales.

How we loved those stories! Tales full of amazing giants with seven heads, witches, genies and imps or a marvellous phoenix, together with sultans, sultans' daughters, sheikhs and wizards. When it got really late we would hear the distant noise of jackals. These were awesome, like the barks and howls of the night itself.

The handyman's wife would tell us, 'The jackals, they swim across the stream, they do. They sneak into the farm. Beams come from their eyes. One look at them chickens and they fall off their branches. They have magic in their eyes, jackals do.'

My brother and I would lie trembling in bed, gripping each other tightly, trying to huddle up close to each other. We'd pull the cover over our heads in fear, listening to the barks and howls of the jackals from the other side of the river but getting closer. It seemed that these were the sounds of creaking bones or of witches escaping from their fairy dimensions with a shriek, haunting screams from the graveyard or perhaps the howls of evil magicians.

So much happened at that farm. Some days we would have visitors from the city. Tables would be laid beneath the great mulberry trees, and the guests would be offered fresh farm butter, milk and eggs. Then my mother would show the ladies the farm, and later in the afternoon they would all wander around the red, green, purple, yellow and white vegetable gardens.

We would run off with their children, playing Mothers and Fathers or just scattering into the fields. The girls would lift their skirts up sufficiently to run after the boisterous boys who would have raced ahead. They would have hundreds of questions – and receive hundreds of cocky replies. Yet if they spotted a yellow field snake slithering out of the hot sun they'd run screaming back to their mothers, where they would have to be given sips of water and reassurance. Once they had calmed down a bit they would tell their mothers of the forked tongue of the huge, horrible snake, how it had chased them, how it had hissed at them, how its eyes were aflame. Then they would get carried away with their own tale and, believing they had convinced Niyazi and me, proceed to boast to us of their bravery in the face of such dangers.

The male guests would always sit separately with my father and converse in lofty tones. I'll never forget one day when an elderly gentleman, whom even my father respected, was inspired by the grains on a sheaf of wheat. 'This is truly a piece of heaven on earth!' he proclaimed. 'Honestly, my son, you have no idea how fortunate you are to be living in the lap of Nature. Ours is no life! There we are, all crowded on top of one another in soulless, immoral cities . . .'

But there are also bitter memories.

The farmhouse had been left by Greeks or Armenians, and I wasn't too sure from whom my father had rented it. It had a huge outhouse with a big black padlock hanging off the door. With its windows reminiscent of a pair of eyes and its door which had been locked for years, the outhouse seemed to be concealing some great secret.

I have no idea what was said, but one day our neighbours convinced themselves that they had persuaded my mother to let them open up the outhouse. She was indoors at the time, ironing my father's clothes. Niyazi and I were making paper birds, that is to say, kites, out of coloured paper.

We heard loud noises coming from the direction of the outhouse. 'Run and see what's going on,' ordered my mother.

I rushed out. The neighbours had opened up the building, and women and children were swarming all over it. Pots and pans of all sizes, copper bowls, porcelain plates, fruit baskets, colourful lampshades, picture frames, curtain rails, water jugs were being passed around. I joined in the mêlée. Everything was covered in dust. Confused cockroaches scuttled away in drove, spiders froze on the dusty trunks, the occasional rat ran from one end to the other. I remember a large, towering mirror in particular, its glass covered in thick dust, sending shivers down my spine. And all those crates. And the books, including foreign volumes, beautifully bound, lying impressively in their huge cases. And also handwritten notebooks. But those books . . . Books, books, so many books . . .

I had been distracted by a toy furniture set I found in one of the cases when I realized that the commotion had died down. I looked up, and there was my mother, standing by the door, her face pale, full of fear. 'What have you done?' she cried. 'What have you done? Do you want to destroy me?'

The neighbours approached her. 'Oh, madam, please, you're a good lady. May God look kindly on your soul, madam. It's all foreign stuff anyway. Let us have a few things . . . You'll be doing a good deed, and we'll pray for you.'

My mother had shrunk inside her white nightdress. Her face full of anxiety, she paused awhile. 'Listen,' she pleaded. 'Please take pity on me. My husband left strict instructions. When he gets back in a few days it won't be you who suffers. He'll take it out on me!'

They had already carried off all they were going to anyway, so they started to leave in ones and twos. My mother pushed me out as well, pulled the doors to and locked them back up. But after that she lived in fear, lost in her thoughts. It was obvious that she was dreading what was going to happen, that my father would hear of the incident or be told of it sooner or later.

About a week later, sure enough, what she feared came to pass.

We knew he was due to return around midnight. My mother had sent away the handyman's wife and the maid, Gülizar, and had told us all not to let slip anything about the outhouse being ransacked. 'Otherwise,' she confided, 'your father will kill me!'

We were asleep. We jumped up in bed to the sound of the door banging as if it was being broken down. Niyazi and I shot out of our room. Unfortunately the lamp had blown out.

We heard my mother cursing. 'Damn you, stupid matches. Where are you? Children, open that door. He's gone off on one again! No, wait, leave the door . . . Have you seen the bloody matches?'

The door was coming off its hinges.

'Damn. Bloody things! God Almighty!'

My father was shouting his head off, banging on the door, swearing loudly. Then the dogs started to bark. Finally my mother must have found the matches because she lit the lamp and ran to the door. My brother and I watched her from the banisters.

She opened the door. My father burst in like a cannonball. He had tall patent-leather boots on. He set upon my mother, violence personified, and grabbed her by the hair. She rolled over with a scream. The lamp in her hand fell to the floor and smashed, and everything around her instantly burst into flames. Flames . . . Red, orange and yellow flames and my mother screaming . . .

The stairs shook as my father bolted up them. 'Lamp!' he yelled. 'Find the other bloody lamp instead of staring like an idiot!'

In the yellow light of the flames, bouncing off the stairs, I found the matches, got the other lamp out and lit it and ran back over.

My father was trying to smother the flames with a blanket. Now and then a flicker of orange fire would reach up from the corner of the blanket and my father would stamp it out. The house filled with the smell of resin, oil and smoke.

Finally my father grabbed hold of my mother and pulled her up. Her face looked as white as her nightdress as she swayed on her feet, her hair in disarray.

'Tell me,' asked my father, 'is what I heard true?'

My mother collapsed on her knees. She didn't reply.

He nudged her with the toe of his boot. 'Tell me,' he repeated, 'is it true what I heard?'

My mother whimpered. 'I . . . I don't know. What have you heard?'

'That you emptied the outhouse?'

'As God is my witness,' she started, 'it wasn't my fault . . .'

My father grabbed her by the hair, dragged her up and down the anteroom, up and down, up and down . . . Then he kicked her and kicked her, crushed her under his feet and disgustedly shook off the handful of hair from his palm.

My brother and I were huddled together, trembling in our long nightgowns, too afraid even to cry, frozen. My mother was no longer moving. She lay on the floor, passed out, or . . . It occurred to me that she might be dead. I looked at my father with a terrible feeling of revolt welling up inside me. But there was his dark furrowed face . . . He was a giant and so powerful!

He didn't even glance at her. He paced around the room, making the floorboards squeak, occasionally mumbling oaths. Then he paused for a moment. She was lying face down, and he leaned over and grabbed her by the arm and harshly jerked her up. She looked at him, her eyes slowly widening with ever-increasing terror. She covered her face with her arm.

'Tell me,' roared my father, 'who do you think you are to do such a thing? Did you not think . . . did it not occur to you that my honour, my reputation is at stake? What if they take you away and lock you up tomorrow? What if they don't just take you, they take both of us, and drag us through the courts? I cannot believe how stupid you've been! How could you break a government seal? How could you dare?'

He divorced my mother that evening and sent her to my uncle's house first thing the following morning. That night my grandmother and my youngest aunt arrived at the farmhouse, and together they quickly went over everything in the house. Then my grandmother tucked the edges of her skirt into her waist, gave orders to the maids and had the house scrubbed from top to bottom.

They were delighted. They laughed out loud at everything. 'My God, would you just look at this filth! You wouldn't wish her on anyone!' Or 'My poor son must have had the patience of a saint! Most men wouldn't have put up with such a slovenly woman.'

I never forget the two of them went up to my mother's – my kind mother's – oatmeal chest, one on either side, and took out everything she had from her dresses to her stocking elastics and laid them out on the floor. They gave some of the stocking elastics to the handyman's wife and the maid Gülizar.

One day my youngest aunt turned to the handyman's wife who had laughed a bit too much. 'I don't want to see your teeth,' she snapped. 'You're not with that servant-minded woman now. Know your place. And don't forget it in front of your betters.'

I think it was about two months later when my father, despite all my grandmother's protests, renewed his vows with my mother and brought her back to us. It was then that we found out that my grandmother and aunt had been working on him. 'Your wife,' they had told him, 'got together with the locals and ransacked that outhouse. The whole town is talking about it. Apparently the police will raid any day now. Just so long as you know . . .'

My mother had long since forgiven my father. 'He can beat me,' she had said. 'He is the man. It's not his fault; it's all those other so-and-sos. So long as he understands, so long as he listens, what can I do? I have to take what's coming to me.'

5

I only really got to know my father in the partisan struggles.

It was troubled times. The streets were full of crowds, united by their hatred, applauding speakers they often didn't even understand. Crowds, crowds, always crowds. Magnificent crowds, in shoes, in clogs, barefoot, all treading the cobbles, a thrilling sight, as if they came for Judgement Day.

I remember us living in one of two large townhouses that faced each other across a narrow street. They were like delicate models constructed by a talented schoolboy, with ornate eave-boards, bay windows, railings and carvings. Our house was also my father's political headquarters. The ground floor was paved with heavy white stones. I was always afraid of the ground floor; maybe because it used to be owned by Armenians: I had the impression the rotting doors to the two adjacent stables would crash open, revealing Armenian corpses staggering towards us. I imagine it was because of the stories I'd been told, but I always thought of Armenians as fearsome and yellow-skinned with bedraggled long hair and beards – even though I had never seen an Armenian in my life.

It was on this ground floor that they would hold their partisan meetings. Angry fists would trace tight arcs through the smoke-filled air. What type, what class of people were these? What did they want? What did they think?

As I positioned myself to see through the knot-holes of the floor above, I heard speeches being addressed to a medley of people I assumed were of the same class and them clapping, and shouting 'Hear, hear!' in response to what was said. I became aware that I was the son of the man inspiring the crowd. I also knew that my father was a man who wrote lengthy articles which stretched all the way to the advertisement pages. However, I was uninterested in both his leadership and his overlong articles.

I would take his articles to the printer's, bring back proofs and return there with my father's corrections. Some days he sat up until dawn with the thick tomes, then he would turn to me with a frown over his bloodshot eyes and shove pages of writing into my hands. 'Take these to the printers now,' he would order. 'Leave them there, and hurry back with a newspaper.' In spite of his warnings I would always find something to delay me. I wouldn't actually look for distractions, but there is much on the streets to keep a young boy from his errands: football, swordplay with sticks, the possibility of getting hold of chocolate . . . I knew

I'd be beaten when I got back, but I would lie so eloquently on my return that my father, who knew me well and refused to listen to me on principle, would often end up believing me despite himself. And the times I couldn't convince him I would be in deep trouble. I couldn't begin to tell you how many canes he broke on my back or how many times he kicked or slapped me.

One day – on a grey morning – my father woke me up very early. He sent me out to purchase some aspirin. I bought the pills and was making my way back. I turned a corner, and there he was! He was in his heavy black coat and brown hat, carrying his yellow briefcase, looking even more awesome and frightening than usual. He was flanked by two of his friends.

I hurried to his side. When I reached him he took the aspirin off me, told me to keep the change, looked up and down the street and kissed me on the cheek. 'Be good now,' he said. 'Carry on going to school, and work hard.' I perceived something unusual in his manner – something that suggested he was going far, far away.

I ran home. My mother was in tears. I asked her why, but she wouldn't say. I think it was about a fortnight later when I, along with everyone else, found out that he had 'safely crossed over'.

A child should be upset to be deprived of his father. Not I. I was glad. Why? I'm not sure. I suspect my youth had little to do with this uncaring attitude.

6

I had declared my sovereignty among the household. What I said went. I could beat up my siblings to my heart's desire, and when I returned after sunset, my football under my arm, no one would question where I had been, why I was so late or whether I had skipped lessons and gone off to play football. I would climb up on the roof with my kites of various colours and sizes and issue decrees to the sky.

My mother was in no state to cope with me. Every day she would rush from the courts to the solicitors and to land registry offices, anxiously trying to sort out the house left to her by that father of mine. She would usually return sweaty and exhausted. Mind you, I'm not sure she could have coped with me even without such worries.

That year I failed at school.

This didn't have the slightest effect on my sovereignty. My mother moaned a few times and then gave up. 'Do whatever you want,' she said. 'You're old enough; I can't be bothered.' With that she handed me my own leash. I was happy: I thought my reign would continue. Then one day we received a long letter from my father. He wanted us to apply for passports immediately, sell everything we could and set off straight away.

I was astounded. My cherished freedom was about to be annulled.

Farewell, blue skies; farewell, sweet shops; farewell, chocolates, team-mates and dusty pitches . . . Goodbye, Little Memet! The cats, the dusty dogs, the little sparrows, the bats, the big mosque, the clock-house, the market . . . Goodbye to them all!

Then one evening, frustrated to the point of tears, we boarded a train. I could have cried at the slightest thing. As the train departed I was in the deep, dark depression of someone who has just had to bury his dearest sweetheart with his own hands.

7

I spent the night huddled into a corner of the third-class compartment with fearful nightmares about what was in store for me.

My mother was relieved to be handing over the worry of providing a living to its rightful owner. Niyazi and my sister were relieved to be free of my tyranny. No longer would I be able to force Niyazi to play in goal, to get the girls to scratch my back for ages or come back home whenever I wanted . . .

They were laughing and chatting away to each other. The train, as if in league with them, was tearing through the darkness, flying along, travelling faster and faster.

My inner pain was getting worse. I thought of Little Memet and of the pink house in which his family lived, of the dusty pitches, of the horse-drawn carriages going through the streets and of the greengrocers pushing their carts through the neighbourhood shouting 'Dill, parsley, radishes, onions!' And I thought of my friends Kurd Ado, Lizard Sureyya and Tekin.

8

We lived in Beirut. As we weren't Lebanese my father wasn't allowed to practise law. So he sold off my mother's bracelets and with a capital of ten gold liras opened a small restaurant under a tall apartment building, facing on to a narrow street leading to a square.

He rarely visited the restaurant. A Turkish refugee called Sureyya cooked the food, and Niyazi and I waited on the customers and did the washing up.

I was seventeen and perfectly happy with my new lifestyle. I forgot my home town, football, Little Memet and the others. Niyazi and I would leave home at dawn. At that hour even the green trams of Beirut were few and far between. Only the workers, those masses who slept less than everyone else the world over, they would be on the streets, that crowd of men and women, walking in groups. We would join them. We would have our jackets hung over our shoulders just like they did, proud to be people in work, to be treading the same paving stones as them.

I think my shoes must have been fairly new. One day, so that they would look less smart, I cut them up a bit here and there with a knife and scuffed them up. I got the most extraordinary beating from my father.

I had tired of being the son of a well-known partisan leader, a lawyer and a reporter. I was sick of being told not to walk around the streets, not to talk to rude children, to talk nicely. I had often fantasized about being the son of a rag-and-bone man or refuse picker.

The restaurant was so good . . .

'Four soups!'

'Place for the gentleman!'

'Get those dishes done!'

'Peel those onions!'

And on and on.

Niyazi and I had agreed on the division of labour. In the morning he would do the dishes and I would wait on the tables. In the afternoon I would do the washing up and he would be waiter. In addition I would go to the market and I would carry water from the public fountain. It was obvious that I came off worse from this deal, but we had deliberately arranged things this way. Niyazi was weak; he had suffered a number of major childhood diseases. Some days he would be too tired to wake up and would arrive at the restaurant long after I did. Most evenings he would leave long before I did.

Our restaurant was surrounded by tall apartment blocks. There would always be women wandering up and down the street in garish makeup and colourful low-cut dresses, cigarettes hanging out of their mouths, full of uninhibited laughter, occasionally bickering with one other. Shiny cars would frequent the street. They would pick up a few of these women, then leave.

A woman called Naciye, said to be the daughter of a famous military commander, lived in the apartment block next to our restaurant. She had the makeup and the cigarettes of the others, but even though she was no prettier than them her Turkish was excellent. We immediately became friends, and she told us her life story. She was the daughter of one of Sultan Vahdettin's generals. Her father had fled the country, and they had gone to Egypt, I think, and then Damascus. Her father had died there. So she had been left alone with her mother and siblings. From Damascus they had travelled all over the place, the usual stories . . . Mind you, she told her story with such innocence, and she was so sincere . . . At one point she cried and almost had us crying with her.

I really adored her dark eyes, those sparkling, moist eyes. When she walked into the restaurant even the cook Sureyya became a changed man. His ever-present frown would soften. As for Naciye, she would pull up a chair, sit down and cross her legs or look at herself in the mirror above the basin or walk over to the pots to see what was cooking. I suspected that Sureyya was a bit jealous of me because of our friendship. Whenever she came he would send me to the market or to fetch more water, or even if he didn't send me somewhere he would come up with something for me to get on with. Not that I minded the work, but I would rather not have had to do it in front of Naciye.

There again, it wasn't as if she paid him any attention. For all his efforts she would insist on coming up to me to stroke my chin and my cheeks and talk to me. I'd catch Sureyya out of the corner of my eye; he would be livid.

Niyazi didn't even enter into it. One day Sureyya had gone to the market, so he and I were alone in the restaurant. He was washing up some bowls, and I had wet my hair and was combing it in the mirror. Naciye arrived. I saw her in the mirror. She wore a white low-cut dress, showing off rather too much bosom, and had a huge pink bow in her hair. She came up to me, wrapped her arm around my neck, pressed her face up against mine. We stood like that for a few moments, frozen in front of the mirror. I was shaking and burning up.

'Are you embarrassed?'

I didn't reply.

'Today,' she said, 'you can bring me my lunch. All right?' She pecked me on the cheek.

Niyazi was at the back of the restaurant singing to himself.

'Who's that?' asked Naciye.

'My brother,' I said.

We went over. There he was, lost in his song, doing the washing up.

'You're doing a good job there,' said Naciye.

Niyazi spun around, confused. When he saw it was Naciye he blushed a deep red. He was wiping his wet hands on his apron, staring guiltily at the floor.

She stroked his hair and looked at me. 'Do you wash up, too?' she asked.

I don't know what possessed me. 'No, not me,' I said, looking straight at Niyazi.

He went purple. 'Did he just say no?' he asked. 'No?' He turned to Naciye. 'He's lying. I do the washing up in the morning;

he does it in the afternoons,' he explained. 'He's just trying to impress you!'

I thought I would shrivel up and die.

Yet Naciye hadn't thought it mattered in the slightest. She wandered over to the cooking pots, lifted their lids and inspected the food, gave a low whistle and walked away.

We were left alone. Niyazi knew I would have a go at him. He was still by his washing up, standing there, looking anxious.

'What did you think you were doing?' I demanded.

He was afraid I would give him a smack. 'Well, you wash up, too,' he mumbled.

I could have slapped him a couple of times, but there were greater things at stake. I was not so naïve that I couldn't imagine my father's outrage when it came out that I had beaten up my brother because of some whore.

The delivery lunches were prepared for our regulars. I grabbed Naciye's tray. Would Niyazi let it go? 'Leave that one,' he said. 'Let go.'

'I'll take this one today,' I said. 'You take that one.'

Sureyya the cook wasn't having it. 'No, no . . .' he said. 'What's this, a new tradition in an old village? The kid can't do the long runs!'

'But it's always me doing the long runs,' I protested. 'He always takes the nearby ones and pockets all their tips!'

Niyazi stared. 'I swear they don't tip me,' he said.

I was so angry though I swore at him. Even Sureyya was amazed.

My brother started to cry. 'You just wait. I'll get Dad to sort you out.'

That put the fear of God into me. What if he did tell our father? I took the tray from the bar and left the restaurant. Niyazi and I didn't speak to each other all afternoon. That evening, after all the customers had eaten and the regulars had dispersed, I was about to get down to the washing up when Niyazi, looking at me darkly, called out to Sureyya, 'Goodbye!'

He left, muttering something like 'He'll sort you out' to me. I left the washing up and ran after him. It was night-time, and the city was sparkling with lights. The green trams sped along, and little bursts of blue lightning on their wires travelled with them. Crowds milled on the pavements. I caught up with him in front of a bar. He was buying bananas from a man selling them off a cart. I grabbed his arm.

He looked up and viciously yanked it back. 'I dare you not to beg,' he said.

Well, I was always up for a dare, but . . . I went after him again. He was being awkward. I gave him some money, I bought him some walnut halva and eventually convinced him not to go to our father.

I really wish I hadn't. From that day on he tyrannized me. The boy who used to do everything I said without question and obeyed my every diktat now started to answer back and do as he pleased.

'Bring me a glass of water, would you?' I'd say.

'Something wrong with your legs? Go get your own drink!' he'd reply.

Then one day he turned to me. 'You can do the morning washing up from now on. You can't just sit around combing your hair. You have to work.'

'Why don't you talk to him?' I implored Sureyya the cook. 'At least get him to carry the water.'

Sureyya shrugged. 'That's for his dad to say.'

My hopes were dashed. It was as if Niyazi came to the restaurant just to pass the time of day. He would laboriously comb his hair, take a chair out on to the street and put his feet up. All he did was deliver the trays for Naciye and the other regulars who lived near by and pocket the tips; whereas I didn't get a moment's rest from cleaning tripe, carrying water or doing the dishes.

I confronted him one day. 'Come on, Niyazi. At least do the washing-up in the morning.'

He shrugged. 'You know I'm weak. I tire so easily, and anyway Dad told me not to strain myself.'

'So what's going to happen? Are you just going to come here to sit around all day?'

He couldn't care less. 'What can I do? It's what my dad said . . .'

Your dad, eh? You and your dad . . .

I had nothing left to lose. Even the chair that I had occasionally put out on the street to sit on had been completely taken over. One day when Naciye was there he turned to me. 'Go and wash the dishes then,' he said. 'What are the customers going to eat off?'

'Watch your mouth,' I said. 'You little shit!'

'You know, I haven't forgotten what you said to me the other day.'

This had all gone too far. I had to put a stop to it as quickly as possible. And when it did stop, that had to be an end to the matter.

Another week went by. That night I was a bit late returning home. Niyazi had been taken ill, so he was lying in bed. My father was at his bedside holding his wrist. He saw me come in.

'Why is this kid sick?' he snapped.

'I don't know . . .'

'Don't know, eh? I'll give you don't know. God knows what you did to him, you little viper.'

Something snapped. I pulled my mother aside. 'Niyazi is getting overtired at the restaurant,' I said. 'He sweats, then he catches a chill, and he's weak anyway. I think it would be best if you didn't send him out to work.'

'He told you this?' asked my mother.

'Many times. He says he's too scared of Father to bring it up at home.'

My mother considered this. 'But, darling, then you would have to do everything.'

'I don't mind,' I said. 'So long as my brother isn't making himself ill.'

From that day onward they never let him come to the restaurant. I admit that meant a lot of work, but it was worth it.

9

It had been over a month since the restaurant had gone bankrupt. We sold heaps of pots, pans, knives and forks. We were very careful in how we spent the money we got from the sales and from the few pennies that Niyazi brought home from his job.

Niyazi was working as a peddler. I had no work. One of my father's acquaintances had promised that he would find me a job, but we had heard nothing from him for the past two weeks, so I went back to fishing.

It was a Sunday. It was cloudy and cold. It was the olive season and the locals, long sticks and woven reed baskets in hand, were off to beat the fruit off the tree. I had my rod on my shoulder and my hands in my pockets as I walked. I shivered as I battled against the cold humid wind.

I walked down towards the quay past huge apartment blocks, each building as pretty as a child's toy. Rows of fishermen sat along the concrete quay. I walked to the right, towards the rocks just past the aeroplane hangar.

The sea was wild. Ashen waters foamed as they swept forward, hurtled themselves on to the rocks and broke apart in huge roars. I buried my wet shoes in some sand the water couldn't reach and proceeded to climb to the highest rock. I hooked a worm on my line and cast my lead weight as far out as I could.

It started to rain, spitting at first, then, gradually, coming down in torrents. My cloth jacket got soaked, and the steely wind made me shiver uncontrollably. I pushed the end of the rod into a hollow in the rock, left my line dangling in the sea and stood up. I found myself some shelter in a café by the hangar. The proprietor was a man with a bushy moustache who looked me up and down disapprovingly and said something in Arabic.

'*I don't speak Arabic*,' I said in Arabic.

The man grew annoyed. He put down the coconut water-pipe he was holding. '*Are you Armenian?*' he asked. '*Go away. Get out of here.*'

It was pouring down outside.

'*No . . .*' I said. '*Me Turk.*'

The man relaxed and patted my shoulder. 'Boy, where you from?' he asked in broken Turkish.

'Adana.'

'Very good. In war I soldier there.'

He took out a lump of hashish from his pocket, broke it up in the palm of his hand, spread it on top of the tobacco on his water pipe and lit up. As he inhaled deeply his eyes narrowed and his swarthy face grew pale.

We didn't speak any more. He was staring out over the sea and I was in the doldrums, caught up in the bleak grey of the stormy day. I don't know how long we sat like this. I eventually stood up at a point I felt the rain had abated and went to leave.

'*Goodbye*,' I said in his language.

'*Farewell*,' he replied.

I walked back to my fishing rod. It was exactly as I had left it. I gathered in the line. I put a fresh worm on the hook and cast the lead weight once more.

The horizon was a deep shade of purple. I hummed a folk tune and thought of my homeland. My school, Little Memet, Kurd Ado, Lizard Sureyya, the dusty pitch near Little Memet's house . . . My eyes brimmed with tears . . . I was back in Beirut. We had nothing to eat tonight. I should at least take one fish back with me.

I heard my name called and looked around. It was Virginie, an Armenian girl who lived with her sick mother in one of the tin huts around the back of our house. She ran across the sharp rock in her bare feet. Her thin dress was filthy, her hair a mess.

'Look at this!' She wailed. 'I haven't had a single bite since this morning.' She showed me her broken rod.

'How did that happen?'

'The dirty Arab down there, he broke it.'

She was crying her eyes out. I pulled the line off the rod, rolled it into a ball and put the ball into a pocket on her dress.

It was getting dark. Suddenly the siren on the aeroplane hangar started to howl. The seaplane returning from its flight to Europe was now approaching the harbour.

Virginie looked at me with her large, dark eyes. 'Didn't you catch anything either?'

'No, I didn't.'

She turned to the sea, her hair flying in the wind. 'My mother's very ill,' she murmured.

'What's wrong with her?'

'Her chest. She gets these spasms and coughs up blood.'

'Why don't you take her to hospital?'

'We have no money.'

'Relatives?'

'There is no one. I have an uncle, but our relatives are in America.'

'And?'

'They've forgotten us.'

'Why?'

'They became rich.'

'I know that feeling. We have rich relatives back home.'

'Were you rich?'

'We were. We had fields, a car . . .'

'How did all this happen?'

'I couldn't say. God's will, I suppose.'

Virginie's eyes lit up. 'If only my mother could hang on for another three years . . .'

'What happens then?'

'I'd be fourteen!'

'And?'

'This woman, Shinoric, she's like a sister to me and says that once I'm fourteen I'll be able to earn really good money.' Her thick legs were pale and covered in dirt. She continued, 'Apparently she started when she was thirteen.'

'Started what?'

'Earning money.'

'How?'

'She brings men back home at night.'

'That's prostitution. Do you really want to be a prostitute?'

'Oh, no! I . . . I'd just take care of my mother.'

The sea howled. A distant buoy rose on the waves and disappeared over the dark cliffs of the rumbling waters, only to reappear a short time later.

Virginie was watching the sea. At one point she looked at me. She was about to say something when a great wave smashed against the rocks and cascaded over her. The poor girl couldn't keep her balance and was thrown on to my lap. We were both soaked.

'Come on,' I said. 'Let's go. The sea isn't feeding us today.'

Just as we were getting up my rod started to twitch. I immediately reeled the line in and found a large fish on the end of my hook. I was delighted. I pulled it around and cut its stomach open. Virginie admired my handiwork.

I got up. I took my shoes back out of the sand. The wind had become bitterly cold.

Virginie's teeth were chattering. 'I'm f-r-r-re-e-e-ez-ing.'

I took off my wet jacket and placed it across her wet shoulders.

All the city lights were on. We went past the square near our old restaurant and got to Ra's Beirut. As we went past the home of the Turkish deputy consul we saw Niyazi.

'What, just the one?' he asked.

'What can I do?' I said. 'The sea is so rough . . .'

'So I walk around all day, through the streets of Beirut, and His Lordship comes back with one fish.'

I didn't reply.

He began to stride faster, as if he wasn't going to demean himself by walking beside us.

'You're brother's a bit stuck-up,' observed Virginie.

It was now really dark. The Christian grocer on the corner of our street had lit his gas lamp. I reclaimed my jacket from her.

We were about to part company when she held my hand. 'Can I ask you something?'

'Go on then.'

'What if you say no?'

'I might not.'

She sighed. 'My mother will die tonight.'

'Don't talk nonsense! That's rubbish.'

Water dripped off her dress. 'She'll die. She'll die . . . You will do as I ask, won't you?' she said, squeezing my arm.

'You haven't told me what you want yet.'

'My mother has been starving for three days. She hasn't had a thing. If you were to give me your fish I could grill it over a fire, and at least she'd get something to eat.'

I handed it to her straight away. She took it off me, full of happiness, and ran off.

I got home, my insides crushed at the thought of Virginie's

plight, and as I rang the doorbell I felt that I had done a good deed in the eyes of God.

Niyazi opened the door and announced my arrival. My father was inside.

'Come on in then, you laggard,' he said. 'You've just been aimlessly wandering around all day, haven't you?'

'No,' I said, 'I haven't been wandering around. Although I didn't manage to catch any fish either. The sea was terrible.'

Niyazi butted in. 'He only got one. I get sores on my feet from walking around all day.'

My father snapped at my mother. 'What are you lot staring at? Get a move on then! Get that fish on the grill!'

My mother asked me to pass it to her.

'What fish?' I asked. 'I didn't catch anything!'

My father turned to Niyazi. 'What was all that about a fish then?'

'Dunno what he did with it. I saw him walking around, and he had a fish then . . .'

My father came up to me. 'Where's the bloody fish?'

'I didn't catch anything!'

'Oh no?' said Niyazi. 'Weren't you walking back with that Armenian girl? Didn't you say you only caught one?'

I was cornered. 'I gave it to that girl because for three days her mother –'

My father exploded. 'We have no gas, no bread, no sugar, nothing to eat, nothing to wear. I'm here racking my brains trying to think of what to do, and you go giving hand-outs to some silly little tart. What do you think you are, some holy benefactor feeding the poor?' And then he gave me the most perfect beating imaginable.

He went on muttering until the early hours.

I got into bed, pulled the duvet over my head and wondered at the sort of world we lived in. You spend the day in the rain, get blown around, shiver, die, I thought to myself, and then you get a beating and get told off for it . . .

I dreamed of Virginie that night. She was beaming at me with her rows of pearly white teeth.

10

We were living in a bedsitting room in Ra's Beirut. My father occupied the right-hand corner of the concrete entrance as one came in from the street. He kept a crate in front of him, and on it were medicine bottles, small notepads, various powders in torn cylindrical boxes, shoe polish, varnishes, pens and pencils of various sizes, pieces of paper on which he'd written notes, as well as morsels of cured beef rind . . .

The crate rested on a haircloth sack which was white with purple lines. An old cushion lay next to it. My father would tell us that he had had this cushion since he was a child. 'It smells of my mother, of my homeland,' he'd tell us.

He would read until the middle of the night, sometimes later, and seldom get much sleep. We had brought over all his books with us. He was surrounded by magazines in dark covers with names like *The Righteous Way* and *The True Path*, histories of all sizes and dog-eared copies of the Old Testament, the Koran, the Psalms of David and other religious texts. I particularly remember his *History of Politics*, a large tome with a cigarette burn on the side of its red cover, which never strayed far from his immediate reach.

Soon after we moved there he started getting severe pains in his stomach. The doctor at our consulate advised him to take certain medicines, but the pharmacists wanted a lot of money to supply them. So my father had looked up treatments in ancient medicine and herb books and created his own mixture of local herbs. He always swore that this medicine saved his life.

My father had a routine. Every Friday he would gather us together and take us to the countryside. I never liked this habit of his. I didn't like it back home, and I didn't like it in Beirut. We would put all our food in baskets, and off we'd go. When we got out of the city we would often find other Turkish families there like us, picnicking under the trees. My mother and sisters loved such occasions, particularly if a nearby family had daughters of a similar age to my sisters. My sisters would go wild at the freedom from being cooped up in small rooms, pick flowers and make them into bouquets. We would sit in the fields and eat our

Adana-style raw *köfte*. The men would sit apart. They would speak of things back home and of the old days. My father would find a way to steer the conversation to religion, bring out his dark notebook, read extracts from the Koran he had copied out and get all excited at the opportunity to explore their meaning in front of a new audience. And the more he grew excited the more people would come over to listen, their curiosity aroused as they happened by.

Sometimes there would be rabbis, priests or imams in the crowd. Matters that had been gone over time and again for a thousand or more years would once more be dredged up and discussed at length, and hours would pass. The whole day would be whiled away, and nothing would be settled at the end of it.

It was Ramadan. The mansion opposite us was home to a rich money-changer. He was a devout Muslim. We would sometimes be invited over to break our fast with him, and he would offer us a splendid spread. My father would usually feel ill on our return.

The end of Ramadan came in the midst of winter. Our clothes were falling apart. I was still out of work. Niyazi had long since sold off the books of any value my father owned. My parents would do their calculations for hours on end, but at the end of the day we had no work, and nor did we get the anticipated financial assistance from back home.

On the eve of the Eid festival I was late getting back. I knocked on the door, dreading punishment and wondering what it would be this time. There was an unusual silence in our house, while all the lights were on in the mansion across the road. I could hear a voice reading from the Koran and someone in wooden shoes walking along the marble floors.

My middle sister opened our door in a white head-scarf, her anxious face a sickly yellow. 'Hurry. Our father's dying!'

I ran in. The room was darker than usual, my father was lying in bed.

'Oh, my poor children. Oh dear me.' My mother was sitting next to him, wailing, my sisters were crying, and Niyazi was by his side. He was crying, too.

At one point my mother gave my father the news of my arrival. 'Look, your son's here. See. You've been asking . . .'

He peered up through bloodshot eyes. 'What? Where? Which one?'

'Look, right here. Your eldest.'

He reached out towards me. 'Son,' he said. 'Your father's dying. You'll be orphans. I have treated you harshly. I've often beaten you. Please forgive me. I haven't left you any worldly goods . . . But, then, that's life . . . Now, get your head together, do as your mother says; be good to your brother and sisters. Look after them. Whatever you do, don't leave each other . . . Write to your relations back home, say your father's dead, tell them there's no one to look after you and ask for some money. Go back home!'

My mother and sisters started to cry even louder. As for me, I probably felt much more than they did, yet I was standing tall, wanting to cry but unable to bring myself to let go. I thought it wouldn't be right. On the one hand, I thought crying was childish, but, on the other, I appreciated that, given the circumstances, it seemed inappropriate to be standing like a gatepost while all around me were sobbing their hearts out. I turned my head to one side and dabbed some spittle under my eyes. At least I wouldn't get called callous.

'If at all possible,' continued my father weakly, 'take my body with you. Don't leave me in this foreign land.'

For weeks now, as the festival approached, he had been growing more and more depressed, despite my mother's attempts to cheer him up. He had been very hard on himself for not getting the children new clothes for Eid. Apparently he had been walking along the square with my little sister that morning and had seen families laden with parcels and packages, their children milling around them joyfully. At least, that's how it appeared to my father. So he had been put in mind of the good old days and how things used to be for us . . .

Suddenly his eyes clouded over, everything went topsy-turvy, and he collapsed. My sister started to cry. People ran up to them. Then, some time later, an Armenian driver who recognized my father brought them home.

'So where did you get the money to pay the driver?' I asked.

'Oh dear,' said my mother. 'We really didn't think of it, and he didn't ask.'

We waited by my father's bedside until dawn. He would drop off now and then, stir and mumble a bit, fall asleep once more, come to again, kiss us and ask our forgiveness.

The morning broke with a damp coldness. My mother got my little sister dressed first and cut a red strip off one of the scraps of cloth and tied it in a bow around her head. The other girls put on their tatty old pale pink print dresses that they wore week in, week out. My father was sitting up in bed, his blanket draped around his shoulders. We tried to appear happy and carefree, hoping that he would get well again that night.

There were hurried footsteps in the streets. The faithful were rushing off to Eid prayers.

At one point my father looked at my mother. 'Well, woman, isn't there a bit of coffee somewhere?'

She was staring into the sack of scrap cloth.

'I so fancied a cup . . .' he murmured.

We children had thought we might go over to the moneychanger's mansion to pay our respects. Neither of our parents suggested it, but I am sure we had all thought of going across, kissing hands in respect and perhaps getting a little spending money in return.

But first we had to kiss the hands of our parents. We lined up according to age, as we always used to. I was first, Niyazi behind me, then the girls. In turn we each kissed first my father's hand and then my mother's. They kissed us in return and wished that 'God would always grant us such pleasures'. My father looked brave. My mother tried to hide her tears.

We went out on to the street. The sun reflected back off the wet paving stones. The doors of the mansion were wide open. Lots of people, coming and going . . . The doorway was guarded by a pair of doormen, large men with broad moustaches, each wearing a fez.

We went through the door and slowly started to walk across the white heavy paving slabs that covered the broad courtyard. We were just about to ascend the stairs when the doormen rushed over and blocked our way.

'Be off with you! Go on!' they said. They must have thought we were beggars.

The great big mansion spun around above my head, and everything started to go dark. My two sisters had immediately turned to head back. My youngest sister was trying to climb the stairs when one of the doormen grabbed her by the arm and deposited her by the street gate. Niyazi was standing by the gate, stunned.

I left, too. I waited, shamed, stripped of my self-respect, my humanity trampled underfoot, feeling as if I had sinned unforgivably. What didn't go through my mind? Many things flashed through, some – it must be confessed – involving dynamiting the mansion together with everyone in it.

I was lost in thought. Then I noticed that my youngest sister wasn't with us. She was standing across the street, next to the tray of a halva seller, looking at the sweetmeats. Before I got a chance to call her back, a man approached the seller. He had two children in tow and bought them a piece of halva each. He must have taken to my sister because he spontaneously turned and gave her a piece, too.

She ran across to us. 'Look, I've got halva . . . That nice man gave it to me.'

The streets were growing crowded. A truck sped past, accompanied by children's songs and laughter. Drumbeats and music wafted across from a distance. The bright sunshine started to warm the air.

We returned home. My father was still in bed, my mother at his side, and they were talking. She was tearful. He didn't ask us what had happened, but I suppose they must have read it in our faces, for their eyes went dark.

'Damn them!' exclaimed my mother.

My little sister went up to my father, halva in hand, 'Anyway, what sort of daddy are you?' she lisped. 'Everybody else's daddies are nice!'

My father tensed as if he'd been shot, his hollow eyes froze . . . Apparitions of fear and despair flew around the room.

My father spent the following two and a half months bedridden, running a temperature, mumbling to himself.

11

The streets of Beirut went in straight lines, as if they had been drawn with a ruler and laid out by some giant hand. We would wander these crowded streets without a penny to our name, staring in at the windows of toyshops for hours on end.

With hands in my pockets and cap pushed back on my head, I would walk the streets engrossed by the beautiful things around me while never entertaining any thought of possessing them.

I would wake up early each morning and, to escape the oppressive atmosphere of the house and my father's disapproving looks, go into the streets in search of employment. But there was no work to be found. Who would take on a dreamy, vacant kid who spoke no language other than his own? Even though I felt as strong as Jano and as nimble as Yanik from my favourite book *Two Friends Travel the World*, and, although I was bright enough to laugh secretly at the piggy eyes and the multiple chins of would-be bosses, people like that somehow scared me. So I would end up wandering the Armenian quarter, nipping over to the priests' school within its orange grove, then making my way to the shore, strolling over to the pier where the fishermen would fish in rows, and not return home until it had gone dark.

It was another one of these days. I had reluctantly returned home, my mind full of the bright sunshine, the blue skies, the clear sea and the huge apartment blocks I had been admiring all day.

My father was in his usual place, in among his piles of books and newspapers. They hadn't yet lit a lamp. In that dusky light he looked like a living heap of hate and abuse.

Just as I was sneaking in past him he turned. 'Don't go off anywhere tomorrow. Ibrahim effendi is coming around. He's found you a job.' I was so happy . . . It was as if they had said, 'Get ready. You're off to Adana tomorrow.'

I was full of joy as I regarded the owner of those lips that swore at me every time they opened, the owner of that angry face, the sonorous voice. Suddenly they all seemed endearing. I decided I wouldn't think ill of him any longer; nor would I swear at him inwardly. I regretted that I had once felt I wouldn't care if he died. I had forgiven this man, the man who told me I now had a job; forgiven all his abuse and insults. So much so that I felt the urge to wrap my arms around him and exclaim, 'Oh, Dad, Dad . . . You have no idea the things I thought about you', and confide in him all my thoughts and feelings and beg his forgiveness, kiss him, burst into tears. I could hardly contain myself.

But in his dark corner he had already lost himself in his books again. I don't suppose he was aware of the delight making my heart flutter, of the thoughts racing through my brain.

He lifted his head up and regarded me for a few moments. 'What?' he asked. 'What are you standing around like that for? You don't like the thought of having to do some work, do you? Lazing around has become a habit. Now listen here. No father is under any obligation to feed a seventeen-year-old son! You'll go with Ibrahim effendi tomorrow, and you'll start your job. Now off you go!'

All my warm feelings towards him smashed into smithereens, like a sheet of glass dropped on a marble floor. I wish he hadn't been like that . . . If he hadn't been like that I might have continued to love him. And after that? Bad, bad feelings . . . I didn't care if he lived or died. I didn't love him. I had no love for him at all.

Trying to keep my lips firmly shut so as not to swear, I walked into the room where the rest of the family were. It must have been past midnight. My mother and sisters were fast asleep. I heard the occasional cough from the other side of the door.

Niyazi and I lay side by side, talking in whispers.

'What's he like!' I exclaimed.

'Well, what can he do? He's only thinking of us.'

'Leave it out! Only thinking of us! Even to you . . . There you are, walking the streets all day long . . .'

Niyazi was glad to have someone to share the burden with of feeding seven mouths. 'Come off it,' he said. 'At the start of the week we'll have our allowance in your pocket, and we can go off to the fields.'

'Of course we will. It's not as if he can say anything about us playing football then!'

'Of course he can't. It's not as if he's still feeding us. We'll stand up to him . . . Won't we?'

'We certainly will,' I agreed. 'All he does is shout. I get so annoyed!'

'What about me? I get back from work, and he doesn't even ask if I'm tired or hungry. How much money am I giving him? That's all he's interested in.'

'He told me that old Ibrahim effendi had found me a job. You know, I was so happy. Fantastic, I thought. I didn't tell him all the things we've been dreaming about – our mother baking nice food again, mixing up all the ingredients . . . "Mum," I'm going to say, "Let's have a dessert . . ." You'd like a bit of that, wouldn't you?'

'What a stupid question! The thought of having dessert after a meal!'

'Once they see I'm an honest worker they'll probably put up my wages.'

'Of course they will. Integrity, that's what they want.'

'Oh, Niyazi, I can't wait till tomorrow!'

I don't know whether he fell asleep first or I. When I woke the sun was on the white curtains of the room.

12

'Fine . . . The father owns a printing press, so the son just walks into a job,' I remember my father saying and trying to hide his deep distaste as he talked to Ibrahim effendi, spitting out his words bitterly. Yet Ibrahim effendi was a smiling, pleasant enough man with thick hair that stood on end, who reminded me of a large cockerel when he stood up straight. When he spoke Turkish he would make guttural 'N' sounds as one would when speaking Arabic.

That day we set off, Ibrahim effendi leading the way, and walked through the sun-filled streets of Beirut. We turned off a square down a steep street. The thoroughfare was no more than a narrow, shady passageway leading down between large apartment blocks. We walked down the alley for some time and reached a dead end, with little shops and taverns and street sellers offering fish and bananas. The place reeked of raki and pickles. We came up to a narrow door, with a marble plate above it inscribed in

Arabic, indicating that the wooden building was a print shop. He climbed the stairs, and I followed. We entered a spacious typesetting room. To a right stood a large machine shaped like a guillotine, used for cutting paper, and on the left another machine, a shiny, sparkling case with cogs and wheels which I later found out was for gilding. Facing us were the typesetting blocks.

Ibrahim effendi waved his hand in greeting to the people there and walked towards a half-concealed door on the left. 'You wait,' he said.

As the print-shop workers toiled with blackened hands and faces, sleeves rolled up past their elbows, now and then they would lift up their heads and glance over in my direction. It was disconcerting. I felt unimportant and small among all that activity. I could hear the rumble of Ibrahim effendi's voice. As the people looked over with their dirty faces I felt that they knew why I was standing there and were inwardly laughing at me. I feared they'd be thinking: Doesn't speak the language, doesn't know a thing about printing. Just wants to pull strings and be mollycoddled.

I had never been given preferential treatment in my life. At primary school I was among the idlers, and for a long time – actually, I think, until I finished school – I struggled to escape that group. But never once did my father say anything to anyone or have a word in the teacher's ear to try to get me through the classes. So when I felt that favours had been involved in me getting this job it embarrassed me deeply.

Finally Ibrahim effendi appeared at the door and came out, followed by a plump and smartly dressed man. He pointed me out to him, but he didn't even look at me, although it seemed to me that he may have fleetingly glanced at my worn-out boots.

Ibrahim effendi was talking, waving his arms about, occasionally turning to the print workers, his head leaning to one side. They were miserably shaking their heads. As they spoke in Arabic I couldn't understand a word of what he said or what replies the plump man made. But I had the impression he was being told that I was the son of a poor refugee and that he was being begged to give me a job, even if there was no need for extra staff.

I was particularly taken aback by a young woman who, looking like a china doll with blonde curls, emerged from a side door, stopped when she saw Ibrahim effendi, listened to what he was saying and turned towards me and looked me up and down. I felt as if I had been mocked and belittled in front of her and had no pride left. I was shaking all over, my hands were freezing, and my ears burned.

Ibrahim effendi must have finally got his way, because he came over to me. 'Well, that's you sorted out,' he said, 'but it's the end of me . . .'

The print workers were staring at us in wonderment. I was lost in the conversation taking place between the blonde girl and her smartly dressed boss. Ibrahim effendi was addressing me, telling me how they had only taken me on as a favour to him, not that they needed extra help. They would pay me a hundred and fifty Syrian piastres a week. The girl kept staring at me. When her serene blue eyes looked into mine something lukewarm poured down through me.

She seemed to attach no importance to the compliments of her smart boss. If she hadn't been wearing a black apron one might have mistaken her for a snooty apartment owner, one who had been brought up on limitless supplies of biscuits, ham, steaks and roast dinners, but she had about her the gravitas and maturity of those who have suffered while young.

She was perfectly serious as the smart boss withdrew to his room, stroking his chin. She looked at me one last time and then left, slipping away quietly through the door through which she had entered. Then Ibrahim effendi left.

I stood there with my pride wounded, confused, waiting.

For whom? For what?

Who knows.

13

My job was to turn the handle on the paper-cutting machine. My supervisor was a thin, tall man who wore a maroon fez pulled over his left eyebrow. He loved a joke. He'd tease anybody and would frequently laugh out loud. He'd keep a bottle of raki in the inside pocket of his jacket, which would hang off a rail on the machine.

He would straighten the reams of paper on the metal table of the machine and push them under the blade. 'Go on!' he'd shout at me. Having done his part he would pull his bottle out of his pocket and take a swig. I would gather my strength together and turn the handle with my scrawny arms, using all my might. He would replace the bottle when the machine finished cutting the paper. 'Enough!' he'd call out.

I would take another deep breath and grab the handle of the iron wheel, which turned at great speed and hurt my hands as it whirled. I would try and keep the pain under control by clenching my teeth, attack the wheel once more and try to wrestle it to a standstill. If it hadn't lost some of its momentum it usually flung me against the wall beyond.

It was obvious that this was a job for a large, well-built person. But I was afraid that if I allowed anyone to realize this they would think: He can't do this job, and there's nothing else here for him. Then they would show me the door. If this were to happen and I did lose my job I knew I would endure the shame back home and have to put up with my father's dirty looks and hurtful remarks. So I put up with the pain of operating that handle.

I would arrive before anyone else in the morning, squat down next to the machine and eat a piece of dark bread and the few olives I had brought over from home. Soon the other workers and typesetters would arrive, and we would all start our jobs.

I worked non-stop all morning and then, after an hour's lunch break, until seven or eight o'clock at night, all the while deeply resenting the machine handle that so hurt me, shredded my nerves and left me drenched in sweat.

When I arrived before the others in the morning I would pray and praise his name. But the iron arm and its wooden sheath would look at me disapprovingly through the nut on the end of the handle, and my prayers would be ignored completely.

To be honest I had noticed that prayers were rather ineffectual in the face of all that machinery. In this centre of massive fly-wheels and cogs, drowning in the rumble of this giant machine,

God seemed as feeble and insubstantial as a strip of muslin nailed to a wall. I could see the heresy in the paper-cutter, how it stood up to God, its calculated ambition recognizing no excuse, forgiving no one and ripping apart any hint of idleness. Its power was unstoppable by prayer. Such power held me in awe. In my fearful admiration I actually grew to respect the machine. It was an extension to a man's arm, the most honest friend a man could have, his assistant, his slave, yet I still feared it.

Life had become a dangerous road to walk down, and I found myself wondering if I could do it. What would happen, I wondered, if my father suddenly died? It seemed that his very existence held the magic that kept the family together. Although I didn't love him I was afraid of him, and although I longed to run off to be free of him I still found in him the strength of a tree one might lean against or a sturdy oak branch stopping one from falling down a cliff.

As I turned the handle I often talked to myself. I would end up lost in an argument with another me, going over these thoughts and similar ones. My supervisor would shout 'Stop!' several times at me, and I would be in a world of my own and not hear him, so he would give me a slap on the neck to snap me out of it.

When our day was over, at around six or seven after some twelve hours of work, I would leave with the others, jacket over my shoulder, hands and face blackened, just like them. In fact I intentionally slung my jacket over my shoulder to emulate them and made sure my hand and face were as filthy as theirs. As I walked home I would feel enormously proud and forget my aching arms.

I would return to the family I was now supporting, feeling as strong and agile as a wild deer, as confident as a man who has no superior, then retire to bed.

I hadn't yet been paid, but my standing at home had risen immeasurably. When I got in from work my father would greet me with a smile, turn to my sisters and say, 'Come on, girls. Where are you? Have you got the water ready for your brother? Ayshe, come and take your brother's jacket. Hayrinnisa, don't gawp. The boy's starving. Get the table ready.' He would have a go at them all and enquire about my day with a tenderness alien to me. 'Oh, they do look sore. I'm sure it must have hurt,' he'd say and lapse into deep thought.

In any case, I was quite happy with the way things were going. As I walked to work early in the morning, through the deserted streets, I would be full of dread, though, as if the day might not end and that I'd never make the evening.

But the days went by.

14

On Saturday, after lunch-break, they started handing out our wages. As well as the workers in our print shop, the women and girls from the chocolate factory next door – which also belonged to our boss – gathered in front of the door of our boss. The blonde girl was among them. I sat on an upturned crate and watched the murmuring crowd babbling away, pushing and shoving.

The women were uninhibited, the girls coquettish. They were all full of anticipation, happy at receiving their pay. Even the older ones were getting carried away, chatting with the young ones, seeming lively and in high spirits, perhaps genuinely cheerful at the sight of others' joy.

Then I saw the blonde girl . . . She seemed prettier than ever today. She had her hair tied tightly in a blue ribbon and wore pretty small red earrings. I don't know why, but I didn't like it. I didn't want her laughing with the others, playing about. My eyes fell on my boots again, and I observed the splits in the sides. I felt that a man with footwear like this had no right to love any girl. I tried to make my feet inconspicuous and placed one on top of the other, but to no avail . . . I couldn't hide the state of them.

She was still laughing and chatting; surrounded by all these people, both young and old. She was enjoying herself like the rest of them, although I had thought she wasn't really the laughing kind.

Even our big-nosed supervisor was laughing.

I felt cross. Her tarty shoes, red earrings, blue ribbon – she had to get rid of them, stop laughing and stop talking to other people! The boss chucked her under her chin. Was that all? Would it go any further? It was awful. Why didn't she reject his advances? She should have spat in his face. I would have backed her up; of course I would. What would they do if I did? Sack me? Oh God! If it wasn't for my father, my mother, my sisters, my brother . . . If only I was alone in the world. One punch on the boss's jaw, then I'd grab her by the wrist, and off we'd go . . . We'd board the three-funnelled ship at the harbour, and the ship would take us to America!

America! As I conjured the name I thought of buildings a hundred storeys high, memorized by staring endlessly at photographs of them, pictured in my mind's eye the fat-bellied bosses of the American movies I had seen and thought of cool woods full of large broad-leafed trees.

I had mainly learned about America from the book *Two Friends Travel the World.* I had wandered through their Chinese quarters, I had punched the Mexican bandits in their bandannas alongside Jano, I had been captured by the Red Indians with Yanik and experienced the thrill of being tied to a stake with him and nearly being burned alive. Jano was the physically stronger one, but Yanik was always that little bit sharper, that bit more agile, more aware. I felt he had the light-footedness of a deer.

I became aware of my supervisor and snapped out of my reverie. He was laughing. He showed me to the boss's room. I got up, and the women surrounding my girl gave way. I thought I felt their mocking eyes on me. I walked past them, my cheeks ablaze. It was the first time I had entered the office. Delicate net curtains hung in the windows, and the chairs were of the finest morocco goatskin. A large glass-topped chestnut desk dominated the room. And, laying on the glass were wads and wads of cash . . .

The boss's face turned sour at seeing me. He mumbled something. It was obvious that he wasn't happy to have an unnecessary worker on the payroll. He took two paper notes and some coins and pushed them across the table with the back of his hand. For the first time in my life I was getting paid.

I approached the desk. As my ears rang, and everything seemed to grow dark, I scooped the money into the palm of my hand and looked up at the man to thank him.

He maintained his sour expression. '*Go on, go on!*' he said.

I walked back to the door. The girl was standing there. She glanced at the money I was holding. Then she looked into my eyes. She curled her lip at the pitiful amount.

The door, the crowd in front of the door, the red earrings in that crowd, they all blurred together in a spin.

I walked on. When I sat back down on my crate my ears were still ringing, and the print shop seemed to be whirling.

So she curled her lip. Curled her lip, did she? What did I expect, the little tart . . . If she wasn't a whore, she wouldn't have let him chuck her under her chin. But she curled her lips at me. Why? Because I wasn't earning enough? I looked at her shoes . . .

I raised my head, and there she was, laughing under her blue ribbon. 'Are you Armenian?'

'No.'

'What then?'

'I'm Turkish.'

'Turkish?'

Her eyes widened, and she grew serious. 'So you're Turkish?'

'Yes. What's so amazing?'

'Oh, I'd been told you were Armenian.'

I had lowered my head once more, but she still stood there. I found myself looking into her eyes. 'You curled your lips at my money!' I said.

'When?'

'Just now, as I was leaving the office.'

She thought about this. 'I don't remember that.'

'Really? Are you saying you didn't curl your lip?'

'Certainly not!'

'Are you Turkish, too?'

'No, I'm Greek . . . You know the lithographer Barba Dimitri?'

'Yes.'

'He's my father.'

'He's your father? He drinks a lot!'

'He does . . . Anyway what brought you here?'

'To the print shop?'

'No, to Beirut.'

'I don't know . . . First my father came, then we followed.'

'Is your father a refugee?'

'Yes.'

'Come on, let's go.' She started to move off.

I pushed past the mocking looks of the crowd in front of the boss's door and followed her out. We crossed the road, then turned into a deserted alleyway.

'You don't earn much,' she said.

'Very little.'

'Do you look after your family?'

'I do.'

'I look after mine, too.'

'What about your father?'

'He's no good. He drinks it all.'

I abruptly changed the subject. 'We used to be very rich back home. Now I feel ashamed.'

'About what?'

'These boots, for one thing . . .'

'Forget them.'

'How can I? Look at the state of them!'

'They're nothing to be ashamed of. I have an older brother, and he always says that if anyone feels shamed by poverty it should be the rich people who look on.'

'And what do you say?'

'Oh, we all say that. My father does, too. Not that it matters . . .'

'What does your brother do?'

'He's a cobbler. He does piece-work. Makes shoes at home.'

'You know, you don't look Greek.'

She laughed. 'So what do I look like?'

'You look Turkish.'

'How did you guess?'

'Your Turkish is excellent.'

'We're actually from Istanbul . . . We went over to Athens during the Exchange. I was very small.'

'Then?'

'Then they imprisoned my brother.'

'And?'

'He escaped from prison and came here. Later we followed.'

'Why did they imprison your brother?'

'Long story.'

We walked for another ten minutes and suddenly saw the sea. In the bright sunshine it looked a placid dusty blue, stretching out for ever. In the distance, a sail; further on were pale-blue ghostly mountains.

'There's our house,' she said, pointing to a small cabin with its back to the sea, covered in reeds.

'You live there?'

'Yes.'

'Why?'

She laughed. 'Why do you wear those old boots?'

'Huh?'

'It not a bad house, you know! Some nights when the sea is rough we hear the breaking waves singing us to sleep. And other things, too . . .'

We approached the cabin. There was a small boat moored by the shore.

'Is this yours, too?'

'Yes.'

'What do you do with it?'

'You ask a lot of questions!' she said with a smile.

'I do. I'm sorry.'

'Wait a minute,' she said as we approached the door. She had stopped. 'What was your name?'

I told her.

'Mine's Eleni.'

She went in and a few moments later came out with her mother. She greeted me warmly. She looked fairly young, but half her hair was grey. Eleni was talking about me non-stop. I kissed the woman's hand, and we went inside. The room was small and dark. In the far corner was a table piled high with books, and a heavily built young man sat by the table on a low stool. He had a wispy beard, and he was cutting out yellow leather uppers for shoes. His curved blade moved quickly and expertly.

'Welcome, lad!' he said.

I liked him. I wondered if I might be as well-built and handsome as he was when I grew up.

Eleni's mother kept asking me about Turkey.

When Eleni's brother found out that my father was a refugee he put down his blade. 'A political exile, eh? What's his name?'

I told him.

'I've heard of him,' he said, 'but what good is he going to do? What could come of that sort of struggle?' With that he returned to his work.

I was annoyed. I felt my father was above criticism. I stared at Eleni's brother with dislike. 'My father's a lawyer', I said, 'and very well read. You should see all his books.'

He paid no attention.

'We were very rich back home.'

Still no reaction. He looked up after a while. 'You,' he said, 'shouldn't attach too much importance to such things. Try to be much, much, much better than your father.' He carefully looked me up and down and turned back to his work.

Eleni and I went back outside to the sun, the sea and the mountains. 'What did your brother mean?' I asked.

'Don't you know?'

'No.'

'You'll find out one day, my boy!' she said and gave me a friendly punch on the chin.

The seagulls were descending on the sea and, like splashes of foam, rising up into the sky again. There was a gentle breeze. The distant sail was still there. I took my cap off. Eleni and I sat down on the grass.

'Do you read novels?' she asked.

'I don't enjoy fiction,' I responded, 'but I love *Two Friends Travel the World*. Have you read it?'

She hadn't.

I looked at her with pity. 'I read all four volumes, oh, maybe ten times,' I said and started to tell her the story.

That day Eleni and I became good friends. We sat on the grass, picnicked with bread, cheese and spring onions, played tag, got covered in sweat, then rested against the wall of the cabin. We sat together watching a glorious sunset as the huge red orb of the sun slowly disappeared behind the darkening navy waves.

She talked of many things.

'I'm going to give you some books,' she said finally. 'Read those. They'll be much more use to you than your beloved *Two Friends Travel the World*!'

By the time I got home it was dark. My father was again in his corner by the entrance, surrounded by his books. The light had been lit early today, and he was in a good mood. As I pulled my pay out of my pocket he asked, 'Weren't you off this afternoon?'

I told him we were late getting paid and placed the money in the palm of his hand.

He took it and waved it around his head a few times. 'I won't die after all,' he beamed. 'My son is earning money!'

15

Even though I had made a decision to hide my relationship with Eleni from Niyazi I nudged him soon after I got into bed. 'Niyazi!'

He had his back to me. Either he was very tired or he was being pig-headed. He was letting himself drift off. I nudged him again. 'Hey, Niyazi!'

'Mmm.'

'Hey, wake up!'

'What is it? What's going on?'

'Don't shout! Turn around and talk to me.'

'Suppose I turn around. Then what?'

'Stop pretending to be asleep!'

'Who's pretending? I said I'm tired. Are you deaf or something?'

'But I can't get to sleep.'

'So?'

'Nothing . . . I just wanted to talk.'

'Not now. I'm tired.'

'I'll pay you.'

'I don't feel like talking.'

'Not even if I pay you?'

'I don't care. I'm tired.'

'Hey, I'm offering money, you idiot.'

'Offering money, eh? How much?'

'I thought you were tired.'

'Well, I am. I am . . . How much?'

'Oh, forget the money!'

'I'm not listening unless you pay. And, I'll call Dad.'

'You greedy little sod! Keep your voice down.'

'Whatever you say. One cry to Dad, I'll say I was asleep; you woke me up; you're not letting me sleep . . . It's up to you.'

'So how much do you want?'

'Ten piastres should cover it.'

'That's too much!'

'If it's too much I'm not listening . . . Just shut up. One more word from you . . .'

'But I can't pay it all now.'

'Oh?'

'Next week, when I get paid.'

'Really?'

I eventually talked him into it – but on one condition. If I welched on the deal he knew what to do. So we started to talk.

'There's this Greek girl at work, Niyazi. If you saw her . . . She's as pretty as a picture.'

'Oh no! Not another girl! Have you lost your senses?'

'What do you mean?'

'You've got into all kinds of trouble chasing after a bit of skirt, and you're still at it,' he said and muttered, 'First it was that Naciye, then that Armenian girl, and now this . . . It's not as if he gets anywhere.'

'That's what you think!'

'What, you did something with Naciye?'

'I was just saying: That's what you think.'

'OK, so that's only what I think. And . . . ?'

'Now . . . Forget that Naciye and stuff. Just her blue ribbon . . .'

'Do you get on?'

'Really well. Everyone was getting paid, and I was watching them. Then she came up to me. She'd been told I was Armenian. I told her I was Turkish. She spoke Turkish beautifully. She's originally from Istanbul, but her family went over to Athens in the Exchange. What a girl!'

'So you get on then?'

'Of course . . . I even . . .' I almost let slip that I had been over to her house.

'So you've known her a couple of days. That's a bit soon to decide you get on, isn't it?'

'Well, my son, these things go like that.'

'*Your son?* Remember that beating you took in Antakya?'

The beating in Antakya! I remembered . . . One day my father overheard me calling Niyazi 'my son' and stood in front of me. Who did I think I was calling him 'my son'? 'Go into the garden,' he said, 'and bring me a good, heavy stick that won't break.'

I went and searched everywhere. I picked up every stout stick that seemed a likely candidate and hid them behind the rose bushes. Then I picked a weak-looking one and took it into the house. My father didn't inspect the stick. It broke in half on the third blow, and I escaped a really heavy beating.

'Never mind that . . .' I said to Niyazi. 'It's just a turn of phrase.'

'You watch your tongue.'

'Her wavy blonde hair . . . You know what she does to it? She takes this blue ribbon . . . But it's the earrings that really do it . . . And those little patent-leather shoes.'

'Oh yeah, sure . . .'

I don't know when we fell asleep.

I woke up in the morning. I had had the most wonderful dream. Eleni and I were together, side by side on the deck of a snow-white transatlantic liner gliding across the deep blue sea. There was a gentle breeze, and seagulls hovered near by. Then a sudden commotion, bells ringing, whistles blowing. The police arrived. There was a deserter on the ship; they were conducting a search. Then the ship came to a halt and smaller steamboats pulled up. I saw the police leave, taking my father away. He grabbed my ear as they dragged him off. Clamped between his fingers, my ear stretched and stretched, longer and longer . . .

It turned out I'd been mumbling in my sleep and my father really had been pulling my ear. Clasping my breakfast bag, I went to work.

16

I kept going next door to the chocolate factory where she worked. One day the boss grabbed me by the ear in front of the girls, dragged me back to my machine and yelled at me. I guessed he was telling me that I'd be sacked if he caught me there again.

I was so embarrassed. It's fair to say that, thanks to my father, I had been given full training in readiness for such an occasion, but I still found it undignified. I felt worse and worse over the following hour, and I had the distinct impression that I had shrunk in size, my cheeks had caved in, my wrists had got even scrawnier and that I had become quite a gruesome sight to behold.

I felt that all the metal, wood, glass, humans and machines in the print shop had ganged up on me and were having a good laugh at my expense. The paper-cutting machine, usually the one to give me the dirtiest of looks, now seemed to be smiling unpleasantly as the bolt on its handle gave it the appearance of sticking its tongue out at me. My boots? They had really fallen apart. For the first time in my life I deeply resented being a nobody and stood there in a daze. I didn't get angry, or, rather, I didn't know how to get angry. I didn't think I had the right to, anyway.

Suddenly Eleni was there, red in the face. 'Don't you worry about a thing,' she said. 'I'll give him what for!' She marched over to the boss's door and walked in without knocking.

I wondered exactly how she proposed to give him what for. I heard angry voices coming from the room. The print workers were laughing to themselves, looking at me and shaking their heads. Eleni's angry voice rose in volume. I, meanwhile, felt ashamed for not doing a thing.

Eleni emerged. 'Did you hear me shouting at him?' she asked me.

'I heard you, but I have no idea what you said.'

'You wouldn't believe what I said to him! I really made him look stupid . . . From now on I'm going to work here, too, on the gilding machine right there!'

'Are you really?'

'Honestly!'

'How did you swing that?'

I never did understand how she managed it, but from that day on Eleni worked at the gilding machine. She would pass me paper, and I would take it, or I would pass paper to her, and she would take it. We'd both have our hands and faces covered in gilding, but we'd work with such zeal . . .

17

One day Eleni and her father Dimitri disappeared. Nobody had any idea what had happened, not even the boss. He asked me if I knew. I decided to go to their house after work, but Niyazi came over, and I had to go straight home.

Not the following day but the day after that – a Saturday – I left work after being paid and finally got to their place. The house was still there, but there were no curtains in the windows, the door was hanging open, and it looked very sorry for itself. I went over to see the family's Armenian neighbours.

The woman there gave me the stunning news. 'Two days ago they were given twenty-four hours to leave Lebanese soil.' She went on: 'I told them this would happen. That son of theirs, you know that son? He'll be the death of them, you mark my words. You know that boat of theirs? He would pile them in, and off they would go. And that house of theirs. Do you know how many times the police raided it?'

At that point, I decided that I really didn't like Beirut. I wandered back through the deserted streets, angry and upset.

That night, I cried myself to sleep.

18

I carried on with my job, but my heart wasn't in it. As I collected my fourth week's wages my boss said a few harsh things, and I realized I was being sacked. I couldn't have cared less, but my father was upset, and my mother . . .

I was unemployed once more; hands in my empty pockets, cap pushed back on my head, back at the seaside, the priests' school, the fields, the pier . . . The days passed.

Even I was aware of my change in outlook. I would get home wearing a long face, not talk to anybody, answer questions only if I had to, mostly just talking to myself and actually beginning to enjoy it.

I was sick and tired of these foreign lands. It had been two years, and I had not ever liked it. I missed my homeland. My homeland, my home town, my school and my friends!

Niyazi and I hardly ever spoke in bed at night. He would get disturbed by my vicious moods. I would turn my back on him in bed and drift off into a land of dreams . . .

All of a sudden I find myself back home, so I run over to Little Memet's house. He sees me standing there and is stunned. 'Wow,' he says. 'Wow, you've grown so much!'

I surprise him with phrases in Arabic. I talk of the restaurant, of Naciye, of the priests' school, of Beirut's sea, of its apartment blocks, of its streets and green trams, of Virginie and, finally, of Eleni.

The things I make up! The girl had been madly in love with me, and we would secretly meet. She had begged me not to return to Adana. But duty called; for my country, for my school, for my friends . . . And one day the boss makes a pass at Eleni, and she bursts into tears and rushes into my arms. She tells me everything. I rise in an incandescent rage . . . Face, hands, covered in the grime and grease of hard labour, I burst through his door. 'You cad!' I exclaim. 'What have you been saying to the girl?'

The boss blanches; his mouth hangs open: 'I . . . Er . . .'

I land one on his chin with my right, one with my left, followed by a good kick, and the creep's out cold.

As I'm telling Little Memet all this Kurd Ado, the teacher's son and Lizard Sureyya appear. They see me and go crazy. We'd be all over each other . . .

Little Memet would say to them, 'So much has happened to this guy. He's done more than any of us! If it had been one of us, no way would we have been able to do everything he's done.' As the others looked at me in awe he'd turn to me. 'Tell them, go on, tell them!'

So I would sit in the middle and retell all in a more cooler, more self-assured manner than when I had told Little Memet. They would listen to me with rapt attention. They had obviously lost some of their stature in my presence.

Then we play a proper game of football. I'd be centre-forward.

I have the ball . . . I run with it. Someone tries to block me, but I dodge . . . then another. I dodge again . . . I'm in front of the opposite goal, and they're all over the place. I'm unstoppable . . . An amazing strike and . . . Goal!

The ball's back in mid-field . . . I get the ball passed to me from my inside-left. I make it to their goal, again dodging my opponents as I go. Another strike, and goal!

The other team's players are objecting. He's not your usual team-mate. He can't play for you; he's too good . . . I smile to myself. Mihriban, the daughter of the family living opposite Little Memet's house, is a high-school student in a black satin pinafore, and she has been watching me excitedly for some time from her window. She keeps clapping. But I have been with so many women, so many girls . . . I am a man who has made love to Eleni. No one else here could have made love like that.

On such nights, when I was fantasizing like this, I wouldn't get a wink of sleep. As my father's frequent hollow coughs broke up my thoughts I'd grow angry and sometimes cry. I knew that the biggest obstacle to my return to Adana was him. Because of him I'd never be able to go home, never be able to tell my friends of my adventures. I was condemned to die in these foreign lands, and it would be the end of the world. (Now I find myself thinking that it would be the end of the world if I die before these memoirs are published.)

Occasionally I would fish, if the mood took me, but it rarely did. I rather hoped that I might benefit from being a rebellious, unruly burden. In spite of my father's swearing, his beatings and the strain I put on the meagre family purse I wanted to continue being a burden, hoping to make them sick and tired of me.

My father would get angry with me time and again, but eventually he would give up, saying that I should just leave and go to hell.

Most evenings I would flick through old sports magazines,

admiring the pictures of famous footballers, rereading the match reports, reliving the excitement.

The fantasies would start up again . . .

I was back home. I had been accepted into one of the clubs. I was due to play in the game that week. Finally, the day of the match arrives. I go out in my new uniform and gleaming football boots. For some reason this is a particularly important game. We must win this one. All eyes are on me. As our team comes on to the pitch to our supporters' applause the captain pulls me to one side. 'Do your best,' he says. 'You're our only hope!'

I act nonchalant and jog on to the pitch. Naturally once we're off I achieve unbelievable tackles, brilliant strikes, classic goals . . . We win and leave the pitch to the applause of the crowd. I'm carried out on people's shoulders . . .

Then my father's hollow cough would bring me back to the present, and reality would hit me like an icy slap in the face. I would bite my knuckles in frustration.

Very quietly, but full of hate, I would make my announcement. 'I'm going to go. I'm not staying here!'

My desire to return home was growing stronger by the day. I felt that first and foremost I was a Turk. And my military service was coming up soon . . . Should I go to the Consulate and ask for their help?

Why not? What are consulates for? Aren't they there to provide help to their citizens in foreign lands? That's it . . .

But then I recalled that people in the Consulate might know my father. They would mention something to him about his son's application or even ask his permission. It was obvious that my father would put a stop to it the moment he heard.

One day I approached my mother. 'I want to study!' I said. 'You brought me all the way here, and because of you I've had no education. I want to study, to learn!'

My mother told my father, and naturally he flared up. 'Don't be ridiculous, woman!' he said, 'I'm not that gullible. You shouldn't believe a word of it either! All he wants is to get away from us so he can do as he pleases. He's got no intention of studying or settling down to something.'

So I had one option left: to escape!

I planned and schemed for days. I thought of different ways and means. I looked into how I could get over to Turkey. I measured the distance between Beirut and Adana in my geography atlas using a compass. I figured I could walk about five kilometres an hour at best and did calculations based on this figure. But, I still felt uncertainty gnawing at my insides. I guessed formalities would be involved, and I'd probably need money or documents.

Were I to make my escape, come the evening my father would wait, then wait a bit longer but finally decide that something must have happened, and then there would be a commotion, a panic, and off he'd go to the police. The rest would follow inevitably: I'd be arrested before I even reached the border.

So what to do? I had no option but to raise the flag of rebellion.

One morning we were about to drink our tea, and my father was distributing stale bread from the day before. He got to me. 'Here, boy! There's a good dog!' he said, throwing me a chunk. The bread hit the cup of tea, the cup went over, and the tea spilt on my foot, burning me. I was frustrated enough to start with; at that point I exploded. I must have said all sorts of things. I went into the room and slammed the door in his face.

For a moment there was a deathly silence. I knew that I couldn't get away with this, that I would pay for my outburst. I simply stood in the room, amazed at myself. Then, just so I wasn't doing nothing, I walked over to the wardrobe and pulled out my bag. I sat on the bed.

'Come here, you!' yelled my father.

I didn't go. Nor did I reply. I waited, feeling ice cold, quaking where I sat.

He called once more. Again I didn't respond.

Another short silence. Then the door burst open, and he stood there in his white nightgown, his face almost purple. 'You little . . . Why, you . . . You come here when I call you!'

'No!' I shouted through my tears. 'And I'm not coming ever again! I'm not going to sit at your table! You treat me like a stepson! You always look down on me!'

My father went pale and let go of the doorknob. And then? Then he quietly withdrew.

As I was packing up my school certificate, my identity papers and various other documents I deemed important, my mother entered the room. She hesitantly came and sat next to me. 'You shouldn't have done that,' she said. 'That wasn't at all nice . . .'

I got mad at her, too.

'No, seriously,' she said. 'A father is always a father. And a son should . . .'

'If he's a father, he should act like one. He's not some god!'

I had packed my things, and my mother eyed my bag suspiciously. 'What's all this? What are you doing?'

'These are my identity papers, my school certificate . . .'

'Why have you packed them in your bag?'

'I just have.'

'But why? There must be a reason.'

'I have decided to go to Adana,' I said with finality. 'If I have to, I'll run away!'

My mother started to cry. 'You'll regret it. You'll never find whatever it is you're looking for, and you'll always regret it. You'll want to turn the clock back. You're going to be desperately unhappy . . .' She continued softly, 'Rebelling against your own father, your own mother! We might be here today, but we won't be here for ever. What you do now will cause you pain until the end of your days.'

My standing at home went up. I had won back the respect I had lost at the restaurant. Niyazi and my sisters were now in awe of me. When he attempted a stand against me I'd give him a slap or push him over, and because he could no longer rely on our father to keep me in check he would cry and withdraw into a corner.

I was aware that the household hated me. But so what? If that's what they feel like . . . I already felt like that about them anyway.

When my anger towards my father got too much I had fantasies.

I would be back home. I had finished my schooling, graduated from high school, and I was an officer in the army. Years had gone by . . . I had been quickly promoted and was now a general. Then we went to war. One day they brought a man to me, a white-haired, unkempt old man. He threw himself at my feet for mercy, begging to be spared. I inspect his identity papers, and I am stunned. The men look on in amazement as I pull the old man up and hug him. 'Oh, Father, Father!' I cry. 'It's me, your son!' It's all too much for him. Sobbing, he collapses into my arms and passes out . . .

One day as I was wandering around Beirut's dock I saw a Turkish ship, our flag high on its mast. This ship, that flag, they're part of my country, a piece of my home. I stayed there for hours. I was bewitched, my eyes fixed on the flag, effervescent with excitement, I paced back and forth, then I ran wildly to the Consulate. I know neither what I said nor to whom. I was still dizzy with exhilaration when I got back home that evening.

I think it was two days later, my father came home that evening. He slumped in the corner among his books. He looked grim. Some time later, without looking at me, he addressed me for the first time since the day I had slammed the door in his face.

'Is it true that you went to the Consulate?' he asked.

'It is,' I replied.

He didn't say anything more.

My mother busied herself lighting lamps. My father remained in his corner and, as the darkness fell, got lost in his thoughts.

19

Every morning I would go down to the Armenians' market and buy stale bread off Bogos the baker. It would cost two piastres less than newly baked, fresh bread and be more filling.

The market, with its Turkish chatter, Turkish jokes and Turkish insults, was like a home from home for me. You might see a grocer, who looked as though his name should be Ahmet, who would start singing a Turkish song in his nasal voice and the butcher next door would join in the chorus, or the cook in the sweet shop would get annoyed with his apprentice and swear at him, flaring up like a Turk, or a vendor might be selling Adana-style stuffed *köfte*.

That morning I went to market again, basket hanging from my arm. I watched the shopkeepers sitting on the pavement on their low chairs drinking coffee and playing backgammon or bubbling away with their water-pipes. I suddenly heard someone call my name. I spun round. It was Virginie, the girl I had taken a beating for after giving her a fish. There was a woman with her. The two came over.

She introduced me to the woman in Armenian and introduced her to me in Turkish. 'This is Shinoric, who I told you about. You remember, that day . . .'

The woman must have been over thirty-five. In spite of her painted face she looked old and haggard. She was one of *those* women. 'So, you're Turkish,' she said.

'Yes.'

'Where are you from?'

'Adana.'

'From Adana?'

'Yes.'

'Which part of Adana?'

'Hurmali.'

'Ah!'

The three of us walked along together. People made lewd remarks as we went by. As for the woman, she would stop in the middle of a conversation about Adana's Bebekli Church, about the priest's garden and the monuments, turn to those making the remarks and respond with equally lewd, snappy ripostes, making them laugh.

'So you're going home?' she said to me. She looked me in the eyes. 'I'm pleased for you. That's good!' Then added, 'Go, my boy, go back to your country. They say that home is where the heart is, but don't you believe it!' She looked thoughtful, brooding. 'As for those in charge, may they never find peace of mind. There was never an issue between us and the Turk!'

We had gone past Bogos's bakery. I went to excuse myself.

'Oh no!' she said. 'The girl has told me so much about you. I insist you come to our house.'

'I can't. I have to take home some bread.'

She planted her fists on her hips. 'You're not put off by us, are you? Just because we're whores doesn't mean we're bad, you know. Whores are God's creations, too. We're only people.'

'I didn't mean anything like that! Honestly, I hadn't even thought . . .'

'Don't listen to her,' said Virginie. 'Go and drop off your loaves, then come over, yes?'

I promised I would. As I was leaving, Shinoric said, 'I'm sorry. I'm a bit crazy. I get down about things.' She grabbed my arm. 'Wait! In case we don't meet again, drink a bowl of water from the Seyhan river when you get back and think of me!' The sun was reaching its zenith, and they left with hurried steps.

I dropped off the loaves and walked across to Shinoric's part of town. It was where poor Armenians lived, and the place looked wretched. Rusty cans, crumbling walls, rotten timbers, a jumble of crooked houses. The narrow streets were covered in mud. Pigs wandered around in herds; rubbish bins had been knocked over. Barefoot children ran along the streets, squelching in the mud, while women gossiped with their neighbours through open windows and a distant gramophone played an old Turkish song.

After walking around for some time I finally found Shinoric's house. My boots were covered in mud, and the splits in them meant my feet were soaked.

They were delighted to see me. Virginie wrapped her arms around me.

'You floozie!' said Shinoric. 'Look at her. She's worse than me!'

We went up a blackened old staircase that creaked ominously with each step. The room upstairs was fairly large, and sackcloth hanging on a clothes-line divided the room in two. A very old and worn Sivas kilim lay on the floor. A table with a broken leg was propped up against one corner. It was covered with empty bottles of raki, washing-up bowls, fish-bones, eggshells . . . The room stank of rotting fish.

'I told her, you wouldn't bother to come and visit people like us,' said Shinoric. Clumsy with excitement but bustling about, she picked up a large coffee-pot and put it on the stove. She went to the cupboard and took out delicate coffee cups with intricate floral patterns. 'These were left by my late husband. He bought them in Paris. The only things I never sold . . .' Then she started talking about Virginie. 'Her mother's dead, so now she's my daughter.'

Virginie was busy pulling out her toy-box from under the bed. 'Look!' she exclaimed. 'Look at my dolls! Look at this one. Shinoric made it, and I made this one . . . Which do you think is prettier?'

I told her the one she had made was the prettiest, and she seemed satisfied with my reply. She showed me little pictures of famous actors and actresses which I knew came free with chocolate bars. 'Dr Altunyan's daughters gave me these . . . And look, I made this doll's dress myself . . . I did! Didn't I, Shinoric?'

Shinoric rested her chin in her hands, elbows on her lap, and regarded the girl. 'Oh, you poor, poor orphan . . . Why don't you leave all that sort of thing to the rich girls and think of ways to make money, eh? You know, money . . .'

I could see Virginie's thick white legs through threadbare parts of her old dress. She was preoccupied with dressing up her baby in its new apparel when we heard noisy footsteps climbing the stairs. A crooked-nosed man appeared at the door. His cap was on sideways, his hair a mess. Shinoric leaped up. They exchanged a few words. I think the man was asking who I was. He peered at me over her shoulder.

He wanted to take Shinoric in his arms, but she pulled back, irritated by his advances. Then they disappeared together behind the sackcloth. I heard their voices and sounds of scuffling. Then I heard a couple of slaps and him swearing.

'Who's that?' I asked Virginie.

'Kegam. Her friend . . . But he's trouble.'

Meanwhile we heard more slaps, wailing and the man laughing.

'He'll be wanting money again.'

The noises died down. I could hear only murmurs.

'So why does he come here?'

'He's a gambler. He must have lost again.'

'She shouldn't give him anything!'

'She can't say no. He'll carve her to pieces!'

I heard a chest opening and closing.

The coffee-pot on the stove started to boil up. Virginie pulled it off the heat and poured the liquid into the cups. 'You don't know what we have to put up with day in, day out.'

'Who from?'

'Drunks mostly.'

'Why?'

'Well, you know how Shinoric takes in men at night . . . When she's doing the business over there' – she pointed to the other side of the sackcloth – 'I keep the drunks happy on this side.'

'How?'

'Oh, really! Don't you know anything? You know! I let them suck on my breast, sit on their laps . . .'

'Sit on their laps?'

'If they pay me to.'

I looked around the room with new apprehension and smelled raki in the air.

Shinoric and her friend returned.

The man seemed to have become almost cross-eyed with drink. He grinned unpleasantly. 'So you're tired of mutton then, Shinoric?'

She reached for his shoulders and tried to shove him out of the door. He held himself steady against the door-frame and pushed her to the ground. He looked at me long and hard. She managed to stand up, went for him again and succeeded in wrestling him through the door. He muttered under his breath, stomped off down the stairs and left.

'Don't worry,' said Shinoric. 'He's a worthless old sod.'

Later we talked and laughed and sang together. Shinoric spoke of her time in Adana, of her parents and of her first husband. Then she told my fortune and said the future held a long journey and that fate smiled on me. She was still trying to find out whether I really was going to go back.

'Look at my girl,' she said. 'She's just right for you. You'd be good friends if you weren't leaving.' Virginie was still engrossed in her dolls. Shinoric continued, 'Rather than have her go to some foul beast . . .'

The sun had started to set by the time I finally left. We said our goodbyes again and again. Virginie cried.

Shinoric asked me to write to her when I got home. As I walked away she shouted, 'Don't forget now, will you. A drink from the Seyhan river, just for me . . .'

20

We were expecting it anyway, and finally one evening my father said to my mother, 'Tell the boy,' as if I wasn't there, 'he's going tomorrow.'

My mother and I exchanged glances. Her eyes watered. I was bursting with joy. I flew out into the back yard. I couldn't have contained my excitement indoors.

I now felt sorry for everybody; even my father. Although Niyazi and I weren't supposed to be talking to each other, I had forgiven him long ago, and I wasn't at all cross with him. In fact, I felt a tinge of regret at having hit him. I became so full of empathy I was ready to burst into tears. I could sense a sadness in everything I was leaving behind. The fountain we had floated paper boats in seemed like it was shedding tears as its water splashed softly down. The rosebuds, the upside-down clothes-pegs on the washing-line, the toy car with its missing wheel, the torn leather of my football, a clog with a broken strap, the rusty woodwork separating our backyard from next door's, they all seemed to share this sadness, this forlornness.

Niyazi's head was lowered, as if he wanted to say, 'Don't leave us, big brother.' My sisters seemed to be silently saying, 'You're leaving us here and going away! What's to become of us?'

I went into the kitchen. I addressed the frying pan that was staring at me with its copper studs. 'Did you know,' I said, 'I'm going to Adana tomorrow.'

I imagined the pots and pans, crockery and cutlery were regarding me with awe and envy. I met Ginger at the kitchen door. He arched his back and rubbed against my legs. I picked him up and gave him a kiss. 'Guess what, Ginger. I'm off to Adana tomorrow!'

He miaowed.

'No, I'm afraid I can't take you. You stay here. Keep them company.'

He miaowed again.

I put him down and rejoined the family. My mother was preparing my bundle, arranging my things on a sheet, crying silently to herself and trying not to let it show. I was upset by that, but the feeling was overwhelmed by my joy at returning home . . .

I went out into the entrance-hall, then back into our one room, from the room into the kitchen, from the kitchen into the back yard, from the back yard to the lavatory . . . I suddenly felt inspired by its recently replaned wood, so I took out my pencil and started to write on it. I dated my graffito, but then, fearing my father would discover it, I scribbled it all out.

My father was the same as ever. He sat among his books, brows still furrowed . . .

That night in bed Niyazi and I talked about all sorts of things. 'Imagine,' I said, 'you were in my shoes. Just picture it. You're about to go to Adana. What would you do?'

He thought about this. 'Well, if it were me, I wouldn't be going.'

'Why not?'

'I just wouldn't.'

'OK, but why not?'

'What do you mean, why not? Don't you feel sorry for him? He has no one else.'

'Huh?' I realized that I was being somewhat cold-hearted but continued, 'Shall I say hello to Little Memet's brother for you?'

'Do.'

'Is there anything else you'd like me to do for you?'

'Go on to the stone bridge and look down into the stream.' He sighed.

'All right,' I said. 'I'll take a good long look for you. Don't you worry. And I'll write to you every week – and send you sports magazines.'

He sighed again.

I woke up next morning to my father shaking me. 'You're off today! Come on. Get a move on!'

I leaped up, as did my brother and sisters. They surrounded me.

My father seemed taken aback. 'What's up with you lot?' he yelled. 'He's leaving you here. What does he care?'

I hurriedly got dressed, my heart bursting with joy. I tried to be careful, but I knocked over the water-jug, whacked the lamp and stepped on the cat.

My father was standing by my bundle. My mother was showing him my clothes. 'Two pairs of underpants, a string vest, two shirts, one undershirt . . . I must say, that's really threadbare now – no good to anybody . . .'

'Take my woollen vest,' said my father. 'Put that in there, too.' My mother got his woollen vest and placed it with my clothes. 'And my gloves.' She added his gloves. And then they put the bundle into my suitcase.

I went out into the backyard one last time. The air was pleasantly cool, the sun had started to rise, and the sky was turning pink. A red-headed nightingale had landed on the fountain and was singing away. Dewdrops shivered on the rosebuds. Ginger had sat in front of the lavatory door and was licking his face. Sparrows were perched all along the washing-line and were twittering among themselves.

'Where are you, you bum?' demanded my father.

I ran inside.

'Where have you been?'

'I was in the lavatory.'

'I don't know . . . For God's sake. How could a son be so happy to leave his parents?'

My brother, my sisters and I kissed for the last time. They were all crying. Then it was my mother's turn. I kissed her hand. She was in tears and kissed me on the face again and again. We hugged, mother and son, and remained like that for a moment. I suppose it was so that he wouldn't have to watch all this, but my father had gone ahead out into the street. He was waiting for me, growing impatient.

Finally, suitcase in hand, I walked out of the door. Those I was leaving behind started to wail even louder . . . My sisters wished me a safe journey, bidding me farewell again and again.

Niyazi and I walked along side by side, and he took my suitcase off me. My father led the way. I noticed his neck. It had started to wrinkle and was thinner now.

It was a long walk. My father didn't once turn to look behind. Niyazi and I spoke quietly to each other. The sun was rapidly rising, and the air had begun to warm up.

My father bought eight bananas at the station. We ate one each on the train, and he gave me the remaining five, saying they were for me to eat on my journey. He didn't look me in the eyes. 'When you get there,' he said at one point, 'tell them that we're destitute. See if you can warm their cold hearts a bit!'

He still wouldn't look me in the eyes. He blew the smoke from his cigarette over towards the station.

The first bell!

I settled into the compartment. Niyazi got on, too. My father was just outside the compartment window, standing on the platform. He seemed preoccupied. He lit another cigarette but didn't look up at me.

The second bell!

My father was clearly upset. He agitatedly smoked the cigarette, inhaling its smoke in short, frequent breaths. He seemed to be on the verge of saying something.

The last bell!

Niyazi and I hugged and kissed; he started to cry and hurriedly alighted from the train. My father had his hand stretched out towards the window, and I took it and kissed it.

'Or maybe,' he said, 'you shouldn't say anything at all. Just think of yourself, yourself and your school. God will take care of us!'

The locomotive's whistle gave off a piercing shriek, and the train juddered and started to move.

'May God watch over you, son!'

The train sped up. My father and Niyazi were at the side of my compartment, running alongside it.

'Write often, and let us know how you are!'

As the train went into a bend, leaving them behind, my father turned and lowered his head. Niyazi was waving a handkerchief.

I suddenly felt very homesick. The train accelerated. Then we got to the mountains, the mountains of Lebanon. And the valleys. Valleys full of banana plantations. We passed numerous stations, green trees, Arab headdresses, fezzes, the sparkling sun, the sea . . .

That was it really.

21

As soon as I got off the train I kissed the ground. My homeland's soil, warmed by the bright June sun. Then, suitcase in hand, I hit the road. I had enough money for a seat in a horse-drawn carriage, but that would have raised me off the soil of my country. And anyway I thought I might travel faster on foot.

My insides were churning up.

In spite of the sun, the dust and everything – everything else – I started to run. I had memorized Arabic phrases with which to surprise Little Memet, and I kept repeating these to myself as I went. My head was a jumble of thoughts about Eleni, Virginie, the print shop, the priest school in the orange grove, the deep-blue sea, banana plantations, the Armenians' market, about all sorts of things from Beirut.

I entered the city. I suddenly noticed how dilapidated my home town looked. Streets devoid of fun, skinny, overheated cats roaming the streets, rows of shops, their owners now bankrupt, watching the streets through heavy-lidded eyes . . .

I didn't care about my grandmother. I could see her later. If I went now I wouldn't get away for ages. I'd face tears and an inquisition about my father, my mother, my brother and sisters and Beirut.

I left my suitcase at a depository and ran to Little Memet's. My excitement grew as I approached our neighbourhood that somehow, on those hot summer days, had always managed to keep the shadows at bay that little bit longer; our neighbourhood, where we played football on the empty plot of land, where snotty-nosed kids would swarm around with glee, through which tired workers would plod through at the end of their shift. That dog-ridden neighbourhood of ours had changed so much . . . Roads stretched out reluctantly into the distance, the houses looked forlorn, and even our football ground had been taken over by piles of red tiles and a small wooden shack and was surrounded by barbed wire.

I arrived at Memet's house: the pink house with its fine woodwork like delicate lace. Its bay window stood proud, the domain of his disapproving mother who relentlessly watched us as we played football on the pitch . . . Its shutter was closed. But that shutter was always kept open, whatever the weather.

The knocker was shaped like a hand with rings on each finger, and I quaked as I lifted it to rap on the wooden door. We went way back, that wood and I. One day, years ago, I had written 'Hip hip!' on it with a coloured crayon. The writing was still there, faded but untouched.

I knocked again but not as hard. I heard shuffling feet inside and a tinkle of a bell. The door opened. A young woman stood at the door. I had never seen her before. She asked me whom I was looking for. I told her. She considered. Her dress revealed too much breast and was very short. My eyes were drawn to her pulsing vein in her neck . . . She told me she did not know of anyone of that name and went back inside.

I saw an old acquaintance walking by. 'We haven't seen you for a while,' he said, recognizing me. 'Where have you been?'

I told him. He didn't seem surprised in the slightest. If only he showed a glimmer of interest, the things I would have told him!

'I presume Little Memet and his family moved . . .'

'Which Little Memet?'

'What do you mean, which Little Memet? You know, we used to play football with him all the time . . .'

'Little Memet, Little Memet . . . Oh, right! Oh, they moved a long time ago. To Istanbul, I think, or was it Izmir? Somewhere anyway. That was ages ago.'

'And Ado?'

'The Kurd's son? Leave it out! You still remember him?'

'And Sureyya?'

He spat on the ground.

'Tekin? The teacher's son? The others?'

He shrugged, and we parted company. The whole country

seemed to be spinning around my head. I felt something, something deep inside me crumbling into dust.

Who was I going to impress with my Arabic phrases now? Who was I going to tell about the priests' school, the boss I punched on the chin, about Virginie, Eleni and the others? Why on earth had I come here?

22

A month later I received a letter from my father. He was sending the family home! His letter gave no details, but I knew he thought an eighteen-year-old son was more valuable than a daughter, and he obviously loved me. However, they didn't make it. The summer went by, and the schools reopened. I restarted secondary school. But the ties between me and schooling had been utterly broken . . .

Come dawn, my grandmother would prepare me for school and send me off, books under my arm, yellow-striped school cap on my head. In spite of her care and attentiveness I would go straight to Yorgi's bran shop.

Yorgi was an immigrant's son whom I had met within a week of returning home. His real name was Ismail, but for some reason everyone called him Yorgi, which seemed to suit him. He was an incurable football addict who couldn't kick a ball, tackle to save his life or take up an intelligent position for someone to pass to. Even so, we all loved him dearly. We had become close friends within hours of meeting each other.

He would make us laugh with his flattened nose and crooked gait. He had a hunch-backed uncle who used a walking stick and constantly complained of his rheumatism. He reminded me of my Uncle Pavli from my childhood. The uncle was a very rich man who had a daughter whom he was, in all likelihood, going to marry off to Yorgi. For this reason Yorgi's love of his uncle bordered on devotion.

Yorgi would store coal behind the shop. He would buy it at knockdown prices in summer and sell it at inflated rates over the winter months. His coal depot was also the clubhouse for our neighbourhood football team. Whatever the hour, the place would be full of factory workers, butchers' apprentices, students, cobblers' assistants, newspaper delivery boys and the unemployed. All true fanatics knew of our clubhouse. In midsummer, while the country baked in the burning heat of the sun, we would sit with the pile of coal cutting leather for our footballs, repair punctures on the rubber inner ball or mend the stitching of the outer balls and talk endlessly about football. We never had to go far to relieve ourselves. 'Just piss on the coal,' Yorgi would say. 'It all adds to the weight.' So we would, and in the summer heat the whole place would stink.

Sometimes Yorgi would scuttle in like a crab. 'My uncle!' he'd warn.

Everyone would scatter. We'd hide behind sacks of bran, inside large dusty crates, sometimes among the coal itself. His uncle would slowly approach, leaning on his walking stick with each step. Yorgi would greet him at the door, sweet-talk him into a chair in the shop and order him a coffee. But, whatever he did, his uncle would always be dissatisfied. There would always be a shortcoming, some opportunity for him to say, 'You're never going to make something of yourself. I don't see how you're going to get anywhere in life.'

We'd sometimes forget to post a look-out at the door, or the look-out would get distracted, and in the middle of intense discussions on the merits of the various players in last Sunday's games Yorgi's uncle would suddenly appear in our midst. He would blow his top. First he would scream and chase us all out, then he would start beating Yorgi with his walking stick.

Watching Yorgi being beaten up by his uncle was a rare treat. While he was being hit this way and that we would stand in front of the shop, watching the spectacle and cracking up with laughter. His uncle would lead the assault while Yorgi would dash from one corner to another, trying to block the strikes raining down from all directions. The more he blocked the blows, the madder his uncle would get. His face would turn bright red, and he would spit out insults to our female relatives as he bobbed around under his hump.

After such incidents Yorgi would supposedly have learned his lesson. He would sit grim-faced, tend to his scales and refuse to let any of us into the shop.

So we would stop talking to him. We would decide we were never going to set foot in the shop again and head for Ahmet effendi's café.

This was directly opposite Yorgi's bran shop. Once he saw us sitting on chairs pulled up close, relaxing under the shade in front of the café, he would go crazy. It wouldn't take long.

'Ismail's calling you guys,' the apprentice from the bicycle shop next door would inform us.

'He can take his shop and shove it,' we'd say. 'We're not going there!'

The boy would leave with the message and come straight back. 'He says to stop messing about and to come on over.'

We'd send him back. 'If he wants us, he can come and tell us himself.'

And he'd come. He would bare his teeth in a broad grin.

'Keep those teeth covered up,' Ahmet effendi would tell him. 'You look like a bloody idiot!'

Yorgi would continue grinning from ear to ear. 'I called you guys. Why didn't you come over?'

None of us would answer. We would be desperately trying to stop ourselves from laughing. Our lips would be quivering under the strain.

'Eh? Why didn't you guys come over?'

Silence.

'What? What about you, Rejep? You pathetic sods! I'll get you for this . . .'

Finally a few snorts would escape, and then we would burst out laughing. Our seriousness would completely evaporate. The whole café would be rolling around in laughter.

Led by Yorgi, we would then set off for his shop. He would suddenly stop, though, as if he had forgotten something and count us all. 'Is this all we have today?' he'd ask and turn and call out to the café, 'Hey! Are you going to take our order or what?'

Ahmet effendi, standing at the doorway to his café, would be unfazed. He would calmly address his waiter. 'Adem, please see to the gentleman's needs.'

Yorgi wouldn't detect the sarcasm. 'Lemonade for all the boys,' he'd start, 'and I'll have a cup of . . .'

'Up yours!' Ahmet effendi would interrupt.

Yorgi would be nonplussed. 'I beg your pardon?'

And we would all crack up again, doubled with laughter.

I was a devoted attendee at Yorgi's bran shop as well as a football fanatic, my mind far from lessons which held no interest for me whatsoever, attending school with an empty head. The school did have a football team, and I was the right-winger in the first eleven, but the school had neither a Yorgi nor his bran shop with coal to piss on!

23

Yorgi was in love with Mendiye. 'I'll marry my uncle's daughter and be rich,' he'd say, 'but keep Mendiye as my mistress.'

She was the maid of the house above Ahmet effendi's café. She was a gipsy girl of perhaps eighteen, skin as white as paper with large, dark eyes. She would smile with a glint of a gold tooth, and her looks would make a wreck of any one of us.

She flaunted her beauty. She would wash the balcony or clean the windows of the house and deliberately flash a bit of leg or a bit of thigh and eye up passers-by in a sultry way.

She would occasionally go out. Purdah was still legal in those days, so she would cover herself in black silk, driving us all crazy. She possessed a beauty that would lead a man to drink and into trouble, and she would majestically glide past us without so much as a glance in our direction.

Whom was she seeing?

'She sees the soap-maker's son,' Salih would assure us. 'I'm telling you!'

'No, no! She goes to Amados's place,' Saim would inform us. 'You know, Amados's eldest son . . .'

We all fancied her. We were secretly jealous of each other. But she was officially Yorgi's mistress-to-be. He would paint such a vivid picture of how he was going to marry his uncle's daughter and be rich and how he was then going to get Mendiye a separate house, what he was going to buy her, how they would sleep together and how he would kiss her that we would just sit there and let the words wash over us, sighing with regret that we weren't rich ourselves.

As time went by we virtually forgot our talk of football. We let training sessions slip by. Although none of us became overweight, we weren't exactly fit either. Until that year we had never drunk wine. As a result of our love of Mendiye, we found out all about drinking. We started to skive off school, pool our money for wine and go to Cretan Hussein's tavern and get blind drunk. You could see Mendiye's house from the tavern, and once we were drunk enough we would wave handkerchiefs at her and express our longings out loud. We often didn't have enough money between us to buy wine but still felt the need to get drunk. We'd watch those who could afford to drink, and should there be an offer of half a glass attack the offering with such ferocity that we'd find ourselves draining the dregs and sucking on the empty vessel.

On one occasion when we were blind drunk we were hanging around Yorgi's shop waving our handkerchiefs and blowing Mendiye kisses. She was in a particularly generous mood. She kept lifting her skirt further up her legs, driving us wild in front of all the curious passers-by. Then she disappeared inside. She walked out of the house shortly afterwards, all neat, tidy and nicely dressed. She set off towards the market, then crossed over to the side the shop was on. She turned and headed towards us. 'Louts!' she called out as she passed.

We froze. She walked off into the distance.

'Louts, huh?'

'We're not louts!'

'She's just saying that . . . I mean, look at her!'

'Well, OK, but are we really louts?'

'Aren't you?' enquired Yorgi.

'What's got into you?'

'Well, look at yourselves!'

'Idiot!'

'Oh, shut up!'

We never saw her again. She didn't come to the house, nor

did she walk around the neighbourhood. Naturally, in time we forgot all about her and slowly returned to our football and our football gossip.

As winter approached, Dodge Ali got some new tenants who had daughters. The eldest sister was a particularly eager widow. After midnight I would sneak upstairs with Dodge. The woman would let in first Dodge, then me. I always got very embarrassed. It was as if she was a teacher and we were her pupils.

We really loved it, but if we came across one another in the street she would look grim and ignore us.

'Hey, guys,' said Yorgi one day. 'Have you heard what happened to Mendiye?'

'No.'

'She was caught with the son of the soap seller. They carted her off, had her examined by a doctor, and they say she's working in a brothel.'

'Hooray!' shouted Saim. 'We can go there and have her!'

24

One of the many football fanatics I knew from Yorgi's shop was Hasan Hüseyin. He was not in our first eleven because he wasn't a good enough player. Initially we were rather formal with each other, but in time we became closer acquaintances and then friends. I would even visit him at home. After a while I became almost part of their family.

Hasan's family lived in a large room of a brick hovel in a narrow alley by the livestock market. The house bulged and sagged, and the alley reeked of burnt dung and animals. This part of town – like many parts in those days – was reminiscent of a rural village, with its sun-dried brick huts, its cows and oxen, chicken scrabbling around narrow crooked streets and the distant noise of machinery. So much so that as the sun went down life would come to a standstill. There was no electricity. The local store would sell salt, woad, paint, nails, and stale sweets to barefoot local children. Its owner would sit out in front in the summer months and doze off, trim round beard resting against his chest.

Hasan and his mother, father, grandmother and three sisters, seven people in all, lived and slept in one room. Hasan would do his homework in one corner. He would get out his ruler, pen and ink and use the lid of their sewing machine or an oil can as a desk.

I had heard a great deal about his family from him. Although his father was in perfect health, the head of the house was his mother. She would sew, do the laundry, sell yoghurt on the streets and, if she had time, visit houses as a laundrywoman. She was only just over forty, but she was doubled over, her hand and face wrinkled far beyond her years. She had a trachoma infection in her eyes. She would frequently complain of forgetfulness and how everything went dark if she stood up suddenly.

She would get up, milk the cow and begin her chores before dawn. Then she would collect the pots of yoghurt she had left to set the night before and take them to Kuruköprü to sell. When she got back she would set the purple kettle with its chipped enamel on to a fire she built with dried dung. Then she would start working with her sewing machine. Although she would try to operate it with as little a noise as possible, Hasan's father would usually wake up. 'Woman,' he'd say. 'Show some consideration! We're trying to get some sleep here. What's the meaning of all this racket from that infernal invention?'

On cold, cloudy, grey winter days he would get up after nine and spend at least half an hour yawning, stretching and rubbing his eyes. He'd then go to the lavatory, return, smoke one cigarette after another, lie down a while longer on their sofa and ask his wife what there was to eat. The poor woman would pass over a glass of stewed tea, by then inky black from being reheated, and some freshly heated pan bread, cheese and an onion.

I usually met him as he left the house later in the morning. He would step through the doorway with a prayer, rubbing his eyes – also inflamed by trachoma – with his fists. He had shiny black trousers and canary-yellow kerchiefs; a navy jacket would hang from his shoulders. His large amber-beaded rosary would dangle from his hand as he held himself tall and sauntered over to the villagers' café in Melekgirmez Street.

This would really annoy Hasan's mother. 'Look at him. His jacket slung any old way over his shoulders, dangling his rosary like that, strutting along – he's a bloody disgrace. If only the government did us all a favour and closed those dens for the lazy. What is this? He's found himself a barn with a never-ending supply of feed. Comes in, eats, drinks, falls asleep – everything on tap – and if that isn't enough gathers up the rest of his useless crowd when the fancy takes him and brings them home for a drink. Is this what I deserve?'

The woman had given up having a go at him directly. 'Cursing him doesn't work,' she would say, 'and I tell him and tell him, and it makes no difference. If I had said as much to that corner-stone there, believe me, it would have crumbled to dust by now.'

Hasan wasn't happy with his father either. 'When his lordship starts to mouth off,' he would say, 'he completely loses it. I wouldn't mind so much, but he actually believes everything he says. I mean, we're originally peasants, right? I was born and brought up in the city, so I don't know any village life or anything, but my mother always told me what things were like. Back in my grandfather's days we had a crooked old hut, a couple of cows, and that was it. But when the old man gets going the hut becomes blocks of flats, the cows become dragons . . . You wouldn't believe it . . .'

Because Hasan was so good at baiting Yorgi we always felt he was indispensable. Whenever we got an offer of a match or whenever we travelled to a game Hasan was sure to accompany us. Sometimes Yorgi would drop him off the list, but the rest of us would gang up together and go on at him, especially me and Gazi, and do whatever was necessary to get him put back on.

The three of us would always try to get on the same table. We would surreptitiously order the most expensive items on the menu and have one dessert after another. We'd end up feeling bloated and in pain and rub our stomachs while we belched sour fumes.

'A feast fit for a king,' Hasan would say. 'Worth sacrificing a stomach for any day!'

One day we were going to travel by train to a nearby province for a game.

'The captain,' announced Yorgi, 'has dropped Hasan from the team.'

We immediately went into an overt display of displeasure and withdrew into a corner. So Yorgi went over to the team captain and made up all this stuff about how we were upset and refused to go anywhere.

The captain came across. He started off angry but gradually softened. 'You're not attached at the waist, you know!'

'Oh yes we are!' we retorted.

He laughed. 'Well,' he said, 'if he gets his own fare together I'll see to it that he gets fed when we're at the restaurant.'

Hasan had taken out his glass eye and was wiping it clean with his handkerchief. When we told him what the captain had said he grew so upset I thought he would burst into tears. 'How am I going to get the money together for the train fare? No one would give me that kind of money!'

There was nothing to do but to raise a collection among ourselves. Saim borrowed some money from the café owner Ahmet effendi, and we managed to get together the fare. Hasan was over the moon. He ran and pulled Yorgi's hat down on one side, threw his school cap into the air and whooped with joy.

At one point he held me by the arm. His long tatty jacket used to be his father's and was far too big for him. 'I can smell lamb chops!' he whispered earnestly. 'Do you think they'll have lamb chops at the restaurant?'

'I don't think they offer chops at every restaurant,' I said, 'but I really don't know.'

He pulled at my arm. 'Don't tell Gazi I mentioned lamb chops, will you?' he pleaded. 'Don't say I mentioned it, but tell them we must go to a restaurant that has chops on the menu, OK?' He paused. 'I'm not going to have breakfast tomorrow morning,' he announced. 'I'll skip lunch, too,' he added, 'and, come the evening, I'll stuff my face!'

The next day we all lunched at home and gathered at Ahmet effendi's café.

Hasan came up to me. 'I haven't eaten a thing all day,' he confided. 'I'm starving, but I'm going to hang on.' He continued with passion, 'Chops, chops, then more chops! And for dessert, baklava, followed by compote . . .'

To save on fares we took the shortcut to the station through the back streets of town. We boarded the train, and it left the station. Songs, fun, Yorgi clowning around . . . Some other passengers joined in, too. Saim was playing a little ditty on his harmonica. Aydın was singing in his bright, clear boy's voice. Our train was flying along the tracks.

We finally arrived. A gunmetal sea, almost dusty in its appearance, stretched off into the horizon. A few ships and boats, resting on this soft grey blanket, dozed gently under the sun.

We got off the train. 'Huzzah!' shouted our opponents, and we shouted 'Huzzah!' back. We set off together down the dusty town roads.

The football clubhouse was a heavy stone building. The windows along its cool dark hall opened out on to the sea, and I could smell the seaweed on the gentle breeze.

We had dispersed into little groups around the hall. Saim was playing table-tennis. Gazi was lacing his football boots. I was next to Hasan, leaning back on a chair, still trying to recover from the stuffed peppers which it seems I had overdone at lunchtime.

'The chops here will probably be quite filling, won't they?' he said.

'Huh?'

'Don't you think? Do you think they'll definitely do compote everywhere?'

'Honestly!'

'But, look, apples aren't in season now, so how are they going to get hold of them for the compote?'

'I don't know!'

'Do you think they keep them over from last winter?'

'Who knows?'

'I think one should eat lamb chops and compote every meal so that . . .'

'You what?'

'Well, it's true. That way people would be much happier. But I guess you would have to be a bank manager . . . Or perhaps an accountant . . . You could still eat lamb chops every day if you were an accountant.'

'Hmm . . .'

'We might see about a pound of meat a week in our household, if that . . . And that isn't even enough for my dad. A pound of meat and a horde of people!' He paused. 'I swore to myself, I'm going to finish school. If I could work in accounts, maybe in one of the banks . . . Look, let me just get into accounts, and I swear I'll eat lamb chops every day.'

'And money for your clothes? Your wife? Kids?'

'I'll look after number one first. Anyway I'm not going to marry unless I have a decent wage. I've had enough of being poor. I've had nothing since I can remember. I'm sick and tired of it . . . You can make compote from apricots, too, can't you?'

'You can indeed.'

'If they have no apple compote I'll have apricot compote.' Another pause. 'But listen, mate . . . A restaurant with lamb chops, yeah?' He looked at the wall clock. 'It's coming up to three. Three, four more hours at most, and then we'll be at the restaurant!'

His eyes shone and he smiled. After a brief shudder he had a long stretch.

We won the game by one goal. We got back to the clubhouse through the cheers of the fans and changed. We quickly showered under the pump one by one, got dressed and were invited out to eat. Hasan had turned a sickly yellow. He was quaking with anxiety that something might go wrong and that he wouldn't get to accompany us to the restaurant.

At one point a member of our team suggested that we forget the meal and just catch the earlier train home.

'Shut up!' snapped Hasan. 'I'm dizzy with hunger. God only knows how I made it this far! We can take the later train or forget about getting any train at all!' He entered the restaurant with me on one arm, Gazi on the other. We sidled over to an unobtrusive table.

'Can we have a menu?' Hasan asked before we even sat down. 'Where is it? Oh, pass us a menu, Gazi!'

'Shush!' said Gazi. 'Everyone's staring. Behave yourself! Even the bloody waiters are wondering what's going on.'

Hasan grew annoyed. 'So what? I don't mind them looking. Hey, waiter!'

'Oi!' warned Yorgi disapprovingly from a distance.

People had started to laugh. The waiter approached with a big grin.

'Lamb chops, my good man!' said Hasan.

Gazi ordered the lamb stew, and I asked for beans with rice.

When the food came Hasan pushed his cutlery to one side. 'Sod politeness!'

Each chop was a small stick with just a mouthful of meat on it. He got through the plate in a few seconds. 'Well, there wasn't much there . . .' He turned to the waiter. 'Hey, pal. Why don't you take this and bring me another plateful? You know, fat and juicy ones . . .'

To cut a long story short, after five portions of lamb chops he had aubergine stuffed with lamb, a double portion of rice, a double portion of beans, a portion of ratatouille and a plate of stew before moving on to the compote.

The rest of us busied ourselves with our own food while the waiter came and went with bowl after bowl of apricot compote. We started to survey the other diners with the ease that comes with a satisfied feeling of having had a good meal. Hasan seemed nervous and looked somewhat guilty. Gazi got up, went to wash his hands and face and returned. Just as I was about to do the same the captain of the other team stood up.

'Friends,' he announced, 'we forgot to mention this before, but we're only treating the eleven players and their two officials. So . . .'

Hasan blanched, and his spoon clattered to the floor.

Gazi and I tried not to burst out laughing.

'Oh my God!' cried Hasan, as if on his death-bed. 'What am I to do?'

Gazi was in tears. 'You'd better bring it all back up, mate.'

'Stop taking the mickey. It's hardly the time . . . You wouldn't leave me here, would you? I haven't a penny! How am I going to find the money? Who can lend me . . . ? Oh, Gazi, please call Yorgi over.'

Gazi was in stitches.

'God, he's still laughing. You sod, the least you can do is show some sympathy!' Hasan then turned to me. 'You go off with the others. I'm ruined! Damn! I think the waiters have sussed me, you know. Look, he's pointing me out to the one next to him. They're laughing. Oh, if only I hadn't eaten any of it . . .'

Those who were not being treated were paying their bills. It was going to be Hasan's turn soon. Gazi disappeared for a moment.

'Do you think he's legged it?' asked Hasan.

'I wouldn't have thought so,' I said. 'No, look. He's over there talking to Yorgi.'

Hasan looked over. 'The bugger's still laughing . . . Here I am, doomed, and he's just having a laugh.'

It was now his turn to pay. 'If you please, sir,' said the waiter.

Hasan swallowed and held on to the edge of the table. He was drained. The waiters were laughing and staring at the floor. I followed their eyes and saw the apricots lying in syrup. Large beads of sweat were dripping down his forehead.

'He's put them in his pockets!' muttered one of the waiters.

'Come on, sir,' said another. 'The bill, please! Let's not keep everyone waiting.'

At that point Yorgi came over. 'Waiter!' he said. 'I'll take that bill.' Then he saw the apricots on the floor. 'What on earth are those?'

The waiter demanding the bill told him. 'They dropped out of the gentleman's trousers, sir.'

Hasan Hüseyin, shoulders stooped, walked towards the washbasins in his frayed jacket.

Yorgi took a look at the bill. 'Wow!' he exclaimed. 'He's eaten a load and a half!'

The waiter added, 'And as if what he ate wasn't enough . . .'

Gazi's hand shot up menacingly. 'You can shut up!' he said. 'What's it to you? Just do your job. You're getting your money. We buy the food, we can eat it or stuff it in our pockets. It's none of your damn business.'

The waiter withdrew. Gazi burst out laughing again. Later, back on the train, we were sitting next to one another.

'I could have died . . .'

'I understand you eating, but what's that stuffing-your-pockets business all about?'

'My right pocket was torn. In the excitement I forgot and put the apricots in there. I was going to take them to my youngest sister Gulseren. She'd asked me specially.'

Our train carried on through the darkening skies, swishing wetly along the tracks, knocking back the telephone poles.

25

We would play football among ourselves; sometimes betting a round of fizzy drinks or fifty kuruş a player.

The whole of Adana was baking under the August sun, and we'd be out chasing a ball. We had burned our skins to wrinkled leather. From first thing in the morning until last thing at night we'd run from one half-time to the next; so much so that Yorgi gathered us together one day. 'I've been thinking,' he said to us. 'I think that playing in moonlight would be good fun!'

And it was . . . The playing field seemed perfectly light under the big bright moon. So all the sessions we couldn't complete in the blistering heat were played out at night.

We would have away games at nearby towns and villages. On such occasions – which usually took place on a Sunday – we would meet up at Ahmet effendi's café before dawn. We'd still be half asleep. Our 26-year-old team captain Memet would get there before any of us. He was a very small man and would walk around with his sleeves rolled up, lost under his filthy straw hat, barking out orders to us. He'd get Hasan sewing up the leather on the ball, and Dodge Ali would be sent off to get oil. He would then anxiously withdraw into a corner of the shop and carefully scrutinize his top-secret papers listing the week's line-up.

We never managed to get everything ready on time. No matter how careful we were there was always something we had forgotten, and Memet would grow irate. He would shout and pace about, and we'd have a terrible time trying to get him on to the truck with the rest of us.

We would raise the money for the vehicle by pooling our allowances. Whoever had some surplus would help out those who were short, and any shortfall would be covered by Yorgi or a loan from Ahmet effendi. The truck would set off to the joyful sound of songs and rhythmic clapping. On the way Yorgi would treat us to his comic displays and make us laugh. A win would mean the losing club would treat us to a meal. This would always be wonderful and make our return journey twice as joyous.

Yorgi would attend these victory feasts, Saim on one side, Dodge Ali or Recep on the other, Hasan and Gazi facing him. Our managers would make speeches one after the other, as if they were in some sort of speakers' competition. We'd ignore them all and tuck in. Occasionally Yorgi would whisper, 'Get stuck in there, Hasan. Come on, it's free!' We'd be unable to control our giggles and totally distract the speaker.

One day we challenged a nearby town to a game. We had already played a few matches against them, so a letter was sufficient to let them know we were coming. In the usual manner we wrote to them stating our challenge. This was given to Cemal to post. That Sunday, half asleep as usual, we gathered together at Ahmet effendi's café at first light. Memet once more sent people hither and thither, arranged and rearranged his line-up, paced around effing and blinding at all and sundry. Finally we made it on to the truck and, to singing and laughter from twenty young men, it took off.

We reached the town shortly before lunchtime. We had been so full of ourselves all morning we hadn't realized how hungry we had become. We couldn't wait to get there.

'I'm going to get through thirty platefuls,' announced Yorgi. 'I kid you not.'

'I'm going to have cream on my apricot compote,' said Hasan.

'Baked semolina pudding . . .'

'Stuffed aubergines . . .'

'What I wouldn't give for a plate of beans and rice right now!'

Our truck rumbled into town, accompanied by the smell of fuel. It was little more than an overgrown village and seemed deserted. Under the blazing sun the streets were devoid of life. The odd curious face appeared at a window.

We halted in front of our opposition's clubhouse. Amazingly a large lock was hanging on its stout wooden door.

‘What’s this?’

Memet was the first to jump out. ‘You must be joking!’ he said, testing the lock. It wouldn’t budge. Yorgi’s widening eyes made me feel sick with fear. Memet, beaten, turned to us.

‘So, what do we do now?’

‘Don’t know . . .’

‘Maybe they didn’t get our letter.’

‘What, from there to here? What could go wrong?’

We remembered Cemal. I searched around for his huge torso and small grey eyes. Well, well! No sign of him anywhere. Yet he had been with us that morning . . .

A few kids had gathered around the truck and were staring at us.

We sent word to the club’s managers and they came down to the clubhouse, but they had not received any letter. In fact, they couldn’t organize a game that day. Most of their players had gone off to some village, the team captain was in Izmir . . . If, however, we wanted to kick a ball around with a few of their players just for fun and a bit of exercise . . .

Hasan was devastated. He pressed his fists into his stomach and squatted down in the shade by the clubhouse. He took out his glass eye and gave it a wipe with his handkerchief. I suddenly felt my hunger hit me with a vengeance. We were not so rude as to tell the club’s managers we were hungry and that we had no money with us. We had no choice but to accept their offer of an afternoon of exercise.

The truck driver was paid, so he drove off, and the managers also disappeared. The various boys surrounding us wandered off. There we were, each of us lost in thought, some peeing gloomily into a corner, some squatting with head in hands, some cursing like there was no tomorrow.

‘What is this? Are we going to have a game on an empty stomach?’

‘Why didn’t they tell us?’

‘How are we expected to get back after the game?’

‘Yeah, there is that . . . The truck driver won’t take us unless he gets paid in advance.’

It was one thirty in the afternoon.

'Lads,' said Yorgi, 'I have a hundred and ten kuruş on me. Let's pool everything we have and at least get ourselves something to eat.'

'No, no,' said someone else. 'We should all put our cash together and hire a truck!'

'We don't have enough money for that.'

'So what's going to happen?'

'God's will, my son. God's will.'

'First, let's eat. We can't do anything on an empty stomach.'

'Of course not . . . We're starving.'

We came up with eighty-two kuruş to add to Yorgi's. Hasan left and returned with warm bread, black olives and halva.

'Two mouthfuls of water is as good as a mouthful of bread, lads. Drink some water. It will fill you up.'

So we drank and drank.

'Thank God for that!' said Black Hasan. 'Well, mustn't grumble.'

'We'll be fine.'

'We'll just keep up a brisk pace tonight.'

'Of course. And we'll have a nice little game.'

'What about an evening meal?'

'You know, lads,' interrupted Yorgi. 'What we should do is to go to the guys and tell them, look, this is what's happened. Let's just tell them. They can feed us or hire us a truck . . . What do you say?'

'Food,' said Hasan. 'They should give us food.'

'Leave it out!' said Gazi. 'Food! They can hire us a truck, and we can all get home.'

'Food's better!'

'Forget food, will you!'

'Yeah, let's go for the truck!'

'No, the food!'

'No, the sensible thing is to get a truck.'

'Food, food, food!'

In the end food won out. A delegation was sent out, headed by Yorgi. They made their request, but . . .

'If only the captain wasn't in Izmir . . .'

'You know what it's like when you're not an official association . . .'

We had our practice match. We scored loads of goals, winning applause; the other team shouted 'Hurrah!' at us, but that was it.

So to the dusty roads!

The players were in a particularly bad way. When we got out of town all eleven members of the team lay down on the damp earth beneath the whispering trees covering the hills. We were drenched in sweat and burning up. Hasan, Yorgi, Rejep and Salih massaged our legs.

The mighty sun was like a giant burning cartwheel in the sky. It had started to turn crimson as it slowly set. There was a cool breeze that drove us crazy. We tied our football boots together by their laces, slung them over our shoulders and started to walk along the dusty track which was the road home.

Aydın was only twelve and was sitting on Yorgi's shoulders. He was singing.

As we hold our heads high
Clouds drift in the sky,
And what gives us joy
Is the journey, my boy!

We joined in feebly. But when it came to the line 'Shake it, baby, set the night on fire' all voices rose together in rebellion against our ordeal. Twenty young lads, voices dulled with hunger and fatigue, shouted out in unison: 'Shake it, baby, set the night on fire.'

The moon appeared quite abruptly, shrunk in size and escaped to the depths of space. Its sparkling light illuminated the night. We passed by reaped fields of wheat. We could see red and orange flames lighting up the horizon. It was a cool evening, full of the crackling sounds of nocturnal insects.

We walked on. We reckoned that if we managed to walk non-stop we would get back a couple of hours after dawn. So we plodded on. There were complaints of cramped legs and increasing numbers of yawns. We plodded on. As we passed a group of oak trees Yorgi glanced at the luminous dial of his watch. 'Eleven fifteen,' he announced.

We no longer had command of our legs, nor of our eyes. We

crept into the shelter offered by the stunted oaks and passed out. We woke to a huge red sun on the horizon, just starting its journey across the sky.

And then? Then we gathered up some grain from the wheat-fields to kill the worst of our hunger pangs. Yorgi sold his watch to a passer-by, and we spent the proceeds at a worksite canteen on our way home.

We were exhausted by the time we finally got back home to a cooler evening breeze.

Not surprisingly Yorgi got a terrific hiding from his uncle, while I underwent a thorough cross-examination by my grand-mother.

The following day the huge oaf Cemal confessed. 'What could I do? It was so hot, I couldn't bear it!' He hadn't posted the letter at all. He had used the stamp money to buy himself a cold drink.

O hunger! How deeply I have felt your ache, in my stomach, my veins, and my very bones. But you, my fellow man, with your humanity and compassion, one day you will feed us all and end that scourge for ever.

THE IDLE YEARS

I

After Yorgi married his cousin and closed down the bran shop, our football team disbanded. Gazi and I went over to a different club and took Hasan Hüseyin with us.

I was good at taking penalties, and Gazi's headers were wonderful. Unless something was related to football, we had no time for it. However, Hasan, in spite of his shabby appearance in his ageing, frayed jacket, stubbornly retained his ties with school so that he might one day become an accountant and be able to afford plenty of lamb chops.

We hung out at a café known as 'the Cretan's'. It stood in the shade of large eucalyptus trees and was a rectangular shape, with rows of windows on each side. It was quite a distance from the city centre. Men who had had enough of the rumble of the city would come out here, place a chair under the shade of its eucalyptus trees and meditate, particularly when the weather was good.

The owner of the café actually was from Crete. Although he was much older than we were, he was a lively and entertaining host. He would speak a broken Turkish with a heavy accent and sell hashish to some of his less savoury customers.

I would leave home every morning, pretending to go to school, with my books tucked under my arm and my striped yellow cap on my head, and I'd head off to the Cretan's. I would wait for Gazi and Hasan at the crossroads. If they arrived first I'd inevitably get grilled about my tardiness. They would have a little go at me, but then we'd laugh and chat together, absent-mindedly throwing stones at passing stray dogs and admiring the sparkling-clean taxis gliding over the shiny tarmac, and slowly make our way to the café. The proprietor would usually be snoring in bed. Not wanting to wake him, we'd quietly sneak in, light the stove, put on the kettle to brew tea and drop into the grocer's next door to get some shelled walnuts and fresh bread.

'Well done,' the Cretan would say, when he woke to find everything on the go. 'Good on you, lads!'

Occasionally he'd come out with some amazing news. For example: 'I was just about to go to bed, and this car pulled up.

Four or five people got out, went inside the house over there, then the car drove off. The people are still in there.'

We all panicked at this. What if they had come over to arrange our marriages? What if the girls' old man said yes? You see, we had become lovers with the girls from the red-tiled house. The house was set in a wheatfield across the road, facing the café. Three girls lived there, and the eldest was going out with the owner of the café. Mine was the middle one, and the youngest was going out with Gazi. Hasan didn't have anyone. That's because he had no intention of having anything but the best. He was saving himself to marry a girl from either a very rich or a very well-known family.

Although he refused to take up with a girl even on a short-term basis, he still bunked off school to be with us. And back in those days, when we beat up other guys for making impertinent remarks about our girlfriends, he would be the first to wade in, hitting harder than anybody. On windy nights, when we would sometimes have to wait for the girls under the old sycamore tree for hours, he would be by our side. Not once did he ask, 'What am I doing here? What's this got to do with me?' During the hours when we separated out to shelter under different trees, thinking only of love and making love, he would stay in the orange grove some twenty metres away, pacing up and down in a steady rhythm, smoking, coughing intermittently and now and then taking out his glass eye and wiping it on his handkerchief.

My girlfriend did wonder about this. 'Patient and loyal, isn't he?' she commented.

'What, because he's waiting there?'

'Mmm, yes, because he's waiting . . . But also because he's not got himself a girlfriend.'

We would signal the girls from under the old sycamore with a lit match and anxiously wait for the response from the sofa by their window, which they gave using a lantern. We would sometimes wait for ages. Then, as we stood under the trees in the wet night, the skies rumbling, lightning flashing and the harsh wind dissipating on the dry branches around us, the girls would eventually come running towards us, emerging from the darkness like nervously flickering ghosts.

Mine would rub her hands in a repetitive, nervous way, grab hold of my hand and hold it to her chest. 'Look, feel that heart-beat! If I drop dead one of these days it'll be your fault!'

One of the others, overhearing her, would whisper, 'If only they appreciated what we do for them . . .'

One night, when they had managed to get their father off to bed and told their mother they were just going over to their neighbour's, they were tiptoeing down the stairs when one of them stepped on the cat. The piercing yowl made their old man leap out of bed. All our arrangements nearly went down the drain that night.

Once they had reached us, each of us would take our loved one by the hand and wander across the slippery damp earth in a different direction while Hasan stayed behind, lighting a cigarette and coughing hoarsely.

We made a new friend one day. He had dark eyes and a shrivelled white face, made us laugh out loud and consistently beat us all at backgammon without losing a single point. Nejip was from Istanbul and was doing his military service. He was due to get his discharge papers and couldn't stop telling us all about Istanbul. The marvellous picture he painted played on my child-hood memories, making Istanbul seem a bright land of promise. It made my home town appear lacklustre by comparison.

'Around here,' he would say, 'you could have all the talent in the world and not get anywhere. You should come over to Istanbul and see what a real city is like! There was this guy Ali working at the tobacconist's. From Sinop he was. When he first started playing football he wasn't even as good as you guys. Now he plays inside-left for Fenerbahçe!'

One day Gazi said, 'What do you say? Shall we just up and go?'

'What about our girlfriends?'

'Don't worry about them . . . There's no shortage of girls in Istanbul.'

'What about my school?'

'What about it?'

'Well, you know . . .'

Gazi looked dubious.

'What are you looking like that for, Gazi?'

'As if you were going to school!'

'All right . . . But what about the fares to get there?'

'Getting there . . . That's a point. Let's say we somehow got hold of boarding passes from Mersin . . .'

'What would we eat on the way? Let's say we arrive in Istanbul. Where would we stay? How would we feed ourselves?'

'Hang on,' said Gazi. 'Let's find Reshat and Ahmet. They can teach us how to work the looms, and we can work for a while in the cloth factory and save some money.'

'Yeah, then we can up sticks and go. Weaving would be a worthwhile trade in Istanbul, too. If we find ourselves a bit short . . .'

'If we found ourselves a bit short we'd do whatever work came our way.'

'Of course we would. Hasan probably wouldn't want to get his hands dirty, but . . .'

'Don't think about him. Remember what Nejip said? About that guy Ali from Sinop who worked in the tobacconist's? Remember? Who knows what we could do?'

'Maybe, maybe . . . If we could get some decent training. But let's not tell Hasan . . . If we're looking at Fenerbahçe we might make the national team eventually, eh?'

'Why not? It's perfectly possible.'

All our conversations now centred on Istanbul.

We decided to start working at the factory.

Later we told our girlfriends of our decision to leave. We painted such a marvellous picture that they, a few years younger than us, grew as excited as we were. They suggested that we all go together. We could all get there, find jobs, save up and go to the movies every Sunday. We'd have children, and we'd educate them and raise them to be decent people. Naturally we would age and grow old together . . . Until death do us part, all under one roof . . .

Gazi's girlfriend clapped her hands together. 'Oh, oh! It would be wonderful! Wonderful!'

'Let's not wait,' suggested my girl. 'Let's go now!'

Yeah, now we'd seen a horseshoe all we needed was three more horseshoes and a horse and we'd be there!

The next day we went to see Reshat and Ahmet, the weavers. They were brothers and had complexions as white as paper. We knew them from Yorgi's bran shop; they were huge football fans, too. They'd been working on the looms for years and would always turn up to play football bleary-eyed and covered in cotton fluff. They were surprised to see us at the factory.

Ahmet listened to our request to be taught how to work the looms. 'What?' he said. 'You guys? Weaving?' He looked over to Reshat.

'Sure, why not?' we said.

'So you want to learn how to weave?'

'Why so surprised? Weaving's no great skill, is it?'

The two brothers chuckled. 'You know,' said Reshat to his elder brother, 'they think weaving's like playing football.'

'So it seems,' said Ahmet. 'Let's see your hands.'

We held them out.

'Why, you poor little things . . . Look at those soft hands . . . Now you look at mine.' His were hard and calloused.

'We don't want to carry on living off our parents,' explained Gazi. 'Just tell us. Will you teach us weaving or not?'

'We don't mind teaching you,' said Ahmet, 'but . . .'

'But what?'

'You wouldn't last a week!'

Having promised us they would have a word with the foreman they sent us away.

A short time later Hasan got to hear of all this and grew extremely angry. 'You,' he said, pulling me to one side, 'shouldn't be going along with him! You should know better than that!'

'I should? What do you mean?'

'I mean don't forget who your father is.'

Gazi, oblivious to the implicit insult, was a little distance away, a cigarette hanging from his mouth, his hands stuck in the pockets of his flared trousers, kicking small stones at an imaginary goal.

2

I got up before dawn the following day and quietly sneaked out of the house. I slung my jacket across my shoulder and lit a cigarette. I struck the match like an experienced weaver and got the cigarette going the way an experienced weaver would. And, with all the arrogance of a weaver who knew his looms I blew a large mouthful of smoke up towards the sky.

Gazi was waiting for me by his door. He had his jacket slung across his shoulder, too.

'How's it going?' I asked.

'Great.'

We hadn't noticed that his father was watching us from the window. 'Huh,' he called down, 'just look at you. See what happens to you without an education!'

As we walked around the corner Gazi cursed and swore at those who got an education. 'Just give me a cigarette!' he demanded.

A little while later we got to the main road, feeling keen and optimistic. Women, men, children, workers . . . A sea of people filled the road, and we dived in among them.

We reached the factory, and as soon as we entered my head started spinning at the tumultuous clacking of the looms. It was as if the whole place was galloping towards me. The factory was one large haze of dust, shaking and quaking with its clatter of noise. Cotton particles were everywhere, and I was hit by a strong smell of starch. Ahmet led me further in by the arm, laughing at my reaction. I felt that the other workers were staring at me incredulously and finding us as amusing as Ahmet and his brother obviously did. I remembered feeling the same way when I first started work at the printing press in Beirut.

Ahmet, in charge of two machines, stood facing me. He couldn't stop chuckling and looked as though he couldn't believe his eyes. Every now and then he would briefly attend to a broken thread, pull at it in an obviously experienced manner and expertly tie a knot before turning his attention back to me.

'What are you staring at?' I eventually asked.

'Nothing,' he replied.

'No, really, what?'

'I was just looking at you and wondering at God's mysterious ways.'

'Why? What about?'

'Why do you think? That the son of such a great man should come to a guy like me.'

I hadn't come across such a deferential attitude before. 'I've worked as a waiter in my time, I'll have you know. And I enjoyed it, too. Forget about all that. We're all equal in the eyes of God, eh? I'm no soft, spoilt kid!'

In spite of my words he was still shaking his head, wondering at the mysterious ways of God.

'This is what we call a shuttle,' he said finally, holding up a small, torpedo-like device. The shiny wooden object had pointed ends and was painted bright yellow.

'Now this shuttle is empty. When it's empty you have to open it like this, take out the spindle like this, replace it with a full one like this, close it like this and throw it from here like . . . that.'

'Uh?'

'That's the tension arm.'

'Uh?'

'The harnesses. Sley . . .'

'Uh?'

I was overwhelmed by the smell of starch, the cloud of cotton fluff and the incessant clattering. I had all but forgotten about Istanbul and the rest of our plans.

Ahmet interrupted my bout of coughing. 'And this is what it's like at our factory,' he said. 'My brother and I have been swallowing this stuff since we were this high. Our lungs must be full of it by now!'

Then we went out towards the lavatories and lit up. My ears were ringing. The corridor was covered in graffiti such as 'The House of Lords', 'Dynamo Salih', 'Sit on this', 'Bekir was here' and all sorts of other stuff. Ahead of us was the row of water closets.

'Why do these lavatories have only half a door?' I asked.

'That's so that people don't waste time here,' explained Ahmet, 'and so that the foreman can easily check them.'

'Why would anyone want to spend lots of time here?'

'You'll see why once you've been around a while. People prefer to waste time on a lavatory than standing around breathing cotton. You start thinking of things when you're here . . . I tell you, once I'm on the lavatory and my mind wanders, I could be anywhere in the world. I close my eyes, and I drift away . . .'

The foreman was blowing his whistle and badgering the workers back on to the factory floor. We threw our cigarette butts into the dirty water that streamed past under the lavatories, and we returned to the machines.

I don't know how I made it to the end of the day. Gazi seemed as tired as I was and covered in white fluff.

'How was it?' I asked.

'Not fun.'

I pointed to the crowd of female workers passing by in front of us. 'How about the one in the middle,' I asked. 'Shall we go for it?'

He gave me a disapproving look.

'What's up? Why the dirty look?'

'Here I am, absolutely shattered, and there you go . . .'

My grandmother was waiting for me by the street door. 'What's this?' she demanded. 'Where have you been?'

'School,' I lied. 'We had a volleyball match . . .'

'Don't you lie to me. You haven't been to school in a long time. I know you haven't. So let's have the truth. Where have you been?'

'I said I was at school!'

'So where did all this white stuff, this fluff come from?'

I gave up. 'I've been working. At a factory.'

'What did you just say?'

'A factory.'

'What factory?'

'It's just a normal factory . . . I'm working on the looms.'

She leaned forward. 'Are you really?'

'Honestly!'

'You're doing manual labour?'

'Yes, I'm doing manual labour.'

She emitted a wail . . .

I went inside, took off my clothes and had a good wash.

My grandmother was sitting on the edge of the sofa, her back straight and rigid. I stretched myself out on the divan. After a while she quietly walked over to me. 'You were only teasing, weren't you?'

I didn't reply.

'I knew you were,' she went on. 'I knew you were teasing. My boy has ambition! He wouldn't stoop to that sort of thing! You know, when you were little your aunts used to ask you what you wanted to be when you grew up, and you would tell them that you were going to be the most famous doctor in Turkey. As if my boy would do manual labour!'

Inside my head I heard Ahmet's clean, honest laughter and saw Reshat's fair, boyish looks. I nearly swore at the old woman. She just pottered off, oblivious, mumbling some prayer to herself.

3

The following day and the next I had to quarrel with my grandmother to get out of the door. Gazi and I would sling our jackets over our shoulders, light cigarettes and march off to the factory. We quickly learned the ropes. Ahmet regularly left the machines to me and went off. I was now as good as he was at tying up the loose ends, pulling the threads through, cutting off the roll of cloth and warping the loom. So was Gazi. And when our day's work was finally over we'd have time to chat about girls.

'Yep. That's all the training you're getting,' said Ahmet one day. 'I'll go now and tell the supervisor, but he'll probably want to test you, so be ready!'

He went and told the man, and he came across. He was a tall, thin, dark-skinned, shifty-looking character, his eyes red with trachoma infection. He asked me to stop my machine. I pulled the disengaging lever and did so. He snapped off four or five threads and asked me to pull and tie them. I quickly did as he requested. After getting me to cut off the bolt of woven material and warp the loom afresh he seemed satisfied.

'Well done!' he said. 'I'll make sure you get the first machine that comes free.'

I soon found out that Gazi had passed as well. But when was a machine going to become available? When were we going to start earning, so we could save up and leave for Istanbul?

None of the machines looked as though they would be freed

up any time soon. And all of the experienced workers had trainees working with them for nothing. Most of these had swiftly learned their job, passed their tests with flying colours, and each had been told that they would get the first machine that became available.

Of course we didn't realize that we were simply considered spare pairs of hands until much later. The managers of the factory had had us trained up to keep the experienced workers in check. I only found out from a real-life demonstration of their attitude, which ended up with me getting my own machine.

It happened two machines away from where we had been trained.

One day the machine operated by Kurd Dursun threw a shuttle, and Albanian Nuri collapsed. We all ran over. His mouth was opening and closing like a fish. It seems that the shuttle had got him in the ear. Someone went and told the factory-floor supervisor. He came, inspected the wounded man and went off in a hurry. He quickly returned with the short, fat chief machinist, the heavyweight administrator, the stubby-nosed managing director and the owner himself, who scuttled along at an angle, carrying his huge midriff on a skinny pair of legs and outsized feet. Everyone started speaking at once, and they started barking out instructions. Meanwhile, our foreman went over to the mains switch and pulled it down. The whole factory came to a halt.

Dursun, whose machine had thrown the shuttle, looked as white as a sheet. The factory owner started shouting and swearing. At one point he looked as though he was about to slap someone, but Dursun grabbed his raised arm and pushed him away. That caused an uproar. Someone went for someone else, people jeered and whistled. It was total pandemonium. I looked over and saw Dursun's boots moving around at head height. The crowd had grabbed hold of him, lifted him up and were unceremoniously bundling him out of the factory.

Ahmet, next to me, swore loudly for all to hear. He pulled me aside. 'Come on. We're off for a cigarette.'

We reached the corridor to the lavatory.

'Well!' I exclaimed. 'What will happen now?'

Ahmet was nervously tapping the ash off his cigarette as if preoccupied. 'What'll happen about what? You saw it: the machine threw a shuttle. Got the man right in the ear. So now they're trying to blame poor Dursun, so that if the man dies or something they won't have to pay compensation. But really . . .' He spat hard at the concrete floor through his teeth. 'Half the fault's with the machines, but the other half's with our supervisor.'

'Why's that?'

'The supplier's a relative of his. All the warp we get has knots in it. When the shuttle hits a knot – whap! Off it goes. Oh, he knows this happens, but he won't do anything about it.'

'Might Albanian Nuri die then?'

'He could.'

'He could actually die? Really?'

'I remember another time when a shuttle came flying off a machine like this. It hit a good mate of mine, Laz Haydar. Bless him, he was a lovely guy and a man true to his word. I mean, if you said "Haydar, let's do such and such" he'd be right in there, come hell or high water. Anyway this shuttle flew off, smacked him right in the ear and caused internal bleeding. The poor guy dropped dead on the spot. You know, I've lost my mother, I've lost my father, but I never cried as much as I did when poor Haydar died. And you know why? Because he was a true friend; always there for you!'

'He died, eh?'

'Dropped dead on the spot. That's what death's like here. Gets you before you know it.'

'Is Nuri married?'

'With four children. His wife's a strong woman, though. He took her from the thread-making section here in this factory. She's from Crete, but she's a true Ottoman.'

'They'll pay compensation to his children if he dies, won't they?'

'That would depend on our statements. Didn't you see what happened? The whole lot of them turned against poor Dursun. And you know why? It's so they can make it out to be his negligence. If he's found negligent, according to the law, and they say that that caused the accident . . .'

'Dursun's going to get dropped in it!'

'That's what'll happen.'

We returned to the factory floor. The owner, our supervisor, the administrator, the chief machinist and everyone else was there. They had gathered the workers around. They all seemed to be arguing. We moved in among them. We couldn't make out precisely what was going on, but there was clearly some sort of disagreement with lots of people raising their voices. Then one of the weavers, whom I recognized from his black glasses, pushed his way through the crowd towards the centre. I could tell from his tone of voice that he was being calm and collected. But people behind him started pushing and shoving.

'We're not!' yelled someone.

Shouts of 'We're not! No, we're not!' started echoing among the crowd. There was sudden confusion. People lunged at one other, and Ahmet bolted forward. Shuttles began flying through the air, and I heard swearing. Men were chasing each other among the machines. One large shuttle whistled past my head and another smashed into one of the light-bulbs. I saw a pair of black glasses fly into the air . . .

This carried on for some time. Then police appeared at the factory doors; seven, eight, maybe ten or more of them. They blew their whistles as they entered, much factory cloth got torn, but eventually things calmed down. Police carted off many of the weavers, most of them with bleeding lips and torn clothes.

Ahmet had acquired a nasty gash on one eyebrow, and his eye was swollen. He was shaking. He darted forward again. He went up to the police chief, said a few things in an angry tone and returned to us.

'You keep an eye on the machines,' he said to me. 'I'll be back shortly.'

'Where are you going?'

'They're taking some of the lads away, and I can't leave them on their own. I'll get them to take my statement, then I'll be right back.' He picked up his jacket from the metal bar where it had been hanging and left.

When the day was over I finally got to see Gazi.

'How about that?' he said. 'Do you think we'll get a job after all this?'

'I have no idea.'

'What do you think of these flying shuttles?'

'Ahmet says that any of us could die at any time. He says you could be dead before you know it!'

'I thought all hell was breaking loose. These factory workers are really stressed out. Between you and me, I was really worried . . . And what if we get a shuttle in the head one of these days?'

'What do you mean? What are you saying?'

'I'm saying there's a danger of getting a shuttle in the head. Got a cigarette?'

'Yeah. You think you might get a shuttle in the head – what if you do?'

'Think about it! Give me those matches . . . What do you think would happen? How would you feel, pushing up the daisies?'

'Well, it wouldn't really be the end of the world if the great Gazi was gone now, would it?'

'Who says it wouldn't be? What would you do without me?'

On our way back we met our team captain. He was cycling along on his crooked bicycle. He saw us and stopped. He harshly demanded to know why we hadn't been to training recently. So we told him.

He said we should be ashamed of ourselves. How could anyone with any self-respect go and spend all day working on a loom? 'Listen, lads. The league games are coming up soon, and you must come to all the training sessions. OK?'

Gazi and I exchanged glances.

'What are you looking at each other for?' asked the captain, 'We'll see you at the club . . . Is that understood? I want you at the training sessions giving your all.'

And off he went on his battered bicycle, becoming little more than a large bottom in golf trousers disappearing into the distance.

'He said that they'd see us all right at the club,' said Gazi. 'You heard him!'

'So? A fiver a week or a tenner, tops. Then what?'

'I know it won't be much, but you've got to think of this shuttle thing.'

'Meaning?'

'Meaning, it's just not worth . . .' he started, and then he laughed.

'That's all well and good,' I said, 'but we'd be letting down Ahmet and Reshat if we left.'

'Leave it out! What, you'd rather die?'

The next day we told Ahmet of our decision.

'I knew it!' he responded. 'I said you were soft! You want easy money, don't you? A desk job somewhere, a nice little pen and a bit of paper.'

We didn't leave immediately. They sacked a whole group of the workers and filled all their vacancies with us, their spares. So, at the end of it all, we did get to work our own machines, but at what cost?

We quit.

4

The league games had started, and so had the athletics competitions. As there was a huge shortfall between the food we ate and the calories we burned Gazi and I lost a lot of weight. We became ashamed of our skinny legs and washboard chests.

That evening I went to bed having eaten just a quarter-loaf of bread sprinkled with a mixture of salt, red pepper and cinnamon. That's all my grandmother could manage, now that it was nearing the end of the month.

We had athletics competitions the following afternoon. I was to run the two-hundred, the fifteen-hundred and the four-by-one-hundred relay.

'Remember, lads,' the team captain said, 'you're not to eat meat at lunch! And definitely no onions!' He felt we couldn't run our best if we'd eaten such things.

We played table-tennis at the clubhouse and chatted. Gazi teased Hasan, and we discussed the races that afternoon, but I couldn't help noticing that Hasan was chain-smoking. There were forty of us, and we knew each other very well. So I went over and stood by his side . . . and saw that the tips of cigarettes were decorated with shiny foil! I mean, us and fancy cigarettes?

'Where did you get those from?' I asked.

'Don't ask. I've set aside your share, so don't worry. But don't tell Gazi.'

'Well, OK . . . But where did they come from?'

'I said, don't ask! For heavens' sake!'

But I had to know. I carried on pestering him. How could I not know? Maybe he'd found some buried treasure or something . . . I cornered him in a quiet spot.

He was sniggering to himself. He reached into the back pocket of his baggy trousers and pulled out a blue packet. 'Look at all these fags! And you've got your share set aside. But please don't tell Gazi. He'd only go and spoil it all . . .'

'I want to know where they all came from.'

'Bloody hell! You don't let up, do you? Look the deal is, you get your share – but no questions asked. Right?'

'Come on . . . You know I can keep a secret.'

'I'm not so sure . . . I want you to swear you won't tell anyone!'

I did.

'The captain,' he explained, 'had forgotten them on the table.'

'So you . . .'

'So I . . . Well, you know . . . Look, I asked him for one, and he said no. Said I'd get breathless and wouldn't be able to run properly this afternoon.'

'What if he notices?'

'No chance. How could he? It's not as if he's short of supplies!'

Just as he said that the captain came running in. Hasan blanched. But there was nothing to worry about. He had brought in our studded shoes and started to hand them out. Then he pulled a fiver out of his wallet. 'Could you do me a favour,' he asked Hasan, 'and go and get me a packet of Bosphorus cigarettes?'

Hasan's colour returned to normal. He grabbed the money and shot off.

Our captain was a complete sports fanatic. He would race around the clubhouse all day like a speeding machine, rush in and out of every room and attend to each and every member of the team. He'd be with you one minute, with someone else the next. He was like that now, explaining for the umpteenth time how to start a race and what would constitute a false start. As Hasan handed him his cigarettes he was explaining what we had to pay particular attention to when exchanging batons in the four-by-one-hundred.

I hadn't eaten lunch. There'd been nothing for me to eat. Well, one slice of bread, but that had been it: one slice of plain dry bread. In the two-hundred I came second by a fraction of a second.

We won the four-by-one-hundred. But my heart was pounding too hard, and my vision was blurry . . . My stomach rumbled, and I felt quite sick. They called me up for the fifteen-hundred, and I knew that the earth wasn't really swaying and that the trees were not changing position.

'This is it!' encouraged the captain. 'This is it now! We have to win this race. If we do – and there's no reason why we shouldn't – overall we'll be ahead on points. Just grit your teeth and do it.'

I broke out in a cold sweat.

'You didn't eat meat this lunchtime, did you?'

'I beg you pardon? Did you say meat? Who, me?'

'Yes, you.'

'No, no, I didn't.'

'Good. Save up your appetite. You can eat whatever you want tonight!'

'Uh?'

My legs were shaky, and my eyebrow was twitching. I think there were seven of us lined up at the start. We heard the crack of the starter pistol, and off we went. The first lap went by, and we were on to the second . . . My vision grew darker, and my stomach felt worse. It was as if the earth was sliding around under my studded boots. What was going on?

Lap three. I was running past the captain, and I was really pushing myself to continue. The others were just a couple of paces behind me.

The captain had a cigarette dangling from his lips, and his pale face seemed even paler than usual. 'Open up,' he yelled. 'Pull away!'

A final effort and I pulled away a bit more.

We were on the fourth lap now. Around the middle of the lap I was still ahead . . . I was approaching the end of the fourth lap when suddenly I felt as if I'd been hit over the head with a tree-trunk and the world went topsy-turvy.

When I opened my eyes I saw a bright moon shining in a navy sky . . . Gazi was by my side.

'What happened?' I asked.

'Stay still!'

'OK, but why?'

'Shut up, and just stay still!'

'Did I pass out?'

'Yes, you passed out and ruined it for everybody!'

I slowly sat up. It was night-time, and the cool air of night made the silvery light of the moon seem cold. My whole body felt stiff. Then I remembered everything and felt my hunger return with a vengeance.

'You'd better stay out of the captain's way!'

'Why?'

'You lost the fifteen-hundred, so we ended up in second place on points, thanks to you!'

Hasan butted in. 'You idiot!' he said. 'What did you have to go and faint for?' He was joking, I presumed. He and Gazi held me on either side, handed me my rolled-up clothes and bundled me into a cab. Hasan gave the driver a doctor's address.

'Why there?' I asked.

'You're ill, aren't you?'

'Who, me?'

'Yes, you.'

'I'm not ill! Forget about the doctor's.'

'Why did you faint then?'

I leaned over and whispered in Hasan's ear.

He burst out laughing. 'Well then! Hey, cabbie! Take us to Silo's Kebabs!'

We entered the crowded restaurant to a tantalizing smell of meat. Hasan turned to one of the waiters with all the airs of a rich man. 'Excuse me! Attend to the gentlemen, please!' What? Was this the same Hasan Hüseyin we knew?

'Hasan,' said Gazi, 'are you sure about this? I mean, I'm totally broke, and so is he.'

Hasan was deadly serious. 'Excuse me, waiter! Attend to the gentlemen!'

We ordered our kebabs. This had really perked us up . . . But how were we going to pay? Hasan offered us fancy cigarettes from his blue packet, which we stuck behind our ears as the kebabs arrived, and all three of us dived into our food in a frenzy.

After we had eaten, while we were washing our hands, Hasan whispered in my ear and explained where the money had come from. 'You know when I brought back the captain's cigarettes? Well, I had all his change, and there was all the commotion . . .'

5

My grandmother wrote to my youngest aunt begging her to take me in, telling her about my weaving job and how the way I was carrying on was very worrying. My aunt lived in an Istanbul suburb and was married to a gentleman in commerce.

She acted immediately. We received a letter from her; it was fifteen pages long and addressed to me.

'You can't do whatever you feel like! What will people say? As soon as you receive the money I'm sending, you're to come immediately.'

I told Gazi first. His eyes lit up. 'Oh, wow, would you believe it? That's brilliant!'

'Yes,' I said, 'but you'll end up staying here.'

'Forget us lot. I'll come along with you though, if you want. I'm fed up with my mother nagging me anyway. We'll go off, get ourselves jobs or else we'll get into Gedikli. That'll be easiest.'

'And when we graduate from Gedikli we can marry our girlfriends!'

'Forget about them. Your aunt's money is enough to get us both there. We'll go by boat, travelling on the open deck.'

Our decision made, we thought of Hasan. We decided to keep this from him. There would be no problem telling the girls though. After all, they loved us and lived for us . . .

That night we went back to the old sycamore and signalled the girls to come out with our matches. They emerged, and we told them our news. Mine started to cry. 'You're lying!' she said. 'You'll forget all about us as soon as you get there!'

How could we? We lived for them, too. What value would our lives have if not for them?

Three days later, clutching the old suitcase I'd brought with me from Beirut, my threadbare bedding and my basket, I left my grandmother's.

When I got to the train station the girls were there and, in spite of everything, so was Hasan. My girlfriend had her head on her sister's shoulder and was crying. Hasan had removed his glass eye and was wiping it with his handkerchief. Then the third bell went, the engine blew its whistle, and the train started to move. Handkerchiefs were waved, and my girl still rested her head on her sister's shoulder.

Gazi was to board the train at the next station. When the train arrived he leaped on; hands and pockets empty and with half a packet of cigarettes. It was his first proper journey anywhere. He was chain-smoking, spitting and, unusually for him, biting his nails. 'My left ear's humming!' he complained at one point. 'What if my father hears of me running away?' he asked a little later.

'What if he does? So what?'

'Could he have me sent back?'

'No he couldn't!' I said. 'You're over eighteen, your father can't have you sent back from anywhere. Don't worry, the law's on our side!'

He paused. 'My poor father,' he murmured. 'He was saying how his vision sometimes darkened, how sometimes he felt dizzy. And he has kidney stones.' He sighed deeply and flicked away his cigarette butt.

When we arrived at Mersin we bought two of the cheapest tickets available and went down to the port. There, some distance over the flickering sea, the ship that was to take us away was busily releasing clouds of black smoke into the evening sky. We were taken to it on a small boat. Once on board we placed my things in a corner of the hold and went up on deck. We looked back at the twinkling light of the brightly lit city of Mersin.

'My poor father!' repeated Gazi. 'What with his kidney stones and all . . .' He rested his head against the iron railings.

The sadness of the evening, Gazi, the shimmering lights of the city, the sea . . . I felt like crying. The slowly darkening sea somehow made me think of death. I felt sad and remembered my little sister who had died years ago when she was only four. I thought of her tiny little coffin, the narrow little grave and her dainty little gravestone. I felt as if we might be lost in these waters for ever.

'How much money do we have left?' asked Gazi suddenly.

'We have seventy-five kuruş.'

'I've no cigarettes left either.'

So I went and bought him a cheap seven-and-a-half-kuruş pack. Then we descended to the hold and across to our belongings. We spread out my bedding and sat down next to one another. Over to one side of the hold an elderly man had turned his cap back to front and was engaged in his evening prayers. Over on the other a young man with a red waistband was drinking raki. There were women in purdah, naughty boys running around and young girls who had to remain kneeling on the floor demurely for hours on end . . . We paid attention only to one family in that entire crowd though. Well, I say family, and we did know the couple from Adana, but . . . The woman was quite old and wrinkled and wore too much makeup, and we knew that the one-armed man she referred to as her 'husband' was a pimp. But who cared? We reintroduced ourselves, and we were soon on familiar terms.

The woman had a beautiful, graceful daughter. The raucous laughter of the mother revealed nicotine-stained teeth, and the daughter was clearly embarrassed by this. 'Mother!' she would exclaim every so often.

The woman didn't care at all. She laughed, chatted, made eyes at us, kept touching us, lit one cigarette after another and generally talked non-stop. Within half an hour we had her full life story; well, the sort of story that one expects from a woman like her. They inevitably come from a noble family, but then their husband cheats on them, so their womanly pride gets injured, so for the sake of their honour . . .

But she was marvellously open-handed. Every time she lit a cigarette she thought of us, and if we tried to decline insisted with a 'Go on, go on.' Even though I wasn't much of a smoker I thought of what Gazi would be like later, so I accepted each cigarette, took two puffs, then stubbed it out and pocketed it.

As I stared at the woman's – Zümrüt's – blackened teeth I must have drifted off to sleep. When I woke up it was morning. A breakfast feast had been spread out, and Gazi, who clearly hadn't even washed his face, was already sitting cross-legged by the food.

'Come on,' he said, when he saw I was awake. 'We're having breakfast. We were just waiting for you to wake up.'

I took one long look at him. Then I left, saying I was going to wash my hands and face. I did not return. Out on the deck the morning breeze was cool and the sea was calm. Our ship was moving along, quite close to the shore.

A flustered Gazi appeared by my side. 'Why didn't you come and have breakfast?'

I just looked at him.

He laughed. 'Leave it out. This is no time for pride. What do you think of the daughter, though?'

'Eh?'

'The girl. Quite something, isn't she?'

'Shame on you!'

'Why?'

'What about her back home?'

He wandered off, whistling.

I stayed on deck until the sun was high in the sky, watching the dolphins. They were chasing the ship, stubbornly tailing us. The wrinkled skin of the sea, now a dull green under the bright sun, reflected the sunlight back, as if it were a mirror smashed into millions of tiny pieces.

I went down into the hold. Zümrüt was still talking. Gazi was lounging around by her daughter's knees, already friends. Knowing that any comment under such circumstances was bound to fall on deaf ears, I ignored them. Gazi seemed happy with that. The others were as well. In fact, I was happy for things to be this way. At least I didn't have the mouth and the cigarettes to contend with.

I went up on deck again.

The next day passed in much the same way.

As soon as Gazi mentioned he was getting hungry the mother and the daughter immediately spread out the sheet to put food down for him. If anything, the mother was keener. And he didn't wait to be asked. He just tucked in.

As for the one-armed man the woman referred to as 'my husband', he was really quiet. He would escort Zümrüt to the lavatories now and again and help put the food out and clear up afterwards, but otherwise he just sat there, listening to her all day.

We didn't mix much with any of the other passengers. Most of them were there for a short time only and disembarked soon after they boarded. Peasants, tradesmen . . .

At one of the small ports we stopped at on our third night a young man called Hasan boarded the ship. He was dark, athletic, good-looking and played the harmonica beautifully. He did the Charleston as well as Caucasian and West Anatolian folk dances. The atmosphere in the hold was transformed by his arrival. He, too, like us, was off to Istanbul in search of a future. He'd wangled himself a ticket somehow, left his girlfriend behind and was off to seek his fortune.

'If I manage to get into Gedikli,' he told us, 'it'll be good. If not, I have this friend in Galata called Nevzat . . . He works shovelling coal. I'll just have to go and live off him. He'll make sure I'm all right.'

'Did you say Gedikli? That's where we're heading.'

'You, too? Really? Well, I'm hoping that this time . . .'

'This time?'

'Five years . . . For five years now I've been going there year after year, trying to get in but getting nowhere.'

'Eh?'

'I live with my poor old mother . . . I don't remember my dad. Apparently he was a fisherman. Lads around our way don't usually remember their dads.'

'Why not?'

'They go fishing throughout the year. So when they leave one morning and don't come back that night, no one's really that surprised. The mothers around our way have to be our fathers, too!'

Zümrüt and her daughter disembarked that day at a picturesque little port set among orange groves. Gazi was leaning on the iron railings, gazing after them, even after they had disappeared long since.

I nudged his shoulder. 'And now?'

He sighed. 'Give me a cigarette!'

I took out one of the cigarettes I had stashed away for him.

'What do you call that?'

I explained.

He burst out laughing. 'Well done, mate!' he said. 'We're ready for anything now!'

'And that girl?'

'Oh, forget about her.'

'Really? Why?'

'It wasn't the girl I was after anyway. It was her mother's cigarettes and the food. That's all that was.'

'Don't worry about being broke,' said our new friend Hasan, 'or about going hungry or anything. If things get a bit tight we can always shovel coal into the furnace in the boiler room. But it won't come to that. We can help traders with their loading and unloading.'

He was right. We didn't end up having to shovel coal. We helped the traders load and unload all along the route. We didn't earn much, but, then again, we weren't starving either. One day, the ninth of our voyage, we woke to the long croaky sound of the ship's horn.

'We're there!' exclaimed Hasan.

We rushed up on deck. The ship was anchoring at Galata.

Istanbul was shrouded in a fine mist. We were facing the Galata Bridge. Trams were shuttling to and fro, and people were milling around, looking like a mass of ants from a distance. The dirty waters of the port were crowded with barges and steamers. The hubbub of voices permeated the blanket of smoke and the smell of coal.

'Well I never,' marvelled Gazi. 'Well I never . . .'

'What's that?'

'Well, I mean, it's Istanbul. Istanbul! Look at how beautiful it is!'

Hasan took us over to the home of his friend, the coal worker Nevzat, in Galata. Hooked-nosed Nevzat was black all over and had his sleeves rolled up to his elbows. He smiled, baring two shiny white rows of teeth.

'As you have nowhere else to stay,' he said, 'you're more than welcome to stay here.' He offered us some bread with white cheese and a few boiled eggs. 'You'll have to excuse me,' he said, 'but I have to get to work. My room is yours.'

It was a tiny, narrow room. The floor was littered with onion skins and empty raki bottles, and there was a pile of filthy pots to one side.

'What do you think of my friend then?' asked Hasan. 'Just like I told you, eh?'

He pointed out a picture of a pretty woman stuck up on the wall with four drawing-pins. 'He used to live with this woman,' he explained, 'until he caught some dreadful disease off her. Anyone else would have murdered the bitch. But not him. On the contrary, he paid to have her treated and then sent her on her way. Never saw her again. He's a good lad is our Nevzat. Sound.'

There's so much in Istanbul to amaze people like us, fresh from the sticks. It's marvellous! For all its wonders, though, what use is Istanbul to a young man who has just stepped off a boat with all of sixty kuruş to his name?

So the three of us set off to Karaköy, went up Bankalar Road and over to Beyoglu. Gazi was wide-eyed every step of the way. He was completely lost for words.

After that we toured Istanbul, that wonderful city of legends. We were so mesmerized by it all that we completely forgot about our girlfriends and the Gedikli Academy. We were ready to die for any one of the stunning women we spotted . . .

6

Eventually we had our fill of the wonders of Istanbul. This was because we were almost always hungry, and beautiful sights didn't fill our stomachs. It was high time we found ourselves some work. Yes, work! But where?

We were free men, as far as that went. We were free to set up a factory or walk into any restaurant in Istanbul and order anything on the menu. But we didn't have the means to set up a factory or walk into, say, Tokatliyan's and order whatever we desired. I guess we just didn't know how to make the most of our freedom.

One day, when we were wandering aimlessly, once more in the grip of hunger pangs, who should we come across in Aksaray but old Cemal. He was the one who had bought himself a cold drink with our stamp money instead of posting our letter.

After hugging and jumping all over each other so much that passers-by began to stare, we started catching up. He had got into Gedikli the year before, so we asked if we might be able to get in. He shook his head sadly. There were many applicants . . . Having said that, our chances were as good as anyone else's, so why not?

'But hang on, guys,' he said. 'You remember Memet; you know, the twenty-six-year-old?'

'Our team captain?'

'Yeah, him. He's here, over in Beykoz. He works in a nightclub that has a restaurant. It's a cushy number. If you're here to work, his boss could probably get you jobs at the Beykoz shoe factory. All the foremen and people from the factory eat there.'

'That's for later,' said Gazi. 'This idiot's too proud to say anything, but we've not had a bite to eat since yesterday. We can't think straight any more. Come on, mate, how much have you got on you?'

Cemal checked his pockets. 'Not much, I'm afraid. I could get you guys some bread and cheese . . .'

'And a packet of cigarettes. I've had it with smoking butts!'

'As we're going for it,' I added, 'a cup of coffee would go down a treat.'

'Leave it out, guys! Forget about cigarettes and coffee, right?'

'Believe me, Cemal, mate, we can't simply forget about cigarettes or coffee!'

The next day we latched on to him, and off we went to Beykoz. When we got there, he led us to a tiny little restaurant, nestling among whispering trees by the side of the road.

'The food here is amazing,' he confided. 'Let's sit down.'

'So the food here is amazing,' Gazi whispered to me. 'Look, you'd better not stop me from eating my fill. I'll eat as many portions as I can!'

'What are you like? You'll totally put them off from doing us any favours!'

'Why should I put them off? I'm fed up with your attitude! Just don't interfere. I'm going to get stuck in.'

We pulled up a chair each. Cemal returned with Memet. And there he was; the captain of our neighbourhood football team. When he saw us he was stunned at first and then delighted. Then he lost his good humour. He had thought that we had come to watch the legendary Fenerbahçe play football and to spend money, but we just wanted to talk about finding some work. Well, yes, he agreed, of course we were friends, but he didn't own the restaurant. He made enough to eat, but that was it. And the boss was an awkward customer. No, he didn't think he'd let us eat on credit. Jobs at the Beykoz shoe factory? We really did come out with some crackpot ideas, didn't we? We should see what it was like outside the gates. There were queues of people desperate for work– and not people like us but skilled cobblers who had once had their own businesses!

I looked at Gazi, and he looked at me. His fists were resting on his waist, shaking.

Cemal bitterly regretted bringing us all the way here. 'Come on,' he pleaded, 'at least put the guys up for a couple of days!'

'To be honest with you, Cemal,' said Memet, 'I don't know if I can. If the restaurant was mine, there'd be no question about it obviously. But I just work here . . . As for the boss, well, he's meant to be my friend from the Balmumcu orphanage, but you have no idea what he's like.'

Gazi, on the verge of tears, grabbed me by the arm. 'Come on, we're leaving!' He indicated the hills in the distance. 'We'll head that way!'

'Shame on you!' said Cemal to Memet. 'Call yourself a friend? Call yourself a human being? You were starving when we found you in Adana. If it wasn't for us . . . Forgotten all that now, have you?'

'Oh, Cemal, of course I haven't forgotten. I know . . . God bless you, how could I forget? You all helped me out so much, but . . .'

'There are no ifs or buts about it. Go and talk to your boss. Now!'

Memet gulped and turned towards the back of the restaurant, looking around.

'All right,' said Gazi. 'Where is he? I'll talk to him.'

Memet gestured towards one of the crowded tables. 'He's the one standing there with his back to us. With the white shirt, holding the tray.'

Gazi strode forward, and Cemal and I followed. Gazi took the man to one side. 'Look, sir,' he said, 'we're friends of that useless waiter of yours. We've come all the way from Adana. We've no work, no money, and, to be frank, we're starving hungry. Could you possibly put us up for a couple of days?'

The boss looked us up and down. 'Did you come all the way here thinking that Memet owned the place?'

Gazi told him the full story.

The man laughed out loud. 'So you lads heard that Istanbul's streets were paved with gold.' He called Memet, who ran to his side. 'Look, they came here thinking you owned the place. They heard the streets of Istanbul were paved with gold. Why are you sending them away?'

Memet blushed.

'Come on now,' said his boss. 'Get them some chairs to sit on and offer them a drink. Now that we're running this charity we might as well look after them! Oh, and feed the poor beggars!'

We took the chairs, feeling small and embarrassed. We carried them out behind the cafeteria, on to the grass. We sat down and lit up.

'Don't let it bug you,' said Memet. 'He always talks that way. You should hear what he calls me!'

We pretended not to care. We sat there an hour, then two, then until it was dark. We talked about Yorgi, about Ahmet the café owner, about Mendiye, about our football games, how if Meatball Ahmet had played in the final against Kubilayspor instead of Croupier Bayram we might have won, how if only the free kick had been taken by Gazi and not Dodge Ali it would have been a dead cert, and how grocer Nuri kept going on about the membership fees he kept paying even though he never got to play a single game . . .

Gazi slapped Cemal's cap playfully. 'You useless oaf! Remember the day you nicked our stamp money to get a cold drink?'

'Yeah . . . Those were the days. Mind you, I was dying of thirst!'

'We had to walk all bloody night because of you!'

'Yorgi sold his wristwatch, do you remember? Good old Yorgi.'

'He was better when he had the bran shop . . . Now he's really rich, in the drapery business.'

'Really?' said Memet. 'So he finally married his uncle's daughter? And what about Saim?'

'He's graduating from high school this year and wants to get into law. Says he's going to be a judge.'

'And Dodge Ali? Salih? Hunchback Recep?'

'You don't want to know about Hunchback Recep.'

'Why? What happened?'

'He died.'

'No, really?'

'Yeah, it was awful, the poor guy . . . His body was crawling with worms when they found him.'

It was getting dark, and we sat silently, listening to the rustling of the leaves and the distant hoots of ships traversing the Bosphorus.

'And what about Hasan Hüseyin?' asked Memet. 'Is he an accountant yet?'

'No, but he will be.'

'He will be, huh?'

'He will.'

Memet sniggered.

'What's so funny?'

'I just remembered the day he stuffed his pockets full of fruit compote.'

'And then there was that time with our captain's cigarettes . . .'

'And that day he ordered us kebabs?'

'Those were the days all right,' mused Gazi, 'stuffing our faces one day, starving the next.'

Cemal caught the last ferry back.

'Right then,' I said. 'Are you really telling me that a city this size, this huge place can't fit in a couple more people like us?'

Memet sighed. 'I hate this poverty! Look, I'm not a bad guy . . . Come on, guys, you know I'm not bad at heart. Not at all, really. But what can I do? A couple of my friends have come all this way, and really I should be able to go and take them out somewhere, put them up, show them the sights . . . I mean, I know I should, but I'm tied down here. I don't have that choice.'

I caught Gazi's expression out of the corner of my eye. I could hear people going past on the road behind me and the lively laughter of children chasing each other under the trees.

Memet's boss had come right up to us, and we hadn't heard him. 'So,' he said, 'you're going to get a job in Istanbul, earn some money and send for your girlfriends? You'll need a decent place to stay . . . Plus, most important of all, you'll need a good strong safe each. That's a must. To keep all your savings in, eh?' Fists resting on his waist, he laughed at us. 'If,' he continued, 'you ever need a cook and a scullion, do let us know. Memet and I are always on the look-out for something better!'

He started to walk away but then stopped. 'The restaurant has an attic. It's not what you might call a guest room, but you'll be OK if you lay down a mat. The weather's warm, so you won't need any covers. The only thing is, there'll be plenty of rats and cockroaches. They might get a bit cheeky, so I'd plug my ears if I were you. Oh, and I think there's a cracked mirror up there, too. You can brush the dust off that and use it. I think it belonged to some Armenian nobleman who used it for his morning ablutions. It doesn't reflect very well; it's a bit warped, and the silver's coming off. Still, it did belong to a nobleman, and even if it isn't worth any money that's got to count for something, eh? What do you think?'

We didn't reply.

He went off, laughing to himself. Then he called Memet over and had words with him.

Gazi, meanwhile, was cursing his poverty and at having to put up with all this.

7

The next morning Memet came up to us. 'I'm going into Istanbul,' he said. 'I'll go to Nevzat's in Galata and bring your stuff over. Why don't you write a note I can give him?'

I wrote a brief message and gave it to Memet.

When he got back, he looked very pleased with himself; suspiciously so. 'I got there,' he explained. 'I found Nevzat and gave him your note. He read it, and he said, "Tell them not to worry about their stuff. It can stay here. I'll look after it. They can pick it up whenever they come back."'

Memet laid on an excellent feast for us that evening, complete with dolma, salad and raki, and quickly got drunk. He started crying. 'Now take me,' he said. 'I'm not a bad guy really, you know I'm not, but this poverty, you know . . .' He was putting his arms around me, then turning to Gazi and giving him a hug, then embracing me again.

We ate, we drank, we sat in the park by the sea and watched the sailing ships, shared our knowledge of stars, made lewd comments about immodest women and finally went to bed in the early hours. When we woke up the sun was reflecting off our dusty piece of mirror.

'What did you make of Memet's behaviour last night?' asked Gazi.

'I don't know. It reminds me of Hasan ordering us those kebabs. If Memet hasn't stumbled on some treasure something must have happened. I'm sure we'll find out sooner or later.' And, sure enough, we did.

It was another day at the restaurant, and we felt we had no chance of finding work. The day went by, and late that night Memet was with his boss stuffing dolma. The smell permeated the whole place. We had not had a bite to eat all day. We were breathing in the smell of the fresh stuffing and staring straight down at the aubergine dolma, which were lined up on white oval serving plates immediately below us.

'I could eat twenty of those,' declared Gazi.

'Don't go getting ideas!'

'No, I'm serious.' We stared at the plates without blinking. 'Later on, we could creep down quietly . . .' he continued.

'And then what?'

'We'd gently lift the glass on the display unit . . .'

'And?'

'Just take one each.'

'Would you really do that?'

'I don't know. You?'

'Me? I don't think so.'

Gazi swore at Istanbul. 'What a place!' he said. 'If my mother was still alive to see me now! Here I am, agonizing over a couple of dolma!'

'What about me? I'll never forget, one day my brother Niyazi turned his nose up at some lamb chops at a meal. So my father forced him to eat a couple of them, and he ran off heaving. We used to have meat delivered by the carcass. Butter was delivered in large bags and cheese in big cans.'

'And that joker's taking the mickey out of us.'

'Who?'

'Memet's boss.'

'Oh, what, that stuff the other day? If we ever needed a cook and all that . . .'

'And all that business about what we'd earn and how we'd need a safe. He's taking the mickey. Hey, look, I reckon they've made a bit too much of that stuffing for the dolma. What do you think?'

'It looks that way. But that's not for us to say, is it?'

'No, but if they have too much stuffing . . . I mean, if it was all eaten at least none would be wasted.'

When Memet and his boss had finished preparing the dolma there was indeed some leftover stuffing, but they got a spoon each and started tucking in.

I bit down on my lips. Gazi swore and let out a cough. They looked up, but we pulled back just in time.

'Are those idiots asleep?' asked the man.

Memet nodded.

'Are we idiots?' whispered Gazi.

'I don't know. I don't think so,' I whispered back.

'You tell that friend Cemal of yours,' continued the boss, 'not to be gathering up all these useless strays and dumping them here. And tell those bums to pack up tomorrow and bugger off!'

Memet hung his head.

'I realize,' said the man, 'that Istanbul's a big city. It's not easy to be broke, to have to wander around with no money. It's hard, really hard. I do realize that, but you know the financial situation we're in . . . I asked you to see Bohor today. Did you?'

'To settle his tab? Yes, I saw him. He apologized and said he'd definitely settle in a couple of days or so.'

'Typical! Whoever we go to, it's either payment in a couple of days or at the end of the month. We owe over a grand ourselves. I don't know how we're going to get through this month. Go and tell those bums that they have to be out tomorrow. I'm not a charity. Let God feed the mouths he created!' This was followed by a long silence.

Gazi looked at me with his sunken eyes and we just sat there, regarding one another.

The next day Memet didn't have to say anything. We politely asked him for the fare money back into town. He pretended to be disappointed that we were leaving so soon. 'Don't think badly of me,' he said. 'I'm not a bad guy. At the end of the day, I'm only . . .'

His boss had come over, curious. 'What's up? Off already? You should have stayed until you found some work. What're you going to do? Have you decided?'

We told him that we had made no decision. Gazi and I exchanged glances. Then, having got enough money for the boat fare, we went down to the port. We went back into Istanbul, over to Galata and found Nevzat. There he was, beaky nose and pearly teeth. It was at that point we found out the truth.

'Short man, beady little eyes, clean-shaven. Came here, gave me your note, so I gave all your belongings to him. Then off he went!'

Gazi was livid and swore and cursed. I simply froze in horror.

Nevzat took a long hard look at us and wandered over to the window, whistling softly to himself. He picked up a large tomato that was on the table. 'So . . . he didn't bring you your stuff?'

'No.'

'What are you going to do now? You've no bedding, no clothes . . .'

'I don't know.'

He looked us up and down again. 'Well, now! That brings me to the second part of the story. I got your note, but – I'm not going to lie to you – I didn't like the look of him. So I did give him your stuff, but I went and followed him when he left here. Out he went, and so did I. Anyway, to cut a long story short, he took your stuff to this Jewish place down the road, left it there, and off he went. So I went straight in, walked up to the Jew and told him that the property had been stolen and that the police would be along any minute. The Jew had a fit. Your mate had pawned your belongings for a ten-lira note, so I gave the Jew the money and reclaimed your stuff. It's all downstairs, sitting there. You can pick it up whenever you want.'

Gazi and I went wild! We put our arms around Nevzat's neck and embraced and kissed him.

'As you lads still haven't got jobs,' he said, 'you can take your stuff or leave it here if you prefer. What I'm trying to say is, the tenner really isn't that important. So only if you ever have the spare cash . . .'

I thought of asking my youngest aunt for some money. So I wrote her a letter explaining the gravity of the situation we were in, that I had a friend with me and asked her to send some money immediately. Nevzat posted the letter himself.

While we waited for the money we were sure would arrive imminently we had nothing to do but wander around aimlessly, stare into shop windows, select our favourites from the luxury cars that drove by and get into pointless arguments about which car was the best. Gazi suggested that as soon as the cash arrived we should go and get ourselves a slap-up meal.

'No way!' I said. 'Bread and cheese and a bit of fruit. We have to make the money last!'

'Is your aunt's husband rich?'

'Fairly.'

'Do they like you?'

'They used to.'

'A lot?'

'I guess so. "You'll be the greatest doctor in Turkey," they would say. So they must have liked me.'

'Then there's nothing to worry about, is there? I'll bet they send you at least a hundred . . .'

'A hundred liras?'

'Sure! They'll think about what you'll need and take into account that you have a friend with you. They'll not want you to be embarrassed in front of your friend. Don't you think?'

'Maybe . . . But maybe not.'

'Don't think "maybe not"! They care for you!'

'Huh?'

We were in Beyazit, sitting by the fountain. It was a warm, sunny day, and Istanbul was beautiful, but we were hungry!

'You know,' I said, 'it might be an idea to do another round of those restaurants.'

'Be patient,' said Gazi. 'Don't abuse their goodwill. Look, Nevzat isn't kicking us out. Let's just grit our teeth for another couple of days and see what happens.'

'You just want to carry on staying there until he kicks us out, don't you? You never used to be like this in Adana.'

'I'm still not like that . . . It's just that we're stuck now, aren't we?'

A tramp was walking past. He shouted across the road to someone he knew. 'Hey, Metroviçeli!' He ran across the road.

I suddenly had a blinding flash. 'Hang on a minute!' I said to Gazi. 'You remember that friend we made at the Cretan's café? Soldier Nejip? Nejip Metroviçeli, he was!'

'Yeah, he was. Soldier Nejip. What was his address?'

'I think I remember it . . . Metroviçeli, Nejip. Working at the docks he was, up the Golden Horn . . .'

'That'll do,' said Gazi, grabbing me by the arm. 'Come on, let's go!'

Off we went. We eventually found the docks and walked around all the tobacco warehouses there. And, sure enough, by lunchtime, there was Nejip, standing in front of us, covered in a filthy brown layer of muck. He stank of tobacco. He could not believe his eyes. He hugged me, hugged Gazi, then hugged me again. Then he went inside a warehouse and asked for a short break. He shoved us into the restaurant next door and told us to have ourselves a good meal.

'I've got to get back now,' he said, 'but when you're finished here you can wait for me at the café. I'll have a word, so don't you pay for anything!'

Gazi had already sat down. 'Don't just stand there,' he said to me. 'Sit down, and let's tuck in!' He impatiently tapped his fork on his plate.

'Let's not get too carried away,' I warned, 'because . . .'

'Leave me alone. I'm so hungry I can't see straight. Waiter, excuse me, over here . . . These waiters are a bit dozy . . . Hey, waiter, over here!'

The waiter came over.

'First,' said Gazi, 'bring me some cold dolma . . . Or, no, wait. I'll have hot dolma, but make sure the chef gives me some big ones!'

The waiter chuckled as he went off.

'What are you staring at?' Gazi asked me. 'I'm going to eat a week's worth. What's it to you? But how did Nejip know we were hungry? Do we look that starved, I wonder? That's what you call a friend. One look at us, and he could tell we were hungry. Good on him!'

The waiter brought his dolma.

'I'll have a bowl of soup, please,' I said.

Nejip came over much later when his shift was done. The streets were full of tobacco workers and their hubbub. I would love to have been one of their rusty-brown, dirty but none the less cheerful crowd.

Nejip kept asking us questions, laughing and being happy. 'We can go and see some games. You wouldn't believe some of the matches they have. Which club are you going to go to? I'd say you should get yourselves into Fenerbahçe. You see Fenerbahçe . . .'

Gazi and I exchanged glances and smiled to ourselves.

'So which hotel are you staying in?' Nejip asked, after we'd had God knows how many coffees. 'Is it a nice, clean place?'

Gazi winked at me. 'Very clean,' he said.

'Well, you can stay with me for tonight anyway. Come on then . . . Do we have to let the hotel know?'

'Not really,' said Gazi and burst out laughing. 'What hotel, mate? How would we be in a hotel? We've been lucky to have a floor to crash on!'

'Whose floor have you been crashing on?'

'We met this guy called Nevzat. We're on the floor in his room.'

'He shovels coal for a living.'

'And I thought that . . .' Nejip began and then stopped. He started walking off and beckoned to us to follow.

Well, whatever he had thought, it didn't stop him being the perfect host.

We accompanied him along some streets, around a few corners, entered a crowded neighbourhood with lots of tiled roofs and bay windows and then into his family's small wooden house. He led us into their sitting-room. The house was shady and cool inside. A white, fleeting image of a woman flickered to and fro, first at one end of the room, then at the other.

The cover of the divan and the curtains in the room had been delicately embroidered in greens and pinks and purples. There were no pictures on any of the walls, just thickly framed large, ornate texts in Arabic.

'My mother won't allow photographs in this room,' explained Nejip, 'because she prays here.'

The floorboards were yellow from years of polishing. I could see the side of a hill out of the window, occupied by a graveyard.

We respectfully kissed Nejip's ageing mother's wrinkled hands. She spoke a little Turkish. She asked us polite questions, as best she could, and we tried to provide answers.

It was getting dark. Nejip's sister, who also worked in the tobacco warehouse, entered the room wearing blue earrings and with her curly hair uncovered. 'Welcome,' she said and went and lit the pink lamp on the sideboard before leaving us again.

Before long we were joined by Nejip's dark-moustachioed father, his plaster-splattered uncle and his elder brother, who turned out to be a carpenter. They all had thick and calloused hands and chatted to us in their broken Turkish. I thought they were wonderful people, particularly the father. He talked about various matters, smoothed his thick moustache in an authoritative manner and swore frequently. Meanwhile Nejip's sister lay out a dining-cloth across the floor, lay a chopping-board down on it, set down little flannels we would be using as napkins and brought in the bread-box. She did all this as if playing a little game, smiling now and then and revealing a sparkling gold tooth whenever she did so. I wondered who she was smiling for: me or Gazi?

After we had eaten our meal, drunk our coffees and chatted about things of no consequence, we retired to the beds Nejip's sister had made up for us. Our beds had been laid out side by side. All the bedding was spotlessly clean, expertly patched here and there and smelling of soap.

We climbed into our beds.

'Ahhh . . .' I sighed. 'This is great!'

Gazi lifted his head up. 'What? You mean the girl? I could get engaged to her immediately!'

I got very cross with him. 'You unscrupulous . . .'

'No, that's what you are! Now, I know that if I don't beat you to it . . .'

'What?'

'Come on, I saw you. Giving her all those leery looks.'

The next morning we had a marvellous breakfast and wandered down to Galata. The day passed.

'Once the money from your aunt comes through,' said Gazi the next day, 'we can invite Nejip out.'

'Yes, that'll be good. We can take him out for a meal.'

'To a decent place. With raki and proper meze.'

'We'll pay back Nevzat, too.'

'Obviously. We'll also have to invite him out as well.'

'We could do that, you know. Take him along to a restaurant with Nejip. We ought to, really.'

'We could order two full bottles of raki . . .'

'If I get about a hundred and fifty or so, then it really won't matter.'

'I wouldn't worry. Your aunt's bound to send you at least

that. Because she does know you have a friend with you as well . . .'

That evening Nevzat handed me the letter I had long been waiting for. I excitedly ripped open the envelope. Gazi and I leaned over and swiftly read the brief note.

I was to leave any so-called friend and come over straight away. There would be no need for me to pay the bus fare – I had only to give my uncle's name. And when was I going to learn not to let every bum and scrounger tag along wherever I went!

Gazi had changed colour. I tore up the letter and threw it out of the window and into the smell of fried fish. First, we sold my clothes and then my suitcase.

'Istanbul is one of a kind!'

You can hop off its trams, hop on to its taxis and entertain whom you want at the restaurant of your choice . . . You can set up a factory, or stay unemployed or open a bank . . . Whatever you want!

'Istanbul is one of a kind!'

Then what?

Well, then, it was first one bit of work, then another. We worked as waiters in cafés around Galata, shovelled coal, did a bit of street selling and occasionally played for some of the useless local football teams, all for no more than a square meal.

'Istanbul is one of a kind!'

Finally one morning, half starving, we bade farewell to the bridge, to the trams, to the dirty sea, to Galata and to Beyoglu and boarded a ship back home, leaving all those beautiful women to the men of Istanbul.

Farewell, then, Istanbul!

8

We saw Hasan Hüseyin the night we got back to Adana. We found out that my girlfriend had gone off with a sailor. Gazi's had got engaged to her cousin who worked as a farmhand in a nearby village, and the Cretan café owner had been busted for dealing hashish and was doing time.

'How about that?' mused Gazi. 'Would you believe it?'

As for me . . . 'What are you thinking?' Hasan asked me.

'Don't mind him,' said Gazi. 'He just can't let things go. I don't know what it is with him – you can't dwell on these things.'

It was nearly midnight by the time I left them. I went over to the old sycamore tree, where we used to light matches and signal our girlfriends. It seemed to be waiting patiently, resigned to whatever fate might bring. I leaned against its trunk. In the distance I saw the two brightly lit windows. It all looked exactly the way we had left it. I gave a loud whistle. I noticed two shadows pause at one of the windows. My second whistle created more of a stir. One of the shadows seem to climb on the sofa. A lamp signalled 'Coming!' My face began to twitch, and my left ear started to hum. I thought of how she would break down and apologize . . . How on earth was she going to explain what she had done to me? How, I wondered? Just how?

She came and stood in front of me without even saying 'Welcome back.' We stood silently for a while.

'Is it true?' I asked eventually.

She remained quiet.

'So it is true?'

Still nothing.

'How did you meet him?' I asked.

She still didn't say a word.

'So,' I said, 'I don't have a chance.'

She raised her head and looked up to the stars, then folded her arms in front of her chest.

'There's no way he could love you the way I do,' I said. 'You're going to regret this, believe me. You're really going to regret it.'

She shrugged.

I flicked away the last of my cigarette and left.

Back on the tarmac I walked under the electric lights, hearing the occasional whistle of a night-watchman. As I went around a corner someone caught up with me and grabbed me by the arm. It was Hasan.

'Is all this nonsense over now?' he enquired.

I couldn't bring myself to say yes.

'Hey, I'm asking you . . . Is it all over?'

'You see . . .'

'Look, mate. There are no ifs or buts about it. You've got to get your act together. You've either got to go back to school or get yourself a proper job.'

'Got a light?' I lit a cigarette.

9

'I'd expect stray dogs in the street to show more common sense than you do!' declared my grandmother. If only I had left my friend and stayed at my aunt's. In this harsh world it was each man for himself. Blah blah blah.

Gazi got a heavy beating from his father, because he went along with some no-good bum and ran away from home. Three days later he was forced to start work at a flour mill his uncle owned in a nearby village.

And about two weeks after that my mother turned up with my sisters. She carried stern orders from my father. He said that I shouldn't have left school in the first place and that I must decide what to do with my life . . .

'OK,' I said. 'I'll go to school.'

'"OK, I'll go to school"?' repeated my mother, shocked. 'Hang on, aren't you going to school now?'

My grandmother took over and went on and on. She ended up where she had started: 'The dogs in the street have more brains . . .'

My mother regarded me anxiously.

My parents, brother and sister had moved to Jerusalem after I left. From what my mother was saying I realized that they had lived in terrible poverty there. They had occupied one small, dilapidated room in a large building full of Bedouin tribesmen. Niyazi had shot up, but he was still very skinny. He walked the streets of Jerusalem all day long selling bits and pieces from a tray. If only he could walk the streets in peace: he wasn't Palestinian, so he had to stay clear of the British police, as did all the foreigners in the city.

Once a policeman chased him. He ran, and the policeman

pursued him. A tram went by. Niyazi jumped in one door, out of the other and fell down. His tray broke, all his goods scattered, his palms scraped along the ground, and he was left covered in blood.

My mother was simultaneously laughing and crying as she told the story. 'Isn't life strange? We tried to bring him up so carefully, like a delicate flower, trying to shield him from everything . . . At his age he shouldn't have to be working or worrying about money. He should be going to school. Mind you, it's not as if children even younger don't work, but when it's your own flesh and blood . . .'

I thought of my brother. We once sat side by side on the edge of the fountain outside our Beirut home measuring our legs with string so that we could establish whose were the thicker. We both had long skinny legs and knobbly knees. Mine had pale, light hairs; his was darker.

'And that's not to mention all the fighting between the Arabs and the Jews,' continued my mother. Not a day went past without people being killed or shops set alight; particularly when there was a curfew. On such days my father would pace up and down the building and get irritated with anything and everything. He always wanted my brother to be back a good hour or so before the curfew commenced, but he inevitably returned just as it began or with minutes to spare, carrying his tray. My father would shout and become annoyed. Niyazi would then just quietly go to the room.

'Didn't Niyazi want to come with you?' I asked her.

'Of course he did. He'd even got his passport ready.'

'And?'

'The last evening he was laughing and messing with his sisters. He was telling them all about the things he would do when he returned to Adana. How Little Memet's brother would be surprised to see him, how he was going to go back to school, play football again . . . He was so excited! But, then, I don't know what came over him. In the morning he'd changed his mind. And his father had insisted, too . . .'

I didn't need to ask why. He wasn't as self-centred as I was.

'Whatever I do,' my mother said, 'I must find some money from somewhere to send over to them!'

We had some fields that had been taken into 'administrative security' by the government after my father had fled, and these were now being used unlawfully by the neighbouring landowners. My mother was going to try to recover them; go to court if necessary, get surveyors along to establish the borders of our property and find people to rent the land to, and then . . .

'It won't be easy,' said my grandmother. 'You think I haven't tried? All through the winter, the storms, in and out of knee-deep mud . . . There was this one time . . . I went and saw that man . . . That Abdülfettah, Gülistan's husband, remember her? Her husband. You should see them now, putting on airs and graces. He used to come and package the tobacco . . . A man you wouldn't have considered worth talking to. But what can you do? Until you get what you want you've got to humour them . . . Mind you, I gave him a piece of my mind, the horrible little man. My son sends his regards, I told him. I told him my son had told us, "Go find Abdülfettah, and he'll sort everything out. He'll get back all the fields for you, work the land alongside his own and give you a rightful share without you having to ask for a thing." When I said that he just cowered in the corner, looking like a stuck pig. "Oh, madam," he said, "we can barely work our own fields. We couldn't possibly manage anyone else's . . . I wouldn't want to do wrong by you. As far as I know, your fields are simply lying there empty. You should arrange for someone to work them."' "Well then, sir," I said to him, "so why is everybody telling me that our fields are being worked by Abdülfettah and his brother?" You should have seen his reaction! He exploded. He looked like he was having a fit. "Look here, my good woman," he said and started coming towards me . . .' It seemed my grandmother had taken particular offence at being called someone's 'good woman'.

So now it was my poor mother's turn to try her luck. 'I have no choice,' she said. 'I have to talk to him, take him to court if I have to . . . The family's in terrible poverty.' Then she turned to me. 'And you, young man, are going straight back to school!'

10

My mother threw herself into sorting out the problem with the land. Written applications, title deeds, squatters' notices, courts of law . . . Days, weeks, months went by. The results were always inconclusive, and Mother was getting tired. She would return home late at night, drop the fat file of official papers in a pile and throw herself down on the sofa. In order to save money we sat in the dark. Her hair had turned white almost overnight, and, this, together with her newly sunken eyes, made the sight of her depressing to us all.

I had holes in the soles of my shoes, and the hems of my trouser legs were frayed. Most days I went to school without so much as a five-kuruş coin in my pocket. In spite of my father's strict orders, my yellow-striped school cap and the incredible madhouse that was 3B, going to school still didn't appeal to me, and the bond between me and my school weakened as time wore on.

I was no longer a child. While my brother and father subsisted in appalling poverty, my white-haired and sunken-eyed mother struggled though knee-deep mud, and my sisters lost weight all the time, it was clear to me that my secondary education was a luxury we couldn't afford. I felt I had no right to allow this to continue.

Our fair-weather friends gradually deserted us. People no longer found pleasure in our company, and the things we discussed made others feel ill at ease.

'Why did my father have to do it? Did he think that he could single-handedly right the wrongs of the world? Look at what he's done to us, all for the sake of strangers . . . It's each man for himself out there.'

'Goodness me,' said my mother, 'you're forgetting what a respected man your father was! It wasn't that long ago that people like these wouldn't have been able raise their heads in his presence.'

Whatever anyone said I was aware that we were in a rapid decline. What were we going to hold on to? We were all alone, isolated in a mass of people who simply didn't care; people who shrugged and thought only of themselves. There was certainly plenty of evidence of this.

On one of those days when we didn't even have bread and black olives – the mainstay of the poorest households – my mother went to ask a very close relative of ours for a small loan.

'I'll ask for at least ten liras,' she said to me, 'so I can at least get some bread and olives and maybe a little tea and sugar. It'll keep us going for a while. After that, we'll see what is God's will. If the girls wake up keep them occupied. I'll try to get back as quickly as possible.'

We had gone to bed hungry the night before. My mother was late coming back. The girls woke up and asked where she was. I told them she had gone to get some bread and olives and that she should be back any minute. They were delighted. Our youngest sister clapped her hands in excitement. 'Oh, good old Mummy! I'm so hungry!'

It was a damp, grey morning. It had rained heavily earlier, and now there was a steady stream of water flowing down the roads. Mother returned eventually. Her hands were empty. She looked completely drained and absolutely forlorn.

She started to climb the stairs slowly. She made it to the top, but just as she was about to enter her room she swayed and clung on to the doorframe. 'A little water . . .' she croaked. 'Let me have a sip of water.' But before we could rush a glass to her she collapsed in front of the doorway. What was going on?

The girls ran to get our landlady. She arrived in her white headscarf muttering prayers. She held my mother's wrist. 'Eau de cologne!' she demanded. We had none. 'A little floral infusion, perhaps, or even some vinegar.'

'Huh?'

'Don't you even have vinegar in the house?'

We don't have any, we don't have any, we don't have any! We don't have anything! This abject poverty was driving me mad, and the ground felt as if it were melting beneath my feet.

'Don't you even have any vinegar?' our landlady repeated.

'No, we don't even have vinegar! We don't have a home, we don't have a car, we don't have property, we don't have land, and we don't have vinegar!' My fists were planted firmly on my hips. Was it some great social wrong, this failure to have vinegar?

The landlady went away and came back with some eau de cologne. She brought my mother round. She stared around in confusion at first, her face ashen, then . . . She pulled her knees up, rested her forehead on them and started sobbing uncontrollably. She cried and cried. And, although we tried to find out, she did not tell us why she had fainted.

We found out only much later that when she went to our relative, our close relative, she had been treated very badly. She hadn't even been asked in. They kept her at the street door as they asked her business. My mother told them she wanted to borrow a little money.

And the woman – a close, indeed very close relative – said, 'What's the point? There'll be no end to this.' She told my mother that my father shouldn't have been involved in politics, that everyone had to bear their responsibilities in life and that he shouldn't have harmed his nearest and dearest for the sake of strangers. He should have been thankful for what he had and looked after his family properly.

'But the children are hungry,' pleaded my mother. 'I don't want to dredge up things from the past.'

'Right,' said this woman, this close, extremely close relative. 'So you don't want to dredge up the past. Well then, let's close the book on this whole sordid affair.' And she slammed the door in my mother's face.

II

When I found out about this our dilapidated little room spun wildly around me. Should I go along to our relative who had closed the book and burn her large mansion down, beat up her son – or just turn up at their door and create a scandal? Could I do that? Maybe . . . But then, I thought to myself, to what end? What would it achieve? The mansion might go up in smoke, the kid might be injured or she might be mortified with embarrassment. So what? The end result was bound to be negative. Status quo, with the law on its side, would not sympathize with a brave lad waving his fists at a cliff. I realized that waving my fists at a cliff would be a pointless gesture.

Gazi was still at his uncle's mill and under strict control, Hasan was in the third year of the college of commerce, and I was at 3B in my secondary school. The girls were in 3A, and the eldest was barely sixteen.

In 3B were Hamlet Saim, Pipe Ziya, Black Sadri, Bear Mumtaz, Kurdish Sermet and the like, and even the youngest of us were old enough to have children of our own. Yet when I looked around I might see Bear Mumtaz drawing a caricature of our history teacher on the blackboard, while Kurdish Sermet pinned a paper tail to his backside. The class would roar and shout until Bear cottoned on, at which point he would start effing and blinding at whoever pinned the tail on him. Meanwhile Kurdish, clutching his stomach in pain from laughing so hard, would be ready to run away from any punishment Bear might decide to mete out. As soon as Bear realized who was responsible there would be a chase across the tops of the desks, and the whole class would break out into a dusty riot. The shouts and guffaws and the loud banging of the desk tops would last for some time, until the door would silently swing open, revealing the silhouette of a large and irate headmaster. The chaos would instantly end. The class would be a frozen tableau of respect, smiles wiped clean off all our faces.

The headmaster would look around the class for a time, scrutinizing each of us in turn. 'I have yet to decide,' he would say, 'on whether this is a class, a barn full of animals or a den of criminals. Now listen to me, boys . . . This sort of behaviour is totally unacceptable. If you do insist on behaving like animals, I have to warn you that I will not hesitate to treat you as if you were.' In fact we never were treated like animals; at least not while I was there.

I didn't take pleasure in any of the classroom antics though . . . I just didn't feel involved. I kept thinking of my mother, my sisters and particularly of my brother Niyazi in Jerusalem, with shredded knees from tumbling off the tram. If some of my family were in abject poverty there and the rest were in abject poverty here, it really did seem to me that secondary school was a luxury we could not afford. You couldn't put education before food. I was feeling the burden of responsibility falling on my shoulders, and this feeling was intensifying by the day. What would a secondary-school diploma give me anyway? Even if I got the piece of paper – and in those days a diploma virtually guaranteed a job – who would be foolhardy enough to give 'that exile's son' employment?

I had to start working, but doing what? Should I go back to weaving? Or labour on building sites? Should I do back-breaking farm work in the cotton fields or during the harvest under that baking Çukurova sun?

It seemed to me that the easiest thing would be to become a fruit-seller, hawking melon, watermelon and grapes. Now that sounded good. Depending on the season I might sell lemons, oranges or sugarcane or whatever else was available. I'd be sure to earn a living. Well, of course I could earn a living. But in my home town? In front of all my friends and – in particular – in front of those oh-so-clever folk who knew not to put the interests of strangers before that of one's family? All these people thought of my father's principled life as some form of stupidity. But look at them. Having decided 'you only live once' they wanted to dress well, eat well, travel, enjoy themselves . . . They had no interest in why others weren't able to do the same. They wanted the wheels to keep turning the way they always had done. And they couldn't care less about what enabled those wheels to turn . . .

I felt I carried this immense burden of shame, with my holed shoes and frayed trousers. A stupid father would have a stupid son. The standard by which we were judged was their standard. By that standard I was stupid and ugly and pathetic. Therefore I had to escape from them, to hide, to remain out of sight with my disreputable shoes and ragged trousers. I felt uncomfortable when I walked past their disapproving stares and snide whispers.

I became more and more self-conscious. I started to feel embarrassed about my hooked nose, my withered hands and my gaunt face. Whenever I felt people staring at me my hair would stand on end and I'd get a cold and uncomfortable feeling creeping down inside me. My ears would hum, my vision would blur, my hands would go cold and clammy, and I'd feel as if I was shrinking and that my hooked nose was curving down even more and that I was becoming even more monstrous in appearance.

After a time I started to feel uncomfortable even when I walked past shop displays. It was as if all the shiny new things for sale were specifically for those people who dressed well, ate well and who could afford to travel. I felt that when I got too close the items on display would glare at me disapprovingly. So I ended up avoiding them and staying clear of all those attractive, shiny new items.

It had all been easy when I was a kid. Was this what growing up was all about? It felt as if all around me was now in dark shadow. I wanted to see a light at the end of the tunnel; I wanted to feel that there was a way out. I wanted a complete change. I did not want anyone to look down on me, even if I sold melon, worked in a factory, went about with shoes in tatters or frayed trousers. I didn't want anyone to look on disapprovingly. I didn't want people to give me dirty looks because of my hooked nose or my spindly hands.

But there was no chance of that. In time the disdainful looks and the snide remarks made me withdraw into my shell like a pathetic little mollusc. So I took to going out of town and spending my time in empty fields. The fields! The open air! Yet I felt unable to appreciate fully the beauty of the blue sky arching like a giant dome over knee-deep green-covered fields, framing a space filled with buzzing bees and fluttering butterflies, and with the sparrows and doves flying about in the bright sunshine. I knew I didn't have to withdraw into my shell like a snail, but I felt as if fate was conspiring against me.

I'd often lie on my back on the grass, stare at the passing wispy clouds and wonder about God's mysterious ways. It was God who saw even the tiniest step of the tiniest dark ant, even if it was walking on a dark piece of ground in complete darkness, and it was he who had ordained at the very start of time that it be so. He was the ruler of our fate, the master of the universe and the creator of good and evil and of the devil. What did he want from our family? Why had my father gone into politics and been on the losing side? Why had we ended up in poverty, having to go around with shoes with holes in them and trousers in rags? Why was I the target of disdain from all those around me?

It was clearly because God – he who saw even the tiniest step of the tiniest ant, he who was the ruler of our fate and the master of our universe – he had ordained right at the start of time that this was to be our fate. This was obviously the case. But why? What evil had we done to deserve such a fate as ordained by him? Why the disdainful looks? I had no say over my own fate. And if he was actually on their side it would be appalling.

One day, seeking answers to my questions, I raised my head to his blue skies. 'What are you trying to tell me?' I asked out loud. 'Tell me, why are you doing this? Why? Where's the justice in it? It doesn't seem right. What do you want from us? You're laughing at us, aren't you? Just like the others, you're laughing at us!'

I never would find out whether God heard my words or whether he laughed at me or not. But I could see that I was like a scorpion surrounded by a ring of fire. If I walked the paved roads of the city I would be in the ring of fire created by those who thought they were placed on earth only to eat as much as they wanted and to travel afar for pleasure rather than through necessity. Yet when I ran into the open fields I was in the ring of fire made by God. I had no third place to which to escape.

I started watching the ants. I admired the endless hard work of which these tiny animals were capable. I felt inspired by their collective will, as they united in vast numbers and moved a dead earthworm. If only I could be an ant . . . Anyway, what was God up to? Why make me human, make them ants and make the others flies, horses, elephants, tigers or fish?

Hours would go by. The clouds would acquire a pink tinge, and the sweaty labourers would return from the vineyards. No matter how long I thought about things it made no difference. I had no chance of solving the riddles of creation. Just as I thought I might be approaching an answer I'd see another impossible conundrum, and under the now dark skies I would feel deflated. I would then helplessly start making my way back to the city and to that ring of fire, my arms dangling hopelessly by my sides.

I did occasionally drop into school. One day the headmaster called me, Kurdish Sermet and Bear Mumtaz to his study to tell us off about our absenteeism. He had the three of us lined up, but it was me he stared at most. 'As for you,' he said in conclusion, 'especially you, number one hundred and thirty-six, you are the worst!'

I had my eyes lowered to the ground and felt dizzy. My ears were buzzing. Me, number one hundred and thirty-six, especially me. The chick thrown out of the nest, the fruit too bitter for even the frost to spoil. Why did I remain in this ring of fire? What did I expect from such people? Their 'easy money' certificate? Among them I was just a snail shrivelled up in my shell.

Leave their diplomas to them, I decided. I'll go and do my own thing.

So I quit school.

12

When I announced that I had left school my mother cried for a long time. 'Oh my God!' she wailed. 'This is exactly what I feared most! Do my sons have to become little men, obliged for ever to kowtow to others? Oh, to think of all the high hopes I had!'

I felt indignant. 'I shall never kowtow to anyone,' I announced; 'not for anything!'

I felt a load lift off me, as if I had finally made an opening in the ring of fire. I felt as though my father and Niyazi were looking on approvingly. 'Well done, son,' I imagined my father saying. 'You've finally given up on building castles in the air while the family is starving.'

'So now you've quit school and you haven't got a job either,' my mother said a few days later. 'You might as well get going and try to sort out this problem with our fields for us.'

She was right. My mother was absolutely right, but those fields . . . Rain, knee-deep mud, nettles in the summer, the dirty tracks of the village, irate hounds and that man Abdülfettah, with his ruddy face and grey-blue eyes, calling my grandmother his good woman! What if he chased me, too?

'You're a man!' my mother said. 'They're going to think twice before trying anything with you. After all, I'm only a woman!'

One morning, in the dark purple pre-dawn haze, I joined the queue at the bus stop and about twenty of us piled into a ten-seater creaky old minibus. We headed off to the crow-ridden town where I'd been born. I was going to the old farm for the first time in years. I wondered whom I would see there: Would I see Sister Senem, who had helped us through the long winter nights, tucked us in our cosy beds and sent shivers down our spines with her tales of the king of the fairies, of genies and of the emerald-green phoenix; tales full of snakes, centipedes and wise old exorcists? The snotty-nosed son of our household servant who taught us to eat raw aubergines? Or perhaps the chicken Niyazi and I had hung from branches in our attempts to teach it to obey us?

The inside of the minibus stank of feet, garlic and cheese. I felt the weight of Abdülfettah's steely blue-eyed stare. The vehicle clanked and creaked along, rounding bends and somehow managing to hang together despite its load. There was no lid on the radiator; it had been replaced with a piece of wood, and steam hissed angrily from the small gaps around its edges.

I kept my eyes on the kilometre marker stones. I had done this route often with my father. He would be at the steering wheel, and I would sit next to him. Every so often he'd get me to hold the wheel so that he could light a cigarette. While he was preoccupied with getting it going I would push down the advance and acceleration levers as far as they would go. The car would shoot forward at incredible speed. Suddenly aware of what was going on, my father would grab the steering wheel and pull up both levers. 'You idiot!' he'd yell. 'You'll flip the car over!'

The roads were still the same roads, and the kilometre markers hadn't changed. Over in the distance stood the same ancient mountains rising up in waves and peaks. Finally the old town appeared in the distance, at first little more than a long, dark horizontal strip. We were getting closer. As we entered the town we were almost scraping against the sun-baked walls flanking the narrow road. Our minibus limped along the unevenly paved street, managed to reach the taxi rank and juddered to a halt. I jumped down. My feet were numb. I headed off towards the market-place. My hands were in my pockets feeling for the few coins I had. No one paid a blind bit of notice to my holed shoes, frayed trousers, hooked nose, bony hands or gaunt face. Not a single person so much as glanced in my direction. This was real freedom. I loved the people of this town, these lovely people who ignored me.

I passed the Albanian's open-air café on my left. I remember how my father's red 1927 model Ford would be parked in front of the café, and the young Arab who looked after the car would be there, too, holding his spanner, tightening something or other or cleaning the sparkplugs, and my father would have sat there, or perhaps there, talking to his friend, the bearded retired general, discussing wheat, barley or cotton prices and doing calculations on the back of his cigarette box with a pencil. They would look at each other now and then, smile and wink knowingly.

The red-bearded general was a hard, harsh man. He would wave his arms around, creating huge arcs as he talked. He would transfix us with his amazing tales from the War of Liberation. But sometimes he and my father would talk of things that did not interest me in the slightest. Then I would stretch and yawn and stare past the café door at the painting of a noble horseman inside and get absorbed in that or else count the number of posts holding up the wooden frame outside the café.

I was comfortable walking down this road. I went past the Albanian's café and past the grocer's, the barber's and some other cafés. I realized that I knew the stationer standing over by the fountain. I recognized him, but there was no way he could possibly recognize me. He was a flat-headed man from Turkistan. When we were being schooled in the mosque by the market-place we would visit his damp, dank shop to get our books, pencils and paper. He was also the local stockist of the *Anatolian Child's Primer*.

Back in those days they had taught us a marching song which had been written and composed by General Kazim Karabekir. They would take us on long marches and make us sing it all the way.

Arms of steel
Feet of bronze
Will Turks yield?
Will Turks yield?

Turks ne'er yield
Turks ne'er yield
Come what may
Turks ne'er yield

As I slowly walked down the road I felt so relaxed I was softly singing the parts of the march I still recalled:

Army of Greeks
Crawling worms
Will Turks yield?
Will Turks yield?

Turks ne'er yield
Turks ne'er yield
Come what may
Turks ne'er yield

We had a short, dark, rotund teacher who would lead our troop, march to our tempo and sweat like a pig. Red dye from his fez would run with his sweat, dripping down his forehead and cheeks, and make the man look like a clown. We would crack up. I remember once . . .

Suddenly I heard my name being called. Oh no, not someone else I knew! I turned to see. Yes, it was someone I knew all right. And how! He knew not only my father but my grandfather, too. This was the man who, years ago, came over to our farm, talked of the commotion in the cities and counted the grains on a single spike of wheat. He was a former member of the High Court!

It turned out that he now ran a hardware store. He invited me there, offered me a chair and ordered us coffees. He studied me minutely. I was being inspected in a friendly and warm manner, but, not having had such close attention for years, I felt quite uncomfortable. My hands and face became clammy, and I was sure my nose had become even more crooked. What if he noticed that my trousers were frayed?

I avoided his gaze. I found it difficult to accept that the eyes looking at me were friendly. I was withdrawing into my shell, occasionally sticking my head out uncertainly. I thought he might say to others, 'What a skinny, ugly child! And his father was so good-looking, too . . .'

In fact, he was just chatting to me pleasantly. He spoke of my father's childhood, of my uncle who had died of tuberculosis, of my aunts, of the sweets one could get in the old days and of the parties and celebrations that followed the fasting at Ramadan. I slowly extended my head out from my shell. I was warming to the man; the wall between us was disappearing. I started to relax.

'You're not like your father, though,' he pronounced all of a sudden. 'The great man couldn't get through a normal doorway, but you're all skinny!'

I immediately withdrew into my shell again, and the wall between us started to rise once more. I began to feel a chill on my face and hands and a slight twitch in my left eye.

His next remark came down like a second blow. 'I take it you finished high school?'

Oh no! I started to feel overwhelmed by my own feelings of worthlessness. I was certainly the ugliest, skinniest person in the world. What if he found out that not only had I not finished high school but that I hadn't even made it halfway and finished middle school? I didn't know how to reply.

'Let's go over to my house,' he continued, 'and let my wife see you. She'll be astounded to see how you've grown.'

One disaster after another! He didn't even give me time to come up with some excuse for not accompanying him. He picked up his walking stick and his felt hat, and we left the store.

'You're quite reserved, my boy,' he said to me. 'I knew not only your father but your grandfather. There's no reason to feel uncomfortable. Your father, now, he was such a man . . .'

I was following behind, a little to his left, trying to adjust my step to match his slow gait. I felt I had a diffidence about me, and the image of my mother floated in front of me. 'Look at you!' she was saying to me. 'You have turned into someone who kowtows to others!'

I shook myself. I undid the buttons on my jacket and increased my stride. I drew level with the man. My mother disappeared. No sooner than I had got rid of that burden it dawned on me that I had no right to be walking at his side. After all, he was attached to the High Court, and there I was, not even a middle-school graduate! I fell back a little and buttoned up my jacket. My mother reappeared . . .

We arrived at his home. It was a two-storey solid house built of stone. He smartly rapped the door-knocker twice in succession. I heard the shuffling of slippers behind the door. It opened. An elderly woman, wrapped in a white headscarf, peered out before withdrawing. We entered, and she pulled back further.

The man cackled to himself knowingly. 'See if you can recognize the young man, dear!'

The woman, a good Muslim, was clearly nervous as she raised her eyes to gaze at a stranger. 'Well, dear,' she replied, 'I'm not sure . . . He seems a bit familiar, but . . .'

The noise of a fractious young child and of a young woman trying to calm the infant came from the room next door.

'Come on, you know who it is!'

There I was, standing in front of an impatient old man and a confused old lady who stared at me. The reassuring lullaby ceased. 'Shadiye, girl!' he called out. 'Leave the child and come here a minute.'

Oh dear. I shrivelled up inside my shell again. I knew that the young mother about to join us would be taken aback by my ugliness. I was ashamed, ashamed, ashamed. My trousers were frayed, my shoes had holes . . .

'Yes, Father?' A pair of jet-black eyes, an ever-so-white face and a tangle of hair appeared.

My heart was pounding. I felt a warm rush of blood to my face. Her white headscarf had slipped down on to her shoulders, revealing too much, and I noticed her firm bosom, her full chest . . . I saw no possibility of this young woman finding anything appealing about me.

'Your mother didn't recognize him. I want to see if you do.'

The young mother must have been around my age. She was not inhibited in the least and inspected my face closely. The hook on my nose pained me like an open wound. I assumed she thought: What an ugly person!

'Well, to be honest, Father, I'm not sure . . .'

'Hah!' exclaimed the old man. 'I recognized him the moment I set eyes on him!' He put them out of their misery.

The elderly lady, who had been shrinking back a little because of a strange male in her midst, undid her scarf in obvious relief. 'Goodness me, look at you!' she said. 'To think that I thought . . . My, my. You have grown, haven't you?' Then she turned to her husband. 'He doesn't look like his father, does he?'

'No he doesn't. You couldn't get his father through a doorway!'

I felt as if I was floundering in open space, falling endlessly. Oh, my skinniness, my hooked nose, my withered hands, my lack of education, my this, that and the other . . .

They asked me all sorts of questions about my father, my mother, my aunts . . . Shadiye had gone into the kitchen to cook up some eggs with beef, and we sat in their dining-room at the table by the light of their gas-lamp, talking. Well, I wasn't talking so much as being questioned.

The food arrived, and we started to eat. I manoeuvred ridiculously so that Shadiye didn't spot my withered hands. In my haste I let food drop and missed mouthfuls. Occasionally our eyes met. How I wished I was the most handsome man in the world!

'Our Shadiye,' explained the old man, 'has been widowed at a young age and with a young child, too!' Someone's son had shot the old man's son-in-law last winter over a land dispute.

The fact that she was a widow gave me some hope. There was no escaping the fact that I had many shortcomings. But, on the other hand, she was a widow. If she liked me, and we got married . . . Well, I'd never beat her child. But how could we? There I was, unwaged, ugly, with holes in my shoes, frayed trousers, uneducated . . . Could it work? My eyes fell on my withered hands for the umpteenth time. I withdrew them from the table and concealed them on my lap.

'What's up, my boy?' the old man asked. 'You've got to eat . . . Look at you, you're all skin and bone!'

I stiffened. I felt as if I had been whacked with a stick in my most sensitive spot; in front of Shadiye, too. How could he? I would have run out of their house there and then except it would have been ill-mannered. A cold feeling oozed out of my forehead.

The old woman whispered a question to her husband.

'No, he hasn't!' said the man. 'He hasn't even finished high school!'

Oh, the value these people attached to the 'easy-money' diploma!

'What about middle school?' asked his wife.

'Well, he's bound to have finished middle school!'

They turned to look at me. I somehow had to end this line of conversation. 'Sir, did you ever read *Two Friends Travel the World*?'

The old man looked surprised. 'I can't say I have. So tell me, young man, what do you do? Do you have a job? Maybe we could find you something around here. You can't just walk around doing nothing, you know. Bring your middle-school diploma with you when you're next here, and we'll try to arrange something with the local authority, yes?'

This was as much as I could take. 'Did you say job?' I said, raising my head firmly. 'Thank you, but no. I have taken a bank clerks' examination . . . I'll be starting in a few days.'

The man seemed taken aback again. 'Oh? Well done. Well, then . . .'

'Yes, indeed.'

'At a bank, you say?'

'Yes, at a bank.'

'So high-school graduates didn't take the examination then?'

'There were twenty of us doing the exam. Five were high-school graduates and three were fully fledged accountants.'

'Well done! And I thought that . . .'

He had thought that this emaciated, ugly, shy middle-school graduate was worthless. What did he know? Now I had fired the starting gun I was going to run for all it was worth!

'I came here to sort out our land. We have lots of fields, but a few of them are being occupied illegally at the moment. I'm here to sort these out. In fact, we don't really need the income from them all. There isn't really the need for me to work with all that money coming in, but I thought I'd get a job anyway. You know, better than being idle . . . It seems there's this man Abdülfettah . . .

He was particularly rude to my grandmother. I'm going to go and deal with him. I deliberately put on my old shoes and frayed trousers for this trip. I mean, obviously, I have plenty of shoes and clothes to choose from . . .' How I made it all up! How important was a banking exam under the circumstances? 'I shall take my final exams, and then I shall attend university. Later I may take the European exams.'

The old man winked at his wife. 'Oh, that's so good. What an intelligent and keen young man!'

'Just like his father, eh?' said the woman.

I looked at Shadiye with pride. I thought she rather fancied me, and my bravado had reached the level of insolence.

We adjourned next door. The room had white curtains, white covers on the divan, a walnut crib, a laundry box decorated in yellow tin and dresses hanging from the walls. Shadiye started to breast-feed her baby. Occasionally she lifted her head up and smiled at me. I felt confident now. I was managing to return her looks. I experienced warm sensations inside. Finally her father said he was going to the café and left. I really relaxed then and started telling her all sorts of things.

I pulled out a cinema magazine from my pocket, and Shadiye came and sat next to me. We looked at the pages together. Occasionally our heads would touch lightly, causing sparks to fly. We stared at a picture of an actress in a swimming costume. Shadiye's mother was on the divan and had already started to snore. I edged a little closer to the girl and then closer still. The side of my arm touched her swollen breast. I felt as if my arm was burning. I was quivering, and my eyes were aflame. All of a sudden I dropped the magazine and put my arm around her waist.

She flipped out of my embrace like a fish and ran over to her baby's crib. 'You impudent little man!' she snapped angrily.

My fragile confidence shattered completely. I immediately withdrew into my shell again and shrivelled up. The wall rose between us. My hooked nose, my disreputable shoes, my withered hands, my gaunt features and my frayed trousers all rose up to taunt me. So did my mother. 'Oh, darling! Oh, my poor dear!' she was saying.

Shadiye had turned her back on me and wasn't even looking

in my direction. What should I do? Should I get up and leave? No, that wouldn't do. Her father would ask why I had left, and she would tell him everything, wouldn't she? But if I stayed . . . What would I do?

What if she told her mother? 'That dreadful boy, he did so-and-so,' she might say. And what if her mother said to her father, 'Do you know what that awful boy was doing to your daughter?'

I felt totally out of place. I was in a terrible quandary. Just then her mother woke up and sat up, rubbing her eyes. The daughter turned to me, glaring with hatred. I prayed to God that she wouldn't tell her mother. The old woman and I went upstairs. She swiftly made my bed, bade me goodnight and left me alone.

How could I have a good night? The window of the bedroom overlooked the street so I gazed out, absent-mindedly sucking on a finger, thoughts racing through my brain. There was an ice-cold moon in the sky. Rows of wet houses huddled together. Yellow lanterns illuminated the frozen silence.

What if she told her mother? And what if her mother said to her father, 'Do you know what that young man of yours was up to? If you insist on bringing home tramps off the street . . .'

I imagined that her husband would listen to it all sadly and comment on how times have changed, how children were no longer like their fathers or their fathers' fathers. 'But,' I kept saying to myself, 'will she say anything to her mother?'

She might or she might not. How could I tell? I took a five-kuruş coin out of my pocket. If she was going to tell, make it heads, and, if she wasn't, make it tails.

I shook the coin in my cupped hands, threw it in the air, and it landed heads up. So she was going to tell! In which case she must have done so by now. Her mother was probably just waiting for her father to return home. But, hang on, how could I be so sure? I tossed the coin again. Heads again! I was now certain. The girl must have told her mother. And she would tell Shadiye's father. Heads, twice in a row!

I thought of God and the fate he had ordained. He had clearly preordained all this back at the beginning of time. This is why this was all happening. He had ordained one fate for me and another for Shadiye. We were each on our own separate paths obviously.

But forget fate and God, I thought. I was about to disgrace the whole family. What could I do? I could quietly sneak down the stairs, listen at their door and try to hear what they were saying. But what if Shadiye or her mother came out and caught me?

Two heads in a row! She was bound to have told! And the mother . . . Well, she was just waiting for the old man. When he heard about it he would say 'Shame on you. I treated you like a human being, I let you into my home . . . And look at how you behaved.'

I was still standing by the window. Bats were silently fluttering in the air, silvery-grey in the moonlight. I heard an owl hoot in the distance and assumed that the occupants in the thatched brick houses were fast asleep.

I got undressed and into bed. But how could I possibly get to sleep?

Two heads. She must have told. What was I to do?

I covered my head with the quilt and felt even worse. When I closed my eyes my gaze was directed inwards. The inner me and I started a conversation.

'What will you do if she tells?'

'Heads came up, so she's going to. In fact, she probably has already.'

'You think so?'

'She would have, by now.'

'How do you know?'

'I got heads twice.'

'You always end up doing something to make things worse!'

'Why did you attack the girl?'

'Was that uncalled for?'

'More than just uncalled for!'

'Well, it's done now.'

'And you'll just have to suffer the consequences. They let you into their home out of respect for your family. How quickly you forgot that! Who do you think you are anyway? You're nobody. You have neither the looks nor the money to amount to anything. What amazing quality did you imagine they saw in you? . . . And what was all that about a banking exam? You've no shame, have you? All those barefaced lies . . .'

'Huh?'

'What if they see Grandmother and one of them says something like "We saw your grandson, and he told us about his banking examination. How is his job going?" What would she say? "What bank? What exam? Him, work in a bank? He's been lying to you, bragging. Stray dogs have more sense than he does!" she'd say, wouldn't she?'

'Huh?'

'So then the old man would say, "Oh, is that so? To think that we invited him into our home out of respect for you, and we fed him, put him up . . . And all he did was molest my daughter . . ." Wouldn't your grandmother make your world a living hell? Eh? Don't go all quiet on me now. Answer me!'

When I woke up there was a silvery light in the sky, but it didn't look like morning. My struggle with myself flared up again.

'The woman would have said something ages ago.'

'About what?'

'That business . . .'

'Are we back to that again?'

'We are, because the woman will have told her husband. She would have given him all the details. The old man would have felt let down at first, and then he would have grown angry. "That tramp! That scoundrel! That shameless . . ." He won't have slept for hours, smoking cigarette after cigarette, getting more and more irate, waiting for you to show your face in the morning . . .'

'You really think so?'

'I know so.'

'What are we going to do?'

'If you ask me, we should get up, get dressed and get out of here!'

'But it's not even dawn yet. It's still dark outside.'

'All the better. We couldn't make our escape in the morning. The old man would be ready and waiting.'

'So we should get out soon?'

'Immediately. Right now.'

'But . . .'

'Don't waste time thinking about it. We have to go right now. Or else.'

I got out of bed, feeling the cold, and quickly got dressed. I was shaking: my hands, the muscles of my face, all over. I was petrified that I would be caught and things would become even worse. I carefully opened the bedroom door and tiptoed over to the sofa. The white walls looked on sadly. As I crept down the stairs I noticed the knob on the end of the banisters. It was glaring at me. The doorknobs downstairs, the corners of the walls, the windows, all the furniture had come to life, and they were all hostile. They looked as if they might scream out loud and attack me at any moment.

Shaking with nerves, I quickly opened the front door, slipped out and hurried off without even closing the door behind me.

It was freezing cold outside. The streets were muddy, and there was a deathly stillness in the frozen light of the moon. I rapidly walked away from the house, turned a few corners and made my way along the narrow, crooked squelchy streets. Muddy water had entered my shoes from the holes in their bottom. I was turning so many corners and going along so many little streets I didn't know where I was. I didn't know the small town that well, and now I was completely lost. I was afraid I would come across a night watchman who might ask where I was coming from, where I was headed and what I was doing out in the streets at this hour. What would I say? Which hotel name could I give? He would think I was a thief or a fugitive from prison and take me straight down to the train station. The truth would come out there, of course. Word would be sent to my grandfather's friend, and the old man would come rushing over. He would have been livid to start with, and then this would have happened on top of everything else.

'That's him all right,' he'd say as soon as he stormed in, even as he was trying to get his breath back. 'You know who he is? He's so-and-so's son! You wouldn't believe it, would you? No . . . I thought him a decent young man at first. I let him into my house, left him alone with my wife and daughter. And do you know what he did?'

What would I say? They would lock me up. And my mother,

my grandmother, all our relatives, the woman who slammed the door in my mother's face and then my father, all my home town, the whole planet would know I'd been arrested. I would just die. My grandmother would have a field day. 'I told you, didn't I?' she would say. 'Didn't I tell you that stray dogs have more sense?'

They'd say 'He looks shifty. I bet he's a murderer' and who knows what else.

I suddenly noticed the shadow of a large watchman at the far end of the street and hurriedly retraced my steps. I was in a state of panic. They were bound to catch up with me any second now and take me straight down to the station.

I went around one corner, then the next. I heard the watchmen blowing their whistles. The shrill noises started coming from behind, then from in front of me as well and from either side. I was going mad. It was as if all the watchmen of the town had realized that there was a master criminal stalking the streets, and they were united in their determination to capture the villain. I went past a brick house surrounded by a fence, and suddenly a large dog appeared. It came at me growling, baring its sharp white teeth. The watchmen were still after me blowing their whistles, but now they were joined by an ever-increasing number of local dogs. I made it to the fields next to the town. The freshly ploughed ground was soft and muddy, and I sank in up to my ankles at every step. The dogs were still after me, as were the watchmen. I ran. I ran away into the night.

I noticed a yellow light in the distance; the station's lamp. I started heading towards it. The dogs were just a few paces behind me. I found myself crossing a graveyard. It sent shivers down my spine. I ran through the terrible graveyard full of headstones; some leaning, some straight, some fallen over. I was gripped by terror, sweating profusely . . .

I suddenly remembered a rhyme, a little spell taught to me as a child. I said it twenty, perhaps fifty times over, shouting it at the dogs: 'Be silent, be still, and lose all your will!'

When we were young children, that was our spell against dogs. I'd learned it off by heart as an infant in the belief that it would stop dogs in their tracks and bind their jaws. On this occasion the dogs paid no attention to it whatsoever. So, having lost all hope of escaping them I curled up into a ball on the ground, holding my head between my hands. I stayed like that for some time. I then tried to run again but to no avail. I was knee deep in mud; pulling up one foot left the shoe behind, so I had to wrestle my shoes out by hand. Then lightning started to flash, illuminating the dark clouds. A bitterly cold wind sprang up, bringing with it pouring rain with huge, splattering droplets. I was drenched within seconds. A short time later the wind picked up and carried the clouds away with it. The moon appeared. There were newly formed puddles everywhere, reflecting the silvery moonlight. Bright, sparkling puddles . . .

The dogs had long since run off, and I hadn't even noticed. I had gone a good distance and was finally out of the graveyard. A little while later I came to a road and quickened my pace, heading once again towards the station. The yellow light was emanating from a wooden hut in front of the station. I walked right up to it and looked in through the window.

People! Two guards were playing backgammon. I was so delighted to see a human face I started humming a little tune. I felt like barging in and hugging them! I went into the station.

Morning came. The sun was shining brightly, and it was a sparkling, wet but warm and sunny day, typical for the south. The train was six hours late. In spite of the warm sun I was shivering from head to toe. My teeth were chattering. I bought a ticket from the counter, turned around and came face to face with my grandfather's friend. I dropped my ticket.

'Goodness me, boy, look at the state you're in! Fell over in the mud? Got caught in the rain? What time did you leave this morning anyway? My wife is awfully worried. If we'd have known you were leaving so early she could have left some breakfast out for you last night. Ah, you have your ticket. Just a minute, let me get mine.'

I was stunned.

'Come on then. We can talk on the train. I had some business that came up suddenly,' he told me.

'You must enter the high-school exams,' he continued, once we had settled into the compartment. 'Get that piece of paper.

You don't know what might happen. I think you should go into higher education as well. Because your father . . .'

I was so delighted I could barely contain myself. 'Well, that's what I plan to do. Not just university but the European exams too . . .'

'Good on you. That should be your goal. You have to consider the family you come from.'

When I got home my mother gave me dry clothes, made me a glass of herbal tea and put a hot-water bottle down my back. 'So,' she asked, 'did you manage to get anything out of him? Did you see Abdülfettah?'

Oh, no! My God! I had forgotten completely . . . That's why I had gone in the first place! 'I saw him,' I lied, 'but it was no use . . . "If you think you have rights, I'll see you in court," he said.'

The hopeful look in my mother's eyes faded. My sisters lowered their heads. Our youngest turned to one of her sisters. 'Hasn't he brought back any money then?' she whispered. She was only six.

13

I went back to the fields, back to thinking of God and of his mysterious ways. Bad things came from God, and good things came from God. A good fate was God's doing, and so was a bad one. God could be generous, but he could also be miserly. God made you laugh. He also made you cry. God created, God destroyed, and God let the devil have his way. And it was us, his servants, on the receiving end of it all.

My brain was addled with these mystifying dichotomies. I was just twenty, and my only sin was that I was the son of that exiled man.

And so the days went by.

One Sunday morning, our gang of three – Gazi, Hasan and I – met up at the café in the commercial quarter near the cloth factory in which we had worked.

It was one of those days for reminiscing. The weavers Ahmet and Reshat came and joined us, too.

'Are you up for a game, Hasan?' asked Gazi.

Hasan was wiping his glass eye with his handkerchief. 'Of?'

'Backgammon. Gülbahar rules.'

'Sure. What are we playing for?'

'A packet of Serkidoryan.'

'I'm in. Let's see your money.'

They gave me their cash. The loser would place a fresh pack of cigarettes on the table, and we would get to smoke them until they were all gone.

We sat down facing one another. Ahmet, Reshat, I and the others we knew from work crowded around. I noticed a worker at one of the nearby tables wearing blue overalls, dark glasses and reading a newspaper.

'Who's that man?' I asked Ahmet. 'Does he work in your factory?'

'He does,' he replied. 'How did you know?'

'You remember when that shuttle flew off while we were there . . . He stood up to the factory owner. Isn't that him?'

'Yes, that's him all right . . . Master Izzet they call him. He's worked in all sorts of places. A very skilled man. He has a wife, a Bosnian woman; she's very sound, too. Not sure what nationality he is; they say he's Kurdish.'

Gazi and Hasan were making so much noise that Master Izzet had to put his paper down and turn his chair round to watch their game. Just at that point Gazi threw a double-one and went wild. He felt certain that he would now win with a backgammon. He stood up and offered everyone cigarettes in celebration of his decisive double-one.

Hasan was cursing his luck.

Gazi played the double-one, then the double-two, then, as he was playing the double-three, Master Izzet interjected. 'Not there, son,' he said. 'You don't want to do that . . . Bad move!'

Gazi took back his third three. 'Why's that?'

'Think of how the moves will go. You're not going to be able to come out after the third five on the double-five, and you'll ruin the backgammon!' Master Izzet took out his tin of tobacco, started rolling a cigarette and lost all further interest in the game.

Gazi hesitated for a long time. 'Double-three three,' he finally moved, 'and double-three four. Now to the double-four. Double-four one, double-four two and the other two: four! Hah! That was one four for our Hasan here, one four for my future kids, one four for . . .'

Hasan didn't take the ribbing well. 'Yeah, OK. Very good. So you've played your double-four. Get on with it!'

The people around found it all rather entertaining. Hasan's red-striped college of commerce cap had slipped to one side. He swore at Gazi.

'Hey, watch your mouth!' said Gazi. 'Mind your manners . . .'

'I'll leave the bloody game. If you want to play, play properly!'

'You can leave any time you want. The money's safe . . . Was that meant to be a threat? OK, then . . . Now, the double-five. Double-five one, that's the second, here's the third . . . Double-five three, double-five three. Hey, Hasan, how many fives was that? Hmm? Was that the third? Go on, Hasan, tell me. That was three fives so far, wasn't it?'

Master Izzet was still busy rolling his cigarette.

Having played his third five Gazi was stuck.

Hasan turned his good eye towards the café's service door. 'Excuse me,' he called out. 'Could we have a fourth five for the gentleman here, please?'

Gazi turned to Master Izzet. 'Why did you interfere just then?' he asked angrily. 'It wasn't any of your business, was it? What did you think you were doing?'

'You are so right,' said the man. 'I do apologize. I shouldn't have said anything.' He lit his cigarette and offered us tobacco. But Gazi was still angry. He slammed the backgammon board shut and left.

After that Sunday I started going to that café regularly and gradually became friends with Master Izzet, who had first caught my attention on that occasion.

One day, having listened to me rant anarchically for some time, he stopped me mid-sentence. 'So what?' he enquired calmly.

Hadn't he been listening to all the things I'd been telling him? The injustice, the inequality, God, the Devil, people, this, that, the other . . .

'What you're saying,' he continued, 'is that everyone on earth, and the Almighty above, have all stopped everything they were doing just to give you a bad time.'

'Are you taking the mickey?'

'Certainly not. I don't take the mickey out of people. But after painting such a picture this is the impression you've left me with. I hope I'm mistaken, because I would hate to think that anyone could be quite such an egotist.'

'What's an egotist?'

'Someone who's selfish.'

'Selfish?'

'Someone who considers himself to be the centre of the universe and feels that the universe ought to arrange itself accordingly.'

'Am I like that?'

'I hope you can free yourself of that attitude.'

'So I am . . .'

'I genuinely hope you can free yourself from it.'

This was a slap in the face for me. Should I run away in shame or turn on him?

But he left me no time to decide. 'I know of your father and his political escapades,' he said, 'and you've been filling in the gaps for me during these past few days. You are certainly suffering, and, I suppose, like any sufferer you are entitled to your rebellious feelings. But I would strongly advise you not to come here among those who have a far better case for rising up and wallow in self-pity while expressing empty talk of revolt!'

I was completely under his spell and felt crushed. I felt I should say something.

'We all have our problems,' he continued. 'There's no such thing as a problem-free life; particularly in this district. People round here have huge problems. Food is a problem. Fuel is a problem. Sleep is a problem. Tuberculosis is a problem. Malaria is a problem. And God knows what else . . . Let me phrase this in your words: This is the neighbourhood that God forgot. There are many here who have far better reason to be angry than you do.' He relit his cigarette and lost interest in me.

That day went by, as did others. We still talked but now only about inconsequential matters. In fact, he didn't seem that keen on talking to me at all.

Around ten days after his lecture he suddenly pulled me up. 'Why don't you get yourself a job?'

I asked him who would dare to allow the son of an exiled man to work in their business.

'Ah,' he said, 'so you're a millionaire then?'

'No.'

'Well, if you're not, you must have relatives who look after you.'

'Our relatives don't help.'

'There's no reason why they should.'

'There isn't?'

'Of course not. Did they share your father's ideals?'

'No.'

'Well, then . . . So?'

'To be honest with you, I have no idea where our money comes from. I don't know who does what.'

'So, you have no idea where the money comes from? Have you never felt curious? Never felt the need to find out?'

'Well, things are so tight . . .'

'All the more reason for you to find out how you do get by. Have you never thought to ask, "Mother, where does our money come from?" Have you never wondered?'

'You have a very odd way of talking.'

'Is that so?'

The day went by. The following one I was still annoyed. I did not return to the café. I wandered around on my own, thinking, calculating. The day after that, in spite of everything, I went back. Master Izzet was there reading his newspaper. We exchanged pleasantries, he put his journal away and asked me where I had been the day before.

'Nowhere,' I said. 'I had something to do.'

'And what was that? Don't tell me you applied for a job?'

'No . . . As I've told you, I don't even have a middle-school diploma, and I'm the son of an exile.'

'I said "get a job". You're the one who took it to mean "go and work in an office".'

'What else could I do?'

'Office workers aren't the only people on earth. They aren't even major contributors. The majority of the people on earth don't have middle-school diplomas. Yet they all work, earn, live, struggle – and enable those with diplomas to live, too!'

I had not grasped what he was saying.

'Is that not so?' he asked.

'Yes . . .'

'Well, then . . . Let me give you a couple of pieces of advice. First, think about all the different work that people can do, and get yourself a job. Second, get used to listening and allowing others to talk! You washed dishes in Beirut; you could do that here, too. Or – I don't know – you could sell yoghurt.'

I laughed.

'Why do you laugh? I'm being perfectly serious.'

'If we were in another town maybe I could, but . . .'

'But you can't here. Wouldn't want to be seen doing it, eh? What would people say? They'd think: He was such a great man, and now look at his son! Won't they? They'll all look down on you . . .'

'Huh?'

'You value yourself too highly. You think that people have nothing better to do than to concern themselves with you. That's an illness. It's the illness of those who have to get off a horse and mount a donkey or, more accurately, fail to find a donkey and end up having to walk. You must fight this disease, or it will destroy you. All this moaning and complaining, it doesn't do any good at all. It will shut you away in your own mind. You will become a prisoner, trapped in your mind. You have got to overcome this. Furthermore . . . But you must also wonder why I'm taking the time to talk to you like this. Maybe you think me strange. I can see that you're a bright young man. You have got to shake this thing off. Mankind needs bright young minds. That's why I'm making an effort with you.'

We no longer met at the café. We arranged to meet in the fields and walk around in the open air.

'You must rid yourself of your awful self-pity. It will imprison you in your own mind. You will become your own worst enemy. It will ruin you!'

'But what should I do?'

'You should beat that feeling. Try it. First, get yourself a job. Any job. Somewhere out of town maybe. Digging dirt, something like that. You may find it's too much, but stick with it. Try to manage. There's nothing one can't manage if one sets one's mind to the task. If others can manage something and you can't, it'll be your attitude. It's that attitude you have to beat. Then, as time goes by, you can work your way in towards the centre of town. One day you'll realize that no one's paying you a blind bit of notice, and you will have brought down the walls of your prison for good!'

I told him the story of the former member of the High Court and how I had run away in the middle of the night and been chased by dogs.

He burst out laughing. 'You did get in a state, didn't you?'

'Well . . . Don't you think I'm ugly, though?'

'Not particularly.'

'My hooked nose? Withered hands?'

'They're hardly . . .' He paused and continued solemnly. 'Many people are aware of their own faults, but most people would try to hide them. Knowing your own faults is an admirable quality, and the ability to talk about them is another. Particularly if you can be objective about your attitude. Well done. That's very good.'

'Are you saying I'm not so ugly I would scare people away?'

'Certainly not. And you have a perfectly good colour. You have nothing to worry about. But, that aside, you really must find yourself a job, OK?'

Three days later I found myself a gravel-shovelling job at a building site three-quarters of an hour's drive away from town. At five o'clock the next morning I went and stood in front of the radiator of a large double-rear-axle Dodge truck with twenty-two other dishevelled workmen. We clambered up on to the back, clutching our picks and shovels. I stood among these tanned, rough-looking strangers and lit a cigarette as the truck tore through the icy early morning air. It really did seem to be flying along. I stood straight and firm, my shovel resting on my shoulder, taking a perverse pleasure in blowing my cigarette smoke towards the still slumbering farmhouses and mansions we passed. One of the workers was singing a central Anatolian folk song.

I was so excited. It was like the time Gazi and I first went to work at the factory. I wanted to shout out at all those farmhouses and mansions, to announce to the world that I was off to earn my own living now. I wanted everyone to know. I wanted to say: 'Take your diploma and shove it!'

I wasn't thinking of my hooked nose, my withered fingers, my disintegrating shoes or my frayed trousers. My workmates paid no attention to me. They all had their lunch-bags, and most of them were smoking.

Suddenly our truck rounded a sharp bend, and we found ourselves facing a steep precipice ahead. When the truck lurched round the next bend, the precipice was on our left; it was a terrible, steep drop. Meanwhile the sun had started to rise, a red ball behind a fluffy pink veil. Mother Nature was rubbing her eyes and slowly waking up.

Our truck arrived at the site, and we jumped down. Everyone apart from me, all these brown, sun-baked, rugged men, were familiar with the work. They gripped their picks and shovels purposefully. The foreman blew his whistle, and we attacked the gravel. Some of us dug, and some of us shovelled it on to the truck. I was one of those who shovelled. I had made a good, energetic start . . . I was now earning my bread with my own sweat, and I was going to deserve what I earned.

The workmate next to me, shovelling alongside me, noticed my enthusiasm. 'Take it easy, mate,' he said. 'You want to ease up a little.'

But I was off.

My burst of energy didn't last long. I started to feel a pain gripping my shoulders. The truck seemed to take for ever to fill, and the pain grew more overpowering. As it took hold of me I found it more and more difficult to breathe. Then, my ribs started to hurt . . .

Finally the truck was full. We would have a breather until it emptied its load and returned. I sat down under a rock, next to the young lad with whom I had been working.

'What's your name then?' he asked, unenthusiastically.

I told him. 'And yours?'

'Mine? I'm Sugar Veli.'

'Where are you from?'

'Me? I'm from Yildizeli. You?'

'I'm local.'

'Yeah, I'm from Yildizeli . . . I came here last year and the year before. I used to go to Ankara . . . Is this your first time doing this?'

'Yes.'

'It's a tough job, pal. I don't reckon you'll be able to hack it. Couldn't you wangle a desk job or something?'

'I couldn't. So you don't think I can handle it. How come you manage then?'

'You don't want to go by what I can do. I've always done the heavy stuff, me. Brought up that way . . . My dad did this work and his dad before him.'

'How do you know I haven't done heavy work?'

'Look at your hands, mate. Those are clerk's hands. And your face is white. It's not seen any sun, has it? And what are you going to eat for lunch? You've no bread or anything. There's no restaurants around here, you know!' He smelled of sweat. 'Not to worry,' he continued. 'We'll share my food.'

It wasn't long before the truck came back. My arms, my shoulders and my chest were in agony, as if I was wounded. And on the third return of the truck my arms stopped working. It was as if someone had severed all the nerves. I felt sick inside, cold and clammy all over and totally out of energy. No matter what I did, I was unable to move my arms. I stopped.

'Told you, didn't I?' said Sugar. 'You really shouldn't be here, mate. Can't run out of steam now.'

The foreman turned up. He could sniff out anyone not pulling their weight and would start having a go and throw stones at them. He spotted me, shouted and yelled and lobbed a huge stone straight at me. 'What are you stopping for, eh? What are you stopping for? We're paying you to do a day's work here!'

I tried to move but to no avail. He cursed me at some length. I swore back and threw down my spade. Everyone laughed.

The foreman came over. 'Finding it difficult, are we? Why didn't you just stay in Daddy's mansion? Thought you were coming on a picnic, did you?'

'I'm not doing this!' I exclaimed.

'You what?'

'I said, I'm not doing it!'

'Couldn't hack it, could you? Thought it would be like working for your daddy, eh? "I'm not doing this!" Well, you're not hungry, are you? "Not doing this" indeed!'

Although I knew it was not a brave act I set off towards town on foot.

This manual labouring was even harder than weaving on the looms. I realized that the people who did this sort of work weren't built like me at all. They were made of iron or steel or something very similar.

14

'I didn't expect anything else,' said my friend in the blue overalls. 'You went and chose the heaviest work possible. No matter . . . As for what the foreman said . . . Now that doesn't seem to have bothered you at all. I wonder why. He made some quite cutting remarks, didn't he?' That was true . . . I suddenly realized that I hadn't been upset by it.

'Because,' he said, 'in spite of everything, you still believe yourself to be his better. The people who annoy you are those of your own class, aren't they? Those you can't bring yourself to accept as your betters, eh?'

Then, one day, Master Izzet, the man in the blue overalls, disappeared. Where had he come from anyway? Who was he? What was his business? I never knew. But he had had quite an effect on me.

'You have to get used to not getting angry,' he had told me. 'People don't want anger; they want sympathy and love. Try to be like a doctor, not getting annoyed with your patients. Earn a living by an honest day's work. Buy plenty of books. Read a lot . . . You don't need to know who I am. I'm just another human being.'

A while later my mother and my sisters managed to raise enough money for their fares, and they left me in the care of God first, my grandmother second and set off one evening to return to my father's side.

15

I ended up back at the old factory, the one where Gazi and I had woven cloth on the machines . . . but this time as an accounts clerk.

My monthly salary was exactly twenty-four liras and ninety-five kuruş, and I had no doubt in my mind that this gave me complete freedom and the ability to travel, to open my own factory, even start my own bank!

Most of the men in our department were experts at choosing clothes and ties, separating the girls from the women. They all had greased-back hair and carefree laughs. Still, their hearts were in the right place. They wanted to get the most out of life, to live life to the full – be it in a bar, a tavern or a brothel. Books were useful only if they contained explicit sexual scenes or as aids to chatting up girls. Although they would bow their heads and take the most insulting of remarks from the factory owner, the managing director or the chief accountant, they would behave like titans when faced with a bar girl or a waiter.

My line manager was a man about my age who had also left middle school in its final year. He was as highly strung as a taut steel wire. 'I will learn it all,' he would say, 'and one day make it to the top!'

His obsession for learning used to get on the nerves of everyone in the department. No bars, taverns or brothels for him! He had no desire to dress well or to find himself a lover. He just wanted to learn things, whether they were relevant to him or not.

'I was only about this tall when my father died,' he would say. 'And my mother had to go out and do laundry. I had to walk the streets selling milk, yoghurt, pies and newspapers as well as shining shoes . . . But I was studying at the same time. I would have studied more if it hadn't been for my mother's illness. Whatever it is that's wrong with her, I'm going to find out all about it. Why shouldn't one person be able to learn what another can? After all, professors are people, too, just like you and me.'

He would solve the most complicated algebraic equations with ease and took it on himself to know all the calculations and figures from every department of the factory: electricity, expenditure, thread, the yield of the machinery and even the settings on individual machines – absolutely everything!

Although he desperately tried to conceal it, I had seen him spit blood. He wanted to rise, to be on a good income. His aim was to migrate to Switzerland. I asked him once why Switzerland – as opposed to, say, France, Italy, England or America? 'Because,' he explained, 'I consider Switzerland to be the most civilized country in the world. Moreover, they make the best watches in the world.'

The day I saw him spit blood I knew why he wanted to go to Switzerland. But that aside, I did admire his desire to learn. He knew I was an avid reader but wondered what I wanted to do with my life. I couldn't very well turn around to him and say, 'My ambition is to become a person who says nice things to people!' 'Don't waste your time,' he would advise me. 'Set your sights high, and study to get there!' And he would immediately add:

'It takes no skill to be born, so now
You must raise yourself up in the world.'

One of my friends in the accounts department was a guy called Himmet, the son of a lawyer. He was short, skinny and put me in mind of a dried-out carrot. He'd drink wine on an empty stomach with the aim of gaining weight and shave his head all year round just to look different. He was my age. He had lost his father while he was still at primary school. He had been able to continue his schooling only until the second year of middle school, and after that he had to earn a living.

'My father was a lawyer,' he would say. 'I can't stay a two-bit clerk all my life. No one seems willing to take me on, though, so I'm going to have to find a way of making people take notice of me!' He would add that he knew just how to do that. 'When I have a drink I'm really great. I start talking fluently. No hesitation, no holding back. Everyone stops and listens to me. Let me give you a word of advice. Don't let other people get a word in! You've got to talk non-stop.'

'And then?'

'I can tell you that – based on my experience – people give in to you. You tell them all sorts of things, use all the words in your vocabulary, and they might not understand everything you've said, but, believe me, they remember who you are after that! The thing is, eighty per cent of people don't think about what's being said, but they remember who spoke and how things were expressed.'

He worked at the spare-parts section at the factory and, like me, was on twenty-four liras and ninety-five kuruş a month, but he knew the amounts of each and every one of the 2,000-odd items in stock. He could tell you off the top of his head how many had come in, how many had gone out and how many he had in stock.

He would arrive each morning with a prepared speech for me, drag me to one side of the warehouse and start addressing me among the smells of engine oil and machine belts. He would conclude with gusto, and as he wiped the sweat off his brow he would ask my opinion. 'How was that for a speech?'

If I liked it he'd buy me a tea. If I hadn't: 'You,' he would say, 'are not yet in a position to really understand all that I've been saying.'

If I stuck to my guns he would get angry and ask me the meaning of one of the long words he tended to insert into his orations at various points. I knew full well that he spotted these words in his father's old reference books, looked up their meanings in a dictionary, learned them off by heart and questioned me about them later purely to establish the superiority of his knowledge. So I usually approved his speeches and told him I couldn't imagine a better one, just so that I didn't have to sit through his tedious explanations of the terms he had been using. Then he'd be delighted and congratulate me on my perspicuity. 'I can see you're coming along tremendously!' he'd say.

I had now got a taste for getting others to talk while I listened. This development had made me lots of friends, and I found myself becoming very popular. I made friends with some of the other guys in accounts, too; especially with Turhan and Mustafa.

Those two sat at the same desk, doing the same job. They were very close friends, but now and then they would be at each other's throats. Turhan had left high school in his final year and was the son of a bankrupt trader. He was withered and skinny with a very crooked nose. However, he had this thing about how good-looking he was. His drawer was full of eau de cologne, brilliantine and vaseline. He would be forever holding his mirror, freshening himself up and plucking his eyebrows with a pair of tweezers. He would carefully scan those around him, and if he felt he had been spotted preening he would get cross, argue and not talk to people.

Mustafa was completely different. Quite the opposite of Turhan, he was relaxed and would joke, laugh and was generally much more fun to be with. He had only managed to finish primary school. He would follow Turhan around, being his yes-man, always approving his words or actions. One day I asked him why he did this. 'I have to be close to him,' he explained. 'You see, the women he fancies always end up liking me better!'

In fact, their whole friendship revolved around being at bars and the women they picked up there. They both loved the same woman. Or, rather, Turhan was smitten with the woman and the woman fancied Mustafa. Now he was genuinely good-looking. In fact Turhan was only really trying to emulate him, but he couldn't bear the thought of anyone noticing this.

One day he got very angry at Mustafa for no apparent reason. He went almost purple with rage. Mustafa whipped out his pocket mirror. 'Look at that! See how awful you look!' he said, holding it up to Turhan's face.

Turhan went mad. He threw everything on his desk around the office; books, pencils, inkwell, blotter, they all went flying. He swore and cursed . . . And just before he stormed out of the accounts office, his whole body in a knot of rage, he stopped and turned around. 'You bastard,' he said. 'One of these days I'm going to kill you. You see if I don't!'

Mustafa was laughing at him, but he sobered up once Turhan

had left. 'That wasn't nice, was it? Do you think I should go after him and try and make up?'

'What on earth for?'

'Because . . . Well, he is very ugly, and he knows it. It gets to him.'

I went and found Turhan in the thread warehouse. He was sitting between a couple of boxes crying silently to himself. When he heard my footsteps he straightened up and started rubbing his eyes. 'I'm glad you've come. I seem to have got something in my eyes . . . Could you take a look?'

I inspected his eyes, gently blew on them and played along with his pretence that he had something in them.

Turhan didn't speak to Mustafa for a long time after that. He frequently called me to his table. 'You know,' he would say to me, 'it's actually rather upsetting to have to work next to all these uneducated, ignorant people. I do hope I pass my exams and get into university.' As he said this sort of thing he would be surreptitiously keeping an eye on Mustafa, and he'd grow annoyed if he wasn't paying attention. 'He's ignorant,' he'd say. 'The worthless sod.'

On one occasion Mustafa called out to a friend of his across the room. 'Guess what? I'm going to Hollywood soon!'

'To Hollywood? Really?'

'Yeah, really! I've had an offer from Metro-Goldwyn-Mayer, and I'm going to be an actor. It seems they're after a new leading man . . .'

Turhan immediately turned purple, threw away his pencil and stormed out. Mustafa burst out laughing.

'Look here,' Turhan said to me, when the two of them had finally made up, 'today we're off to the bar to drink to your health, so you've got to come along.'

'Me?' I said. 'I've never been to a bar in my life . . . I don't know how to dance either.'

'No problem. You can just have a beer and eye up the girls. I'll introduce you to my one. You wait till you see her . . . Now she is really something!'

At the end of work that day the three of us left together. It was genuinely the first time I'd ever been to a bar. I felt overwhelmed by the loud band, the cigarette smoke, the smell of alcohol, the brightly coloured clothes and the women. I suddenly became conscious of my appearance, my clothes and my nose. I didn't feel as bad as I once might have done, but I still felt rather awkward and out of place.

We ordered beer. There was a flurry of activity which had nothing to do with us, a hint of panic in the bar-keeper's eyes and a preoccupied bustle on the part of the waiters. A few tables were pulled over and set up next to the dance floor. The waiters quickly got the tables ready.

Knives, forks and plates clattered, waiters weaved their way through the crowd, and the owner of the bar, elegant in his tuxedo but looking young enough to be in his teens, nervously hovered around the tables, anxiously checking on his staff. Once he was satisfied that the tables were in order he turned to the band. 'Let's have some music to dance to!'

The band played, and he whirled to the centre of the dance floor, to the enthusiastic applause of the bar girls.

'I guess some rich men are coming,' said Mustafa.

'Who are they?' I enquired.

'You'll see.'

A moment later the outside double doors of the bar swung wide open. A group of large, powerful-looking men sauntered in. The crowed parted for them, and everyone – led by the bar owner and his staff – stood in awe. The bar girls all stood up.

'See the VIPs?' said Mustafa.

They were wealthy men, and they were here to spend. The three in front were visibly tired and drawn, in spite of their imposing girths. They pulled up their chairs and sat down at the tables. The women were called over, and the bar was opened up to them. And I do mean opened up: raki, beer, wine, vermouth, champagne, gin, it was all flowing. They paid no attention to the people around.

'They are spending big time!' grumbled Turhan. 'Big time!'

'Tell me,' said Mustafa, 'what university could hope to award a diploma that would give you all that?'

'I bet they wouldn't know where the Cape of Good Hope is though.'

'Don't have to go that far, mate. You'd only have to ask them what eight times nine is.'

I said nothing. But . . . Could it be fate, giving them all that? Then I remembered my friend in the blue overalls and his advice that this sort of thinking would do me no good and just make me miserable.

By midnight the rich men's drunkenness had reached ludicrous levels. The women were being crudely groped, wetly kissed, roughly fondled and squeezed. Eventually the men decided that they'd had enough of it all and asked for the bill. What bill? They didn't even glance at the paper put down by the head waiter, who had been keeping careful notes of everything going to their table throughout the evening. Large hands sporting numerous gold rings dived into wallets, and these opened to reveal huge wads of money. The men peeled off 500-lira notes. They threw them towards the owner of the bar. He didn't know what to do. None of the men wanted the others to pay, but they eventually sorted it out. The bar owner, magnificent though his tuxedo was, crawled all over the floor on his hands and knees picking up the banknotes as though they were holy scriptures. He carefully arranged their change on a sparklingly clean white plate and presented it to them. But none of the men would touch the change, and, leaving that small fortune by way of a tip, they got up to leave. Everyone in the bar applauded them.

The band started a foxtrot. The bar, as if suddenly remembering what it was all about, sprang back to life.

A little later the girlfriend of Turhan and Mustafa came over to our table, adjusting her bra as she walked across. She stroked Turhan's jaw and winked at Mustafa. Turhan, unaware of the wink, looked at me with pride, clearly pleased with himself, like a man who knows he is loved. The woman pulled up a chair and sat down. She started to freshen up her makeup. 'You're not cross with me, are you?' she asked Turhan.

He was delighted. He immediately leaned over towards me. 'Did you hear that? She's asking me if I'm cross with her! I told you . . . She's knows to show respect.'

When Turhan went to the toilet a short while later Mustafa

leaned over. 'What did he tell you? That she showed respect? You just wait a while; you'll see what happens . . .'

And so I did. Turhan got so drunk . . . He rested his head on the table, swayed back and forth on his chair, then he started to collapse. He ended up on the concrete floor of the bar. He lay on his back laughing out loud, describing huge circles in the air with a shaky finger and shouting out the name of the woman in pink.

The woman was already getting intimate with Mustafa. I went to lift Turhan up.

'Oh, please don't trouble yourself,' she said to me. 'He's the happiest man in the world like this. Especially when I give him one of my shoes.' With that she carefully took off one of her small, dainty pink shoes and dropped it over towards Turhan. He took it, rubbed his face and mouth all over it and started kissing it. Should I feel sorry for a man like that, or should I feel disgusted?

The woman in pink adjourned to one of the rooms with Mustafa. Turhan was still lying on the floor, stretching out towards the shoe that had just been snatched back from him and calling out her name. A waiter marched over, holding a long broom. 'Get up!' he said, kicking him. 'Get out, you disgusting bastard!'

I'm not sure exactly why, but I leaped up and shoved the waiter away. I was drunk, too, and I suppose it hadn't occurred to me that the waiter might have a point. I don't remember quite what I said to him, nor how he responded, but I do remember him eventually saying, 'Look, mate, I'm only human. I know this is my job and everything, but there are limits! I'm sick and tired of this guy. You would be, too. He's like this every bloody evening. And here I am, leaving my pregnant wife alone at home all through the night, just to earn a crust. It's not right!' His eyebrows stretched his wrinkled face upwards, and I noticed the glint of tears on his eyelashes.

Mustafa had sent word, so I went over to the other room to join him. The woman in pink was sitting on his lap, breastfeeding a small baby. I went to leave.

'Come in, come in!' said Mustafa. 'I'm not a jealous man like Turhan. You can have my lady lover, too, if you want.'

My stomach turned, the walls swayed, the floors moved around, and the ceiling started to spin. I mumbled something about there being no need for that much generosity.

The woman in pink called out, 'Mother!' A small, dark woman, headscarf tied tightly under her chin, emerged hesitantly through the doorway on the side of the room. The woman in pink passed the baby over. She was still sitting on Mustafa's lap and obviously saw no reason to get down. The mother, embarrassed not just on her own account but for her daughter as well, took the child and silently withdrew.

'God, I must have drunk a lot yesterday!' said Turhan the following day. 'Still, it was a laugh, eh?'

'Huh?'

'So what did you think of my woman? D'you like her?'

'Yes, she seems very nice.'

'She's lovely. She is so considerate, so willing to please. She'd do anything for me, you know.'

'Huh?'

'You what she likes best about me? The colour of my eyes. They're a lovely delicate hazel, she tells me.'

The only thing that really played on my mind, though, wasn't Turhan's hazel eyes, nor the woman in pink, nor Mustafa. It was that shy, wizened woman who had reminded me of my own mother. I felt awful whenever I thought of her.

I found out from Mustafa that that little old lady had been a teacher and was still getting a pension from her career.

16

Himmet listened to all this angrily. 'It's a disgrace,' he declared, 'an absolute disgrace! A whole generation is being lost to decadence.'

I asked him why he said that.

He gave me a harsh stare. He launched into a history lesson, starting with our valiant ancestors from Central Asia, tracing our glorious path through history, and he really got carried away as he went on with the lecture, barely pausing to breathe. Once he got fully warmed to his subject he became quite animated and started waving his arms in the air and punching invisible targets. To judge by the vehemence with which he spoke, you would think he was addressing an audience of thousands.

We had made it all the way to the reasons behind the fall of the Ottoman Empire when the door opened gently and the tall, large-nosed managing director appeared. Himmet's waving arm and punching fist froze in mid-air.

'Preaching again, Himmet effendi?' asked the director. 'Preaching again? And you, sir?' he said, turning to me. 'What are you doing here? How many times have I told you about this, eh? How many times? Have I not told you that discussing private matters on company time is a form of stealing? Why does no one listen to what I tell them?'

'I was after the inventory records for the –'

'Be quiet! I've been listening from behind the door! The fall of the Ottoman Sultanate is none of your business. You worry about your own fall. Listen to me, gentlemen. This is your final warning. Come on! You will lose your livelihood, lads, so help me you will. You can dream up all your theories, all your projects and all the scenarios you want but not on our company time. We want honest workers, not people who loaf around while others work. We don't want rulers or party leaders or sociologists . . . Go on, the pair of you, get back to work!'

Well, in all fairness, he did have a point about standing around lecturing. As for how much of it was my fault . . . Well, no one was going to take my side anyway. But in terms of standing up against the managing director, well . . . I did need that twenty-four ninety-five at the end of the month.

17

Time passed, and Himmet left the company. Mustafa and Turhan went off to do their military service, and my chief – who had talked for so long about going to Switzerland – passed away. And I, mostly because I couldn't think of anything better to do, fell in love.

The paved road passing in front of the battleship-grey factory gates split into three, its branches leading off into the areas where workers lived. At six o'clock in the evening these streets would fill with all the people working in the commercial district: the girls from the thread factories, the stackers, the labourers, the weavers and the plump old cleaning ladies.

Although our department was meant to work until seven I would almost always call it a day at around half past five and go over to the sour-smelling wine cellar of the cooperative across the road from the factory. I would settle myself down by the street-level window of the wine cellar, fill up a large glass full of their ruby-red wine and light a cigarette and get myself ready to watch the lively crowd of girls leave the thread factory half an hour later.

I would knock back the first, second and third glasses without any *mezes* and notice my vision blur as I became slightly tipsy. This would have a light, mellow effect, and I'd forget all about my withered hands and hooked nose.

Where did half an hour go? Did I really knock back eight glasses just like that?

The girls came out, their black pinafores coated in cotton dust. All the girls who worked on the spinning wheels, the looms and the workbenches, huddled in groups of two or three, sometimes five or more. As they went by in quick nervous steps some of them would subtly glance over, nudge one another and giggle.

One of them – and it was always her I noticed – was a very pretty girl; Bosnian, about fourteen. She would always make a point of obviously looking at me, walking a few steps further and then turning around to look again, smiling each time. She would walk on, stop and turn, smile, walk on, stop and turn, smile – until she disappeared around the corner.

I had no idea how I managed to get out of the wine cellar and stagger after her. I stumbled along the crooked streets between workers' houses, doing my best to avoid the piles of rusty cans and rotting wood. The girls, who were only a few steps in front of me, had huddled together in a tight pack. My insides were churning around like a stormy sea.

My eyes were fixed on her white cotton shoes on her somewhat skinny legs. Her hips were only just beginning to develop.

We were going through narrow, crooked streets, flanked by crumbling brick houses. In front of most doors sat masculine-looking Kurdish women peeling onions, washing their children or lighting braziers and releasing acrid smells into the vicinity. Then we got to a neighbourhood full of decorated eaves, ornate window-sills and women with handfuls of knitting exchanging anecdotes across the street. This was the Cretans' quarter. I knew that behind those windows that opened on to the street there were plenty of Cretan girls giggling and making sure that passers-by heard their exchanges in broken Turkish. They always stared invitingly and were known to be very forward; generous even. But what a useless line of thought that was. Here I was, twenty-two years of age; my girlfriend was all of fourteen, I was drunk, and I loved only her.

A sensuous laugh poured out of an open window I passed. Without turning my head I noticed that behind the white curtain which had been inexpertly embroidered with pink, green and purple thread two women were standing tête-à-tête. They pulled back every time I turned to look, but as I walked on I heard their voices, pitched so that I would only just hear them.

'Ooh, mister! Why don't you come here a minute? I've something to tell you!'

I followed the girls into the poor Bosnians' quarter. A pale, tall and lean weaver, his jacket hanging loosely off his shoulders, eyes drooping with lack of sleep, glanced at me harshly over his dark, thick moustache as he swept by. He paused for a second, weighing me up. I was aware of him staring at me until he turned the corner, but I didn't allow myself to be distracted. After all, I was twenty-two, in love, and I was carrying a polished steel flick-knife in my pocket.

Meanwhile my beloved entered a courtyard on the left, through a pair of ageing wooden doors which were so covered in dirt they looked a leaden-grey. Seeing no reason to hide my quest, I stopped dead in my tracks. There was a long, dusty road to my right which connected the city to the vineyards. I leaned back against an old wall, ignoring the lizards that were darting in and out of it, and turned to face the door to the courtyard. I stood there for some time.

On the road to my right all sorts of people were making their way to the vineyards. Pedestrians, cyclists . . . An occasional motor cycle whizzed past like a bullet and the odd ageing Chevrolet, leaving everything behind in a cloud of dust. The sun was slowly setting behind the ash-coloured soap factory. Everywhere I looked I saw dust, sweat and people in a hurry.

Suddenly my beloved came out. She had different shoes on her freshly washed feet and was wearing a honey-coloured dress. She was clutching jackstones and was accompanied by two friends.

The whole world dissolved around us. I was vaguely aware of various thin, tall men in tatty outfits, women in white headscarves and of young men staring at me suspiciously or hostilely, coming in and out of the courtyard door. None of them mattered.

A little girl quietly crept up to me and glanced around furtively. 'Mister,' she said, 'my sister says, "If he loves me," she says, "please tell him not to wait," she says. "I'm afraid," she says. "My father could get back from the mosque any time," she says, "or my brother might get back," she says.'

'Are you really her sister?'

'No.'

'Then who are you?'

'Her neighbour.'

I left but only as a demonstration of my love for her. I was on the road to the vineyards. After about a hundred, a hundred and fifty steps or so my brain finally took over. 'So what if her father comes? Or her brother? What does it matter? I'm going to marry her, aren't I?' So I went back.

The evening had now really set in. The last of the labourers were hurrying past me in a fair rush. The ashen zinc-walled soap factory had disappeared in the darkness. I returned to the spot where I had been standing, leaned my back against the crumbling wall and began to stare at the courtyard door again.

These sorts of courtyards had row upon row of doors inside, each one leading to a working family's home. The doors to the courtyards themselves always remained open. This one's latch had rotted away, its iron bolts were rusty, and the wood itself had weathered so much that it was no longer straight or even.

When it was completely dark lights started to come on behind the white curtains in the windows. A man wandered down the street, coughing heavily. Occasionally a door opened quietly and then closed again. A child cried near by. As darkness descended the neighbourhood slowed to a halt. The only signs of life in the building were the dim yellow shafts of light escaping from its many windows.

I could no longer see the courtyard door. I went to the street behind the building. My beloved's window would face here. There was a sickening stench to the street, but I spotted the shadow of my beloved flickering up and down behind her curtain as she played jackstones. I became completely focused on her shadow, thinking all sorts of wild thoughts in my drunken state. For instance, I could walk up to their door; saunter into their home with a 'How do you do?' I could do; I certainly had no qualms about it. I'd like to see that tall, terse father of hers try to say anything. It seemed to me at that moment that I could conquer the earth, and I would certainly not hesitate to get blood on my hands and end the life of anyone who stood in my way. But I would never actually go through with anything like that. That type of thought would only ever exist in my imagination, mainly because I felt sorry for the girl and would never want her to end up at the centre of such a scandal.

Then I saw her standing behind the curtain once more. I dismissed my fantasies with a shrug and focused back on the window and remained frozen like that for a number of minutes. Suddenly I heard the heavy footsteps and whistle of a night watchman. I didn't flinch. I didn't have the slightest concern about watchmen coming up to me and asking me my business, suspecting I may be a thief.

Hours went by. The silvery disc of the moon quietly emerged from behind a roof. The filthy street was illuminated in its ice-cold light. Later, having followed its path through the sky, the moon sank away, leaving me in darkness once more. Dawn was approaching. Still drunk and now very tired, I made my way back to my grandmother's home.

She was such a light sleeper that even a passing cat would wake her. I did my best to tiptoe in quietly, so as not to wake her and get an earful of abuse. But I couldn't prevent the slight cracking sound from the door's hinges, nor the creaking of the floorboards. She was sitting bolt upright by the time I was through the door. She stared at me in the dim light of the bulb.

'Oh, you wicked boy! You wicked boy! Have you any idea what I've been going through? I worried about you getting stabbed in some alley . . . I thought you might have got drunk and collapsed somewhere . . . I've been worried sick!'

I was in no mood to reply. I felt the need to whistle a merry tune as I thought about my beloved, her plaits flicking up and down as she sat behind her curtain playing her game of jacks.

'Not only does he tell me he has no money,' said my grandmother, 'and complains about how little he earns, he goes out every night drinking himself stupid! How do you get the raki if you have no money? Tell me that!'

She thought that the only way to get drunk was by drinking raki and that you had to pay up front for every drink you had. There was obviously no way to explain to the woman how things worked. She was simply not going to comprehend that I could get drunk without paying any money out first, nor was she going to have any sympathy with the fact that I was in love with a factory girl. That sort of life was alien to her. There was no way that she would be willing to try to empathize. You see, she was the mother of a gentleman and a mother-in-law to gentlemen. The son and heir of a gentleman could not possibly stoop so low as to show interest in a factory girl. If I were to insist that this was the case she would give me strange looks and her eyes would fill with tears.

'You,' she would say, 'are like your mother. Your mother was just like this. She used to like being over-friendly with riff-raff!'

I don't remember how I got myself into bed or how or when I fell asleep. I woke up just after dawn while the sky was slightly pink. I was still drunk, and my head was full of the two plaits of my beloved, bouncing as she played behind her curtain.

I got dressed. As I was leaving, my grandmother stopped me. 'Don't you have a few kuruş?' she asked. 'It's been such a long time since I last had a hot meal!' But I knew she wasn't that dependent on me.

I was already at the street door. How would I have any money? If I had any, of course I'd give her some; I was not that heartless! But my grandmother didn't know that the only thing payday was good for was renewing my credit.

18

It was evening, and once more I was leaning against the lizard-infested wall, staring drunkenly at the girl's courtyard door.

A short, chubby, sweet-looking woman with a pock-marked face came up to me. 'Are you waiting for her?' she asked.

'Yes . . .' I said. My hand went to my shiny steel flick-knife resting in my pocket.

'What's that? Why have you put your hand in your pocket?'

'Er, nothing.'

'Now, now. You weren't going to pull a knife on a poor defenceless woman, were you?'

'Oh, no. I wasn't going for a knife . . .'

She moved in a little closer. 'Do you really love the girl, or are you just after a bit of fun?'

'I love her, I really do.'

'Do you? Really?'

'I swear to God!'

'The trouble is, there are others who love her, too. I can't see them letting you have her . . . I think you may be wasting your time.'

'Who else loves her?'

'You're asking me who else loves her? Why, almost all of them! Look, this is a workers' district. They're all after a bright young girl like her!'

'But what if she didn't want them? You can't force happiness.'

'Well, I don't know that she is interested in anyone in particular. But her father, now, he has a temper on him . . . He wouldn't care who was interested in who, whether anyone carried a gun or a knife or any of that business. Don't let him catch you here.'

'What would he do?'

'I don't know exactly, but all I'm saying is that it would be better if he didn't see you here. The girl has an older brother who works in our factory weaving cloth. Both these kids work, and once a fortnight they hand every penny they earn over to their father. He was a very influential landowner back home . . . Everyone in the district feared him. Our fathers often told us of how he had sliced the heads off at least a few hundred infidels. So, don't judge him by where they live now . . . He's capable of doing all sorts of work, but he won't. He thinks having a job is beneath him. You should see all the men who come and ask for his daughter's hand in marriage. Why, only the other day the owner of the grocer's in Kuruköprü was here, you know, the one just past Jumali's café. Now that man was crazy about the girl. Promising her a nice house, gold bracelets, diamond earrings, clothes . . . Who knows what else. What have you got? How can you top that? However you look at it, you're just a little clerk somewhere.'

I was mortified.

'See? You've no answer to that, have you? A clerk in some factory. What would the two of you do? You'd have nothing between you. Being young doesn't put food on the table. I heard the man myself. "If only she said yes," he said, "I would put the mansion in her name immediately," he said. What about you? Have you talked to her? Does she like you?'

'No, we haven't talked.'

'If you haven't even talked to her, why are you wandering around after her?'

'I don't know. I don't really know what I'm doing. I'm just following her . . . I can't help it.'

'Give up, son. Just give up. There are lots of men wandering around after this one. They'll corner you in some dark alley, and that'll be the end of you. Don't throw your life away like that. There are those offering your weight in gold for her . . . Honestly.'

Just then my beloved, pretty in her honey-coloured dress, appeared at the courtyard door. She regarded us from a distance. I moved away, all hope dashed to pieces. I turned the corner in deep shame and sped away.

Goodbye, desires, sweet hopes, the moon above, rusty cans, rotting piles of wood, goodbye! Cats, dogs, brick-walled houses,

Kurdish women with masculine faces, crooked little streets and – last but not least – my beloved with your prettily bouncing plaits behind your white curtain, goodbye! And a curse on all the gold in the world!

I withdrew. I didn't go back to the wine cellar, nor to the window from where I had watched her . . . Bitter, dark, boring days went by. One afternoon I was gloomily sitting at my desk. The caretaker came up to me. He told me there was a little girl waiting for me at the factory gates. I went to see. It was the child who had spoken to me the first time days back. She came straight up to me again, just like she had done on that occasion.

'Mister,' she said, 'my sister said to tell you that her father is off to evening prayers tonight and that her brother will be working. She says you should come around to the back window and she's going to tell you something.'

'Who? Her? I don't . . . When? Really?'

'I swear!'

'When? Did you say the back window?'

'Yes. After evening prayers have started.'

I felt as if an inner wall crumbled and I was being filled with sunlight. I wanted to run, shout and tell the whole world. I offered the factory's gatekeeper a cigarette and rather uncharacteristically gave a beggar a few coins. I then went to the grocer's and from there to the barber's.

As I was being shaved I became impatient. I must have been fidgeting under his razor, because he stopped. 'Please, sir! Could you calm down? We're going to have an accident!'

'Oh? You think that's likely?'

The barber gave me a strange look.

'Do you honestly think,' I continued, 'that your razor would be so heartless as to cut the cheek of the happiest man on earth?'

The barber let out a short laugh. 'My, my,' he said. 'Someone's very cheerful. What happened? Did you win the lottery?'

I wasn't going to wait for him to finish off with the rinse, talcum powder, cream or anything . . . 'I couldn't care less about all the lotteries in the world!' I shouted as I ran out of his shop.

The barber called out after me. 'Your Excellency has forgotten to pay!'

'Oh! Oh, I do beg His Majesty's pardon,' I said, turning back sharply.

After that I went into the cellar behind the grocer's. I sat down to eat some pastrami, pickles, a few black olives and a quarter-loaf of bread . . . and to dive into some wine. 'All on my tab, please, Master Grocer' – obviously . . .

I downed one glass then another. Ahh! As I was about to tuck into the generous portion of pastrami I hesitated. It might make my breath smell, and that might put her off. I didn't want her to feel uncomfortable, whatever the cause. The factory working day would soon be over, and I would wait for her at the window. She would come out laughing, glance over at me, walk past, right there, laugh and glance over again. I placed a huge pickled gherkin into my mouth and bit down with my strong teeth. My crooked nose and skinny fingers didn't enter my thoughts. In any case I had put on weight since I'd started work. But, enough of all that . . . I was over the moon. I had only just realized how sweet an effect wine can have on you. Where was that miserable inner me? Nowhere to be found. Hiding. I felt so powerful that the inner me dared not show his face.

Any time now she would come out, glance over, laugh, turn back, glance over, laugh, turn, glance over . . . Time would pass, the moon would come out, I'd go over to their neighbourhood, into that street, into that smell of sewage and stand under her window . . . Life was brilliant, absolutely brilliant!

When the workers left the factory she did, too. As usual, she glanced across, smiled and gave a little signal. I understood.

The hours passed very slowly. Eventually, as the clock in the tower struck nine, I entered the disgustingly smelly street. Her window was dark. I moved in closer. And there at the window, no more than a dark silhouette, stood my beloved.

'You're late,' she whispered.

'Who, me?'

'Yes, you!'

'But it's only nine o'clock! Is that too late?'

'Well, maybe not . . . Anyway, what did that woman say to you?'

'Which one?'

'That mad old one. Her name's Güllü.'

'Oh, the one I spoke to over by the corner.'

'Yes, her.'

'"That girl has many men after her," she said. "You'd better give up on her. They'll shoot you. They'll kill you," she said. She told me the men after you were rich enough to pay out my weight in gold.'

'She said that, eh? Why, the . . . And then?'

'Well, just that there were many men after you. That your dad was a difficult man and that there was no way he'd let someone like me marry you.'

'And when she said all this to you . . . ?'

'I believed her. I assumed you knew she . . .'

'No, I had no idea! So that's why you lost interest in me?'

'What was I to think?'

'Look, I'm not blinded by gold or diamonds. You listen to me. From now on I want to see you there every day, at the cellar window, waiting for me. I want you to be there.'

'Do you really?'

'Really, truly!'

'Who is that woman anyway?'

'No one, really. Just a friend. But she cares for me a lot . . . Come over when my father goes to evening prayers, and we can talk, OK?'

'Well, OK, but how will I know when he's going out?'

'I'll let you know.'

'Write a little note.'

'I don't know how to read or write.'

'Well then, send over the little girl.'

'You make sure you sit at the window now. Just look at me the way you do and smile. The other girls get so jealous . . . Let them, the floozies. Serves them right!'

'Maybe we could go to the pictures one day?'

'To the pictures? Are you mad?'

'Why?'

'That's impossible!'

'Well, OK then, but why?'

'My father would kill me.'

'So your father really is . . .'

'Do you have a mother? They told me about your father. Apparently he's not here, is he? Why? Is he in exile?'

'It's a long story.'

'Who do you stay with? Why didn't you go with him?'

'I did go at first, but then I came back. I'm living with my grandmother.'

'Listen, you wait for me by that window every day, OK? Then, and I'll let you know when, you can have your grandmother come over to ours and ask for me, OK?'

'Huh?'

'OK?'

'All right.'

'You'd better go now. My father will be back soon. But don't forget, I want you waiting by that window, right?'

It was a sparklingly brilliant night, the city was asleep, and the roads were quiet and dusty.

Before long the whole business had spread around the factory like wildfire. Before I knew what had happened I had received four written death threats, one after another. They were going to kill me! I was told that I had to give up on that girl and that there were plenty of suitable girls in office work. Or else . . . Signed by: The Black Crows!

And at the bottom were pictures of a dagger dripping blood, a smoking pistol and a pair of clenched fists. But, in spite of all this, I went to the window of the wine cellar every afternoon. Now and then the little girl would come and tell me that 'her sister' would wait for me that night. I had to walk through many deserted streets to get there. One of them led through an empty park. But I wasn't afraid. It all seemed like a big game.

'I'm afraid!' she confided in me one night. 'I keep having these terrible, terrible dreams. I am so worried they're going to shoot you!'

'Well, what can I do?'

'It's up to you, really. You should have your grandmother come over.'

'Huh?'

'Well, if she doesn't, you'll lose me.'

'Why? What's happening?'

'I think my father's got wind of something. He wants me to go over and stay at my uncle's, in Sivas. And the other day someone threw stones at our window. I'm very frightened. If my father found out for sure . . .'

'So I'll have to get my grandmother to come over. What if your father doesn't agree?'

'Well, at least get her to ask him.'

A few days later, Güllü came to the factory. 'This evening,' she said to me, 'come over to ours.'

'Yours? I don't know where you live.'

'We're two doors down from your girlfriend. Just come over. Don't worry: I'll wait for you by the door. Make sure you come. This is important!'

At nine that evening I went to the woman's house. She was standing by the door. We went in and climbed up four rotting old wooden steps. We entered a small room whose windows had been papered over. A man, her husband who was a construction worker, welcomed me in, shook my hand and offered me a cigarette.

Güllü made us coffee. 'That day,' she said, 'I was testing you. But there really are a lot of young men after the girl. The trouble is, things have got out of hand now. Someone's been sending her father letters, and he's in a complete rage and he's been attacking her. He beat her last night for ages with a big stick, and the poor girl's covered in bruises. She didn't tell him your name, but he's going to find out sooner or later.'

'If you don't hurry up,' said her husband, 'and get your family around there to ask for her, she's going to be sent to Sivas, to live at her uncle's. Either that or the man will kill the pair of you. You know how it is.' And he told me a story.

Back where they came from, a Muslim girl ran off to marry a young Christian. The Christians celebrated. The Muslims were beside themselves with rage. At this time my girl's father had been out in the mountains. When he found out he set a trap. When the boy and the girl got into bed on their wedding night my girl's father crept up to their window and, just as they were kissing, shot them both with a single bullet . . .

I came home confused and dazed. My grandmother was sitting

there. Where would I start? How could I tell her? I knew that she would . . .

'What's on your mind this time?' she asked, 'Lost all your ships at sea?'

'I'm not happy.'

'Why on earth not? You're not hungry, and you're not naked, thank God . . . What's there to be unhappy about?'

'Oh, I don't know. I'm feeling really restless. I don't know what to do.'

'You've been drinking again. Why don't you just stop drinking that stuff?'

It was now or never. 'I can't help it. You know why I drink like this?'

She looked at me slyly. 'No, why? Tell me, then I'll understand!'

'I drink because I'm lonely. I work all day, I get tired, and all I get to do in the evening is to sit in this dingy room.'

'And . . . What do you want me to do about it?'

I laughed.

She laughed, too. 'Go on,' she said. 'Spit it out!'

I laughed again.

'You have to spell it out, son. We can't find a solution unless we know the problem!'

I laughed again and started pacing up and down the room. I felt as if I was locked in by her stare.

'Who is she?' she asked at last. 'Is she from a good family at least?'

I could have died. 'Look,' I managed to say, 'I haven't even finished middle school myself. You know I can't get someone in a high position. The girl I want is . . .'

'Why do you belittle yourself so much? There's nothing wrong with you, is there? I know your salary isn't much, but still . . . And, anyway, you haven't done your military service yet. What about your mother and father? Are they going to agree to this?'

She was perfectly right, of course, but . . .

'So who is she? Where does her family come from? What's their background? Who are they? I certainly don't want you with some loose woman.'

'Oh, no. They're very honourable. And . . .'

'So who is she?'

'She works over where I do.'

'At the office?'

'No.'

'Where then?'

'At the factory.'

'What? A common labourer! Oh my God, what have I done to deserve this? Are you mad, boy? Have you lost your mind? Working in a factory, among all those men. She'll have been through dozens of them! Heaven preserve us!' She mumbled angrily to herself as she got up, washed and prepared for her prayers at sundown.

I ran out into the street.

19

The days wouldn't pass. No matter how much I begged, my grandmother would not budge.

'You need money to get married. Where's your money? When your wife turns around and asks you for something, you won't be able to provide it. You'll end up a bitter and resentful man. You haven't even done your military service yet. Where's your wife going to stay when you're off in the army? Then, and more importantly, there's your father, your mother, your brother and your sisters . . . It's hardly appropriate for you to set yourself up in comfort when they're in the state they're in.'

My grandmother was absolutely right. My beloved was absolutely right, too.

And me? Was I wrong?

I found myself caught in the cogs of a giant machine, being inexorably pulled this way and that. I was unable to sleep unless I was sufficiently drunk to be oblivious to everything. If I did go to bed without drinking enough the inner me would rise up and get into an endless argument with me about how this would lead to that and that would result in the other. Should I sacrifice my father, mother, brother and sisters or my beloved? When I fell asleep I often dreamed of my father. 'What kind of a son are you?' he'd say to me. 'Shame on you! Here we are, in this desperate poverty, and you're off doing this kind of thing.'

I dreamed of the whole family. How they had lost weight, how sunken their eyes were, how pale and ashen they looked . . .

I would wake with a start. The inner me would fan the flames. 'You're a real lowlife,' he would tell me.

Just then my beloved would enter the conversation, with her clean white face and beautiful dark eyes. 'Everyone is talking about me because of you. You've embarrassed me in front of everybody! What's to become of me now?'

Yes, what is to become of you now? And what's to become of my father, my mother, my brother, my sisters, me, you . . . What is to become of us all?

I saw her in a dream one night. She was lying on the floor of a dark basement, hands and feet bound tightly together. A small bulb in the far corner was giving off a pale yellow light. Her father was angrily sharpening a huge broad knife. My beloved was reaching out to me, pleading . . . I woke up with a scream. I was covered in sweat.

'What on earth's the matter, son?' asked my grandmother. 'What's worrying you? Look at the state you're in!'

'It's nothing.'

'Bad dreams?'

'Yes.'

'What happened?'

'I don't know.'

'How could you not know? Something made you scream out loud!'

'I don't know.'

I continued to receive letters threatening to kill me, each one more vicious than the last.

20

'Her father,' said the Bosnian woman Güllü, 'he's going to beat that poor girl to death! If you don't get a move on he may send her off to Sivas, to her uncle's.'

Her husband was sitting on the floor. 'Why don't you send your gran over to ask for you to be married? What are you waiting for?' he asked.

How could I tell them about the factory floozie, the cast-off of dozens of other men? They had invited me over to wrap the matter up tonight, to bring it all to a conclusion. Either this was going to have to go ahead or I was going to have to put a stop to it all.

I was desperate. So I lied. 'I have written to my father,' I said, 'and I'm waiting for his reply. That's all it is.'

'Did you ask for money?'

'No. We have these fields, you see. So I asked for power of attorney. As soon as that comes through . . .'

'What's that?' asked Güllü's husband. 'You have fields?'

'We do.'

'Many? Where? On good soil?'

I told him their location and size.

He got quite excited. 'Goodness me,' he said. 'Did you hear that? So you have that much land? But why don't you farm it?'

I went through a whole story. He listened carefully. 'Listen, young man,' he said. 'You put all of us together, and we can do it. There's me, there's my wife, there's you, there's your girl, your girl's brother, her father . . .' He told me how we could build up a lovely farm. We could have cows, chicken, sheep and goats, so we would have plenty of eggs and milk. Some of the land could be used for growing fruit and vegetables. In time the cows, chicken and sheep would increase, and we could get into selling butter, milk and eggs. Gradually business would expand . . .

'Just get your letter,' he said, 'and I won't ask you for a penny! We can build us a nice little homestead with our very own hands. I'll bring in five or six chickens, a cockerel, plant some lemon and orange trees and vegetables, and we'll be set. I'm sick and tired of brick-laying!'

Güllü was as keen as he was. The two of them came up with such ideas, encouraging each other as they went on, that even though I knew that their talk was completely unrealistic I found myself caught up in their excitement. I decided that the very next day I really would write to my father and ask for power of attorney.

They thought of the whole thing as being settled already. Güllü was so happy that she got up and came over clutching a huge quilting-needle. 'So, young man,' she said, 'are you up for it?'

'What?'

'Being my blood brother?'

'Yes, why not?' I found myself saying.

Her husband intervened. 'We can't do that without celebrating. Let me go and get some brandy and some lemonade, and we can have a toast. Then . . .'

Güllü flung her arms around her husband's neck in delight. 'This is great!' she said, kissing him. 'I'm so excited! Hang on,' she added, turning to me, 'I just thought of something . . . Shall I go and bring your girl over?'

'But you have to behave yourself,' warned her husband. 'Don't go and ruin everything!'

Güllü had run off and was already out of the door. So when her husband went to get the brandy and the lemonade I was left alone in the room. I stared out at the night sky through their window. A red moon was slowly rising in the far distance, a sound like a whisper was drifting over from the factory and a slowly rumbling machine was standing in as the heartbeat for the whole neighbourhood.

I felt uncomfortable, heavy in my heart. I couldn't quite put my finger on it. Yet my beloved would be here in a minute; we'd probably sit side by side, perhaps even exchange looks and smiles. I noticed a cupboard in the room; its door was ajar. I went over and looked inside. It was full of books. I was surprised. They certainly couldn't have belonged to Güllü or her husband. I wondered to whom they belonged and what sort of books they were. Who had put them there? I had just reached in to pull one out at random when the front door opened and loudly slammed shut. I edged away from the cupboard.

It was Güllü, returning in the same mad rush as she had left. 'I've got permission,' she said, 'so she'll be over in a minute. But you must sit nicely. I don't want any hanky-panky . . . I lied to her father, and he bought it. I said we're going to have a drink of sherbet at Beyto's. If it was anyone else he'd have said no, believe me! But for me . . . Well, he'll do anything for me. Loves me like his own daughter. But if only my brother were here . . . Now him he'd die for! If only he were here . . .'

'Your brother?' I asked. 'Who's he?'

'He isn't around any more . . . He's very clever is my brother. Knows all these long words . . . You could sit and listen to him all day.' She opened the door to the cupboard. 'See all these books? They're his. He read every night.'

My curiosity was piqued. 'Where is he now?'

'He's not around any more. He left.'

'Where did he go?'

'I don't know. He just left . . . He used to work at the cloth factory, you know. Used to be a master weaver.'

My jaw dropped. 'What's his name?'

'Izzet. Master Izzet, they called him. Hang on, look, I've got a picture somewhere . . .' She went and fetched the photograph of her brother from the adjacent room. It was him! It was my friend with the blue overalls!

'Hey, I know him,' I exclaimed. 'He's a friend of mine!'

Güllü came over all serious suddenly, and looked me up and down. 'You do? Hmm . . . Do you have books, too?'

'I do.'

'Many?'

'A few.'

She shook her head. 'So he's your friend, eh? Well, if he's your friend, why are you asking where he is?' Her husband came in with the brandy and lemonade. 'Look,' she said, 'what a small world it is! He knows my brother. He's a friend of his.' She took the bottles off her husband.

'Really?' he said. 'He's a friend of yours, eh?'

The couple exchanged looks, chuckled and winked at one another.

'What's up?' I asked. 'What's there to be surprised about? What's the joke? Why are you winking? It's not that weird. I just said I knew him.'

'No,' said Güllü, 'of course it isn't.'

I came out with loads of questions about him, and, although I wanted to get to know something about him, I failed. They seemed to want to close the subject, as if they were trying to hide something from me. 'Did Izzet have a wife and children?' I asked.

'He did,' said Güllü. 'He had a wife. Worked in the factory with us, she did. But she got her arm caught in one of the machines, lost a lot of blood and died.'

'She died?'

'She died.'

'And the children?'

'There was one. Got run over by a train.'

'What?'

'He died under a train.'

'Oh God! How did that happen? How old was he?'

'Only six. Lovely little boy. Thick curly hair, stout kid, bright as anything . . .'

'But how did it happen? How did he end up under a train?'

'Well, his mother had to be at work, and his father was in prison at the time.'

'In prison? Why?'

'Oh, nothing interesting,' said Güllü's husband. 'Stealing chickens, as it happens.'

'The train was going along,' continued Güllü, 'and he was playing on the rails. Poor little mite fell over, and his little foot got stuck. He wanted to get away but couldn't. Got sliced in half. I don't want to be morbid, but right across here, like that . . . They brought him back in two pieces.'

I saw a vision of Master Izzet watching me. 'This neighbourhood,' he'd said to me, 'and I'll say this in words you'd use, is a neighbourhood of people that God forgot. There are plenty of others with far greater right to complain than you have!'

'Have you ever seen a cut-off arm?' asked Güllü's husband. 'It wiggles and wiggles like this. And the fingers open and close, and it turns purple . . .'

'I have,' said Güllü. 'There was this man Süleyman; he used to fluff up wool. An Arab, he was, with dark bushy hair. It was his wife . . . Her arm got ripped off right next to me. I was shocked! I picked up her arm and held it. It was all warm and dripping blood.'

I suddenly felt quite sick. I had visions of amputated fingers and arms wiggling at me. I felt I could almost hear the noise made by the warm blood gushing out of the veins.

Then my beloved turned up. She seemed sulky.

'I'm waiting for a power of attorney to come through by post,' I told her.

'Why? What good is that? Or did you ask him to give you money?'

'I asked him for power of attorney,' I repeated. 'Power of attorney?'

She shrugged. 'What's the use of that?'

I went into the details of the now definite plans for the farm we were going to have with Güllü. She and her husband backed me up.

My beloved seemed to believe me. 'I just hope,' she said, 'that things don't all go wrong before all that comes through.' And she explained that her father was really pressuring her, men were stopping her on her way to and from work and pulling knives on her. She was getting death threats, and people were stoning her family's windows at night.

Güllü handed her a glass of brandy and lemonade. 'Go on, girl,' she said. 'Get that down you. Bottoms up! I don't want to see anything left in that glass or else!' My beloved drained the glass.

Then I drank. Then Güllü and her husband drank. So it went on, glasses being topped up and emptied. After a while, when we were all quite drunk, Güllü returned with her quilting-needle. 'Watch,' she said. 'I'll prick myself first, and then it'll be your turn! Ready?'

She stuck the needle in. A large drop of red blood hovered on the end of her finger. She held it out to me. I sucked it. Then I pricked my finger, and she sucked that. So now I was officially her blood brother.

Güllü's husband was by now very drunk, too. To celebrate he went and got his harmonica. It seems that it had remained in their cupboard since Master Izzet had lost his son. Today, for the first time since that fateful day, he was going to play it in my honour.

So that night we played music, we sang, and we laughed.

Güllü sang us Bosnian folk-songs, and she and her husband danced for us.

My beloved rested her head on my shoulder. I put my arm around her slim waist, which felt full of life. I must have squeezed a touch too hard because she let out a little yelp and looked towards Güllü and her husband. 'Don't be rude,' she told me. 'There's people around!'

Güllü must have noticed because she quickly blew out the lamp. The sudden darkness slowly gave way to the silvery light of the moon streaming through the window. It gleamed and scattered on the metal inlays of Güllü's wooden chest.

She and her husband had started a new folk dance, a livelier one, and were spinning in rapid vigorous moves. I grabbed hold of my beloved and pulled her to me with all my strength.

Suddenly there was furious banging at the street door. She slipped away from me, almost flowing out of my arms. She was clearly terrified. She lay frozen by my feet, unable to get up or move.

'It's my father,' she said. 'It's my father. He must have heard that I hadn't gone to drink sherbet. Oh God, what have I done? What am I going to do now?'

Güllü quickly relit the lamp, and her husband put the bottles away. 'Come on,' he said. 'if it's your father, it's your father! So what? What's he going to do?' He went to the door.

I held my beloved's hands. They had gone ice cold. 'What will we do?' she kept saying. 'What will we do? He'll kill me now!'

Suddenly we heard loud, joyous Bosnian exclamations, laughter and shouting.

'It's my brother!' said Güllü. 'It is, it's him!'

It really was her brother. He staggered exhausted into the room, where he saw me. 'Well, well! Look who's here! Goodness me, what are you doing here?'

We shook hands. Güllü and her husband told him why I was there. Master Izzet listened attentively and looked serious. But he did not ask any questions.

'Sister,' he said to Güllü, 'would you mind heating up a pan of water for me?'

She got up immediately and went to put some water on.

Master Izzet sat silently for few minutes while he smoked a cigarette. 'You'll have to excuse me,' he said. 'I'm too tired now. We'll talk tomorrow. I'll be here for a while now, anyway.' He left us.

'Where do you know him from?' asked my beloved. 'He's a very good friend of my father's. But how do you know him?'

I told her.

'Well, that's good, then,' she said. 'You try to convince him about us. He's my father's greatest friend in the world!'

Güllü's husband had put his harmonica away. He lit a cigarette. Then he got up, too, and we were left alone. I held my beloved in my arms again, but she pulled back this time. Her white headscarf slipped down on to her neck, and she was blushing furiously. 'Stop it,' she said. 'Please, let go. I need to ask you something.'

I let go. 'Fire away!' I said.

'But you have to answer truthfully!'

'I will.'

'Hope to die if you don't?'

'Hope to die if I don't.'

'Right . . . So, why haven't you had your family come over to ask for me?'

She had got me right where it hurt. 'I'm going to,' I said.

'That night,' she said, 'you promised you would get your grandmother to come over. What happened?'

'Well, as I said, I've written to my father . . .'

'You didn't say anything about writing to your father before. You said that you were going to talk to your grandmother and get her to come and ask. Hmm? Why didn't she come?'

'Huh?'

'Why don't you answer? Did you ask her, and she wouldn't come? Did she say "How could I ask for a factory girl to marry my grandson"?'

I felt as if boiling water had been poured over my head. 'Oh no,' I said, 'it was nothing like that.'

'Oh no, it was exactly something like that, wasn't it? I know those sort of people. They wouldn't stoop to a factory girl. They'd say she'd have slept with thousands of men and refuse to lower themselves.'

I tried to hush her.

'No, don't try and stop me!' she said. 'Leave me alone! I know what those people are like. Your grandmother refused to come and ask for me so you . . . Look, I want you to be honest with me. You can't hide anything from me. And, anyway, you've nothing to be embarrassed about. It's true, isn't it? Eh? Isn't that what she said?'

I felt awful.

'Hey, I'm talking to you! Answer me! That's it, isn't it? "She's a factory girl, not good enough for our family; she'll have been with thousands of men." That's what she said, isn't it? Talk to me!' She grabbed my hand. 'Look at me . . . Forget about them. Do you love me or not?'

'I love you a lot.'

'So, then, don't wait on money from your father . . .'

'It's not money; it's power of attorney . . .'

'Whatever. Don't ask for anything. You talk to my father. You could come around one evening and ask for me . . . My father's a tough man, but he appreciates bravery and honesty. So don't worry; come over to ours and tell him . . .'

'What if he chases me away?'

'He won't. Don't worry about the things people say about him. He's not a bad man. He likes straight talking. So you come and ask for me yourself, and forget about other people doing it.'

'If he says no?'

'You just ask. If he says no we'll worry about it then. My brother's heard about us, and apparently he knows you because of you playing football and admires you a lot. He's already said good things about you to my father. So don't you worry. You come over and ask for me, I'm sure he'll say yes. My father's an honest man, and he likes honesty.' Then she continued. We didn't need money. She wouldn't ask me for shoes or clothes or anything. As for my salary, yes, I didn't earn much, and it wouldn't be enough for the two of us. But she would be working, too. We could hire a single room here in their courtyard, settle there, and that would be that! If two hearts were together, what else mattered?

'I do want to ask you something, though,' she said. 'Did you love anyone before me? Have you been with other women at all?'

'No, never.'

'Tell me the truth.'

'I am telling the truth.'

'I don't believe you,' she said. 'You must have been with other women.'

Finally I talked about the Greek girl Helena in Beirut.

She listened attentively. 'She must have been prettier than I am,' she said. 'Come on, be honest. I mean, whatever is past is past. All sorts of things happen when you're young. But now . . .?'

'Nothing like that could happen now.'

'It better not!'

'What would you do?'

'What would I do? You'd find out . . .' Then she questioned me about my father and my family. 'Why did they go there? Who looks after them? Why don't they come over? Couldn't they come if they wanted?'

I talked about them briefly and explained that my brother Niyazi looked after them now.

'Is he younger than you?'

'Yes. About five years.'

'Five years younger? Good on him. What does he do?'

'Sells things on the street. Well, to be honest, he does whatever work he can find.'

'So he's one of us then? If I'd been you I wouldn't have left my mum and dad to come here.' As I couldn't think of a way to explain my reasoning at the time I remained silent. 'I can do lacework, really ornate things, and I can knit. I won't be a burden to you. Come on, come over and ask for me. My father won't bite!'

By the time I left it was very late. I felt happy and at peace, as if I had everything a man could want. The streets were deserted. The lights were all off in people's homes. All the shops were shut up.

Although I tried desperately not to wake up my grandmother, a floorboard creaked under my foot; naturally she was up like a shot. She asked me where I had been. I told her.

'Oh, you crazy boy,' she said, 'you crazy boy . . . A girl brought up among a thousand men. You're going to regret this, but . . .'

I talked to her for a long time.

'No, no, no,' she said. 'I'll not have anything to do with it. If God lets it happen, it'll be his doing. I don't want to know.' She pulled her quilt over her head.

I went to bed. For the first time in weeks I had a long, uninterrupted sleep. That night I dreamed of a sunny orange grove full of sparkling golden birds, with a glittering silver stream running through it.

'Your grandmother is absolutely right!' said Master Izzet.

I objected immediately. 'What? She's right? How can you say that?'

'Yes, she's right,' he insisted. 'First of all, you haven't the money to get married. Second, you don't earn enough. And, third – and this is probably the most important point of all . . .'

'What's that?'

'You have got to accept what the people around you are going to think. As far as they're concerned, a girl who works in a factory cannot possibly be honest and decent.'

'But . . .'

'I said, you have to accept that this is what they think! I'm not saying they're right, obviously. I'm only trying to explain their point of view. This is what they will think, and such thoughts are their handicap. They will also be unaware that such attitudes are their handicap. But sooner or later you will be with this poor girl in their environment. And those people will look down on this girl, as if she had slept around with other men. They will talk about her behind her back and make unpleasant remarks. That will upset both of you. In due course, she will fit in and start to copy them. She'll dress like them, talk like them and start to think like them. Then one day she'll become ashamed of having worked in a factory and of her humble past and be miserable for the rest of her life.' He looked at me attentively.

'I won't let that happen!' I said.

'Well, there's nothing else I can say,' he said. 'It's quite clear that you have made up your mind and that you're not about to change it. So let's drop the subject. You see . . .' And he told me all about my beloved. 'She is a lovely girl, a very dutiful daughter. She works twelve hours in the factory and comes home and scrubs the floors, does the laundry, mends all the clothes, darns the socks . . . She is a sound girl. She will keep your house going single-handed! None the less, the day will come when you will regret ever marrying her. I repeat: you have an inquisitive nature, and you're intelligent. One day you're going to realize the consequences of what you've done and rue this day. I don't know . . .'

That was all we said on the subject. I think it was about three days later he left as abruptly as he'd arrived. I had no idea why or where he went. But he did me a great kindness before he left: he talked to my prospective father-in-law and told him about me and, in particular, about my father. Apparently the old man smiled when he heard my father's name. He'd known him well from their partisan days. 'For his son,' he apparently said, 'I'd give five daughters, if I had them, let alone the one!'

I was taken aback. 'But, Master Izzet,' I said, 'I'll be the one marrying his daughter, not my father! I don't want him to get the wrong idea . . .'

'Well,' he said, 'you can straighten him out yourself. We're going to go to their place tomorrow, so be ready. Come and find me at the Cretan's café at seven.'

We met up the following evening. I was overjoyed. I had just had the perfect shave, I had slicked my hair down, and my heart was pounding with hope and excitement. We set off down the dusty roads. The sun had set. There was no moonlight. The sky was full of dark clouds, and it was windy. We passed through the narrow, winding streets, past the windows overlooking them, past the laughter, the noises from gramophones, the drunken shouts and the watchmen's whistles, and arrived at the courtyard of my beloved. She was waiting for us by the courtyard door with her arms folded. She showed us in. We entered the courtyard. The dark courtyard was covered in small, muddy puddles and stank. As we walked past the rented rooms we noticed curious shadows and heard whisperings. The residents certainly knew what was going on!

My prospective father-in-law greeted us with a toothless smile. We went up the four steps inside their door and emerged into a small room which was immaculately clean with snow-white walls. A lantern with sparklingly clean glass illuminated the room. Güllü and her husband had arrived before us and had sat down in the most prominent position in the room. Güllü was giggling non-stop.

My prospective father-in-law scrutinized me all night long. He talked all about my father, about the party and about the speeches my father had made. I talked about this and that, mostly about Beirut and Antakya.

My beloved got up and made coffee for us. Then, in her nervousness, she tripped and spilled it all over the floor. She was very embarrassed and ran out of the room. So anyway, what with one thing or another, time passed. We drank freshly made coffee, smoked cigarettes, and when we were all done and all that was left in the room was the smoke from the cigarettes we came to the serious matter at hand. Her father became serious and started going on along the lines of 'Well, the son of a great man like that . . .'

'Just a minute!' I said.

Everyone turned to stare at me. They must have wondered what on earth I was going to say. As for me, I came up with such an astounding and pathetic story, full of everything down to the twenty-four liras and ninety-five kuruş, that my beloved's father leaped up and kissed me on the forehead. 'God bless you, son!' he said. 'You can have my daughter with my blessing! And I don't want a thing. Just pick her up and carry her off!'

So that was it then. I had the horse and I had three horseshoes. As for the fourth horseshoe . . . Well, we'd sort something out, eh?

22

How on earth did my grandmother agree to it? You know, I still have no idea. She agreed. I told her how to get to their home. So she went and saw the girl.

'What do you think?' I asked.

'Not bad,' she said. 'She had a pair of black trousers on, and she was doing their laundry. She seems hard-working, pretty and home-loving. But I'm not sure . . .'

We had a low-key engagement (our engagement rings were just simple copper bands), and later we had the wedding.

23

Hasan borrowed a navy suit for me to wear on the day. Gazi got hold of a new razorblade and managed to persuade someone to lend me a pair of patent-leather shoes and a tie. I was getting married, and I had exactly forty-five kuruş, half a packet of village cigarettes and cooperative tokens worth eighteen kuruş.

Long live freedom!

'Hey, Hasan,' said Gazi, 'I only have one-and-a-half liras. What about you?'

Hasan gulped. 'What me? I've got thirty-five kuruş.'

'And you, Mister Bridegroom?'

'I have forty-five kuruş.'

'Hey, so I'm the richest, eh? Now look here, mate, I have a hundred and fifty, Hasan's got thirty-five; that's a hundred and eighty-five. Now you've got another forty-five, so that's . . . Well, you're the accountant. What's that make?'

'Two hundred and thirty,' said Hasan.

'Two hundred and thirty? No, hang on. Forget that last forty-five, this joker here is getting a wife. He might need that. Take away forty-five from two hundred and thirty.'

'One hundred and eighty-five.'

'One hundred and eighty-five, right. You know what we're going to do now? We're going to dive into the Cretan's cellar, and we're going to get drunk in honour of the idiot who's getting himself another mouth to feed!'

'Gazi, you know,' said Hasan, 'sometimes you come up with flashes of absolute genius!'

So we headed for the Cretan's cellar, where in 1937 wine was sold at five kuruş a glass and everyone filled their own glass from a huge barrel.

Gazi lifted up his glass. 'To the idiot who, tonight, gets himself an extra mouth to feed!' We clinked our glasses together and drained them in one go.

'Bloody hell,' said Hasan, 'I mean, look at you! Navy suit, patent-leather shoes, shirt and tie, you look like a right gentleman! Very smart, my man! Look here, mate, I want no showing off in front of the missus, though . . . I swear I'll tell her the suit and shoes and everything are all borrowed. Don't come over all posh on her!'

'Don't you worry,' I said. 'She's already got the measure of me!'

'Oh yeah?'

'I told her all about my twenty-four liras and ninety-five kuruş and everything . . .'

Gazi wrapped me in his arms and kissed me on the cheek. 'Don't get upset,' he said. 'This'll all be behind us soon enough. One day we'll be telling our kids what great men we were!'

We toasted this, drank to that and ended up quite drunk. We couldn't see across the cellar for cigarette smoke, and our laughter cut through the air and exploded like fireworks. Then the old wine merchant joined us, smiling under his white moustache, and started drinking, too. A short time later his large nose was red and his eyes looked swollen.

As he raised his glass for a toast his wife stormed into the cellar. Her fists were planted on her wide hips. 'My, my!' she said. 'So you're here! We have customers waiting for service, and you're here drinking with these kids. You ought to be ashamed of yourself! At your age!'

The large old man raised his glass to toast his fateful day thirty-five years ago. 'Hurrah!' he shouted. 'Bless you, lads!'

We should have had six-and-a-half glasses each, but they let me have their extra half-glass, so I drank over seven glasses. We left together, and they brought me home.

My beloved met me at the door. She was all dressed up and covered in lace, embroidery and sequins. My head was spinning. They were playing music, and women and children were rushing around. I felt ill . . .

They ushered me into a room prepared specially for the day. Chairs and divans, carpets and kilims, wall decorations, colourful dresses on hangers . . . All this was simply not possible on the fifty liras that I'd managed to get the factory to advance me, but still . . . I let myself flop down on to a chair.

'They're about to present the wedding gifts to me,' said my beloved, 'so make sure you pay attention. Look, all these carpets, kilims and dresses – they're all ours!'

'Huh?'

They called her away, and off she went. I was at a loss to fathom how this had all come about.

A little later an old woman's voice came through the door, loud and clear. 'One beautiful gold bracelet from the boy's father. Wear it in good times! From his mother a necklace. May it bring you good fortune! One pair of fine bangles! A beautiful pair of diamond earrings! One carpet, tufted at both ends!'

'Huh?' I couldn't really get my head round this, but I was aware that a small fortune was coming our way. That meant that my father, my mother, all our relatives . . . Whereas I . . .

I passed out. When I came to, my beloved was in front of me. Someone was hammering at the insides of my skull. 'Look!' she said. 'See all these things they put on me? Look at all these bracelets and bangles! And look at this necklace! And what about these earrings? They've got diamonds! These must add up to five or six hundred liras worth! Güllü says . . .'

'What does Güllü say?'

'She says we should sell some of these after a while, and that'll be start-up capital for you, and then you can have your own business. She's right. We won't be dependent on other people then, will we?'

'Yes . . . I could open up a restaurant . . . Or maybe . . .'

'Or maybe you could have a café or a nice clean grocery shop. I like the earrings best.'

'So all these were presents?'

'They were . . . Your relatives were very kind . . . And you'd been telling me . . .'

'I must have got the wrong end of the stick, I guess.'

'Look at these kilims! And have you seen the carpets?'

'Is this dress material yours, too?'

'Yes! And those dresses . . . I'll not be wanting any new clothes from you for years!'

'So we've done pretty well out of this, eh?'

'We've done very well. But, whatever happens, let's not get carried away with spending, OK? And you can stop drinking all that wine. I won't be idle either. We can buy a sewing machine by instalments, I'll learn how to sew, and I can work as a seamstress and earn some money as well.'

I opened my eyes the next day, and my beloved was standing in front of the mirror. I quietly sat up in bed. I took a good look at her. She was combing her hair, plaiting it and putting it in clips. Then she tried on some lipstick and powdered her face. She picked up the earrings, kissed them and put them on. She admired herself, turning first to one side, then the other. Then she turned right round, looked at her back and suddenly noticed me. She shrieked, hid her face in her hands and threw herself on to the bed, right next to me. I held her hand and lifted her up. 'What's the matter, eh? What are you so embarrassed about?'

She was bright red all the way to her earlobes.

'Tell me . . . Why are you embarrassed? Eh?'

She didn't answer and wouldn't look me in the eyes. 'You know,' she said after a while, looking at me with her big, dark eyes, 'I really love these earrings! Let's sell these last or not sell them at all.'

'OK . . . We won't sell them at all.'

'We can cash in the bangles first, then the necklace, and later . . . You know what I'm going to do? I'm going to put on lipstick, I'm going to powder my face, I'm going to put on all my jewellery. I'm going to look just perfect, and I'm going to take you by the arm, and I'm going to walk all through the neighbourhood! I bet my friends will be so jealous when they see me like this. Don't you think?'

'Of course.'

'Let them get jealous, the floozies! Wouldn't come to my wedding, would they? Güllü says to put it all on and let them all see. Let them go mad, she says. Oh, can we have a photo taken, too? We can send it to my uncle. Will you look at these earrings! Oh, they're so lovely! They do suit me, don't they?'

'Everything suits you, my gorgeous!'

Two days later my grandmother quietly took me to one side. 'Son,' she said, 'you know it's our family tradition, and you know I had to keep up appearances for the sake of your father. You tell your wife in a way you think is best . . .'

'What's that?'

'The things I borrowed . . .'

'What things?'

'All that gold jewellery: the bracelet, the earrings, the bangles, the necklace . . .'

'What?'

'We need to return them.'

'What? You borrowed it all? They all belong to other people?'

'What could I do? One has to keep up appearances.'

I felt as if someone had shot me. 'Curse you, and your traditions!' I said. 'Screw the lot of you! You want your wedding gifts back? You go and ask her! Do your own dirty work. I've already sunk as low as I'm going to because of you lot! I won't do it!' I stormed out.

That evening my wife was waiting for me at the top of the stairs. She had none of the jewellery on. No earrings, no necklace, no bangles. We went into our room. We stood in the room, facing each other.

'I want to say something,' she said, after a while, 'but I don't want you to get upset. Please promise me you won't be angry or upset!'

I pretended not to understand. 'Why, what's the matter?'

'No, please,' she repeated, 'promise me you won't get upset!'

'OK, OK . . . Just tell me what it is, I'll be fine.'

'Do you notice anything missing?'

'Such as?'

'Look at my ears!'

'Oh, yes . . . Where are your earrings?'

She threw her arms around my neck. Her eyes were brimming with tears. 'Please don't get cross . . . Don't upset yourself. We're both young. We'll work, and we'll earn money, and we'll make it on our own. It's not as if we were born with diamond earrings!'

'You still haven't told me what happened.'

'Your grandmother came and took everything back. She'd apparently borrowed them all from friends and neighbours, you know, to keep up appearances. They all had to be given back to their owners. But that's only right, isn't it? I mean, it is right that they should be given back, don't you agree?'

I held her under her arms and kissed her. Behind those wet

eyelashes she was bravely trying to smile. 'Tell me,' she insisted. 'You're not upset, are you?'

'No, I'm not upset.'

'And you won't get upset later?'

'No, I promise.'

'Well, you mustn't. You mustn't care about it at all. Forget it. We'll be fine!'

Later, one by one, the bed, all the cloth, the dresses, the carpet, the kilims and the navy suit, tie and shoes were all returned to their owners. My wife laughed out loud at the fact that even the clothes I had worn were someone else's.

'Don't worry, darling,' she said. 'We might not have much, but at least we have each other, eh?'

So we carried on with our lives, appreciating all that we had.

SELECT WORKS OF ORHAN KEMAL

Anthologized short fiction *Yağmur Yüklü Bulutlar* (*Rain Clouds*, 1974), *Kırmızı Küpeler* (*Red Earrings*, 1974), *Oyuncu Kadın* (*The Actress*, 1975), *Serseri Milyoner / İki Damla Gözyaşı* (*The Vagrant Millionaire / Two Teardrops*, 1976)

Novels *Baba Evi* (*My Father's House*, 1949), *Avare Yıllar* (*The Idle Years*, 1950), *Gemile* (1952), *Murtaza* (1952), *Bereketli Topraklar Üzerinde* (*On Fertile Lands*, 1954), *Suçlu* (*The Criminal*, 1957), *Devlet Kuşu* (*Windfall*, 1958), *Vukuat Var* (*The Incident*, 1958), *Dünya Evi* (*Marriage*, 1958), *Gavurun Kızı* (*The Daughter of the Heathen*, 1959), *Küçücük* (*Tiny*, 1960), *El Kızı* (*Foreign Girl*, 1960), *Hanımın Çiftliği* (*The Farm of the Mistress*, 1961), *Eskici ve Oğulları* (1962), *Gurbet Kuşları* (*In Foreign Lands*, 1962), *Sokakların Çocuğu* (*A Child of the Streets*, 1963), *Kanlı Topraklar* (*Bloody Lands*, 1963), *Bir Filiz Vardı* (*There Was a Bud*, 1965), *Müfettişler Müfettişi* (*The Inspector of Inspectors*, 1966), *Yalancı Dünya* (*A World of Lies*, 1966), *Evlerden Biri* (*One of the Houses*, 1966), *Arkadaş Islıkları* (*Whistling Friends*, 1968), *Sokaklardan Bir Kız* (*A Girl of the Streets*, 1968), *Kötü Yol* (*The Wrong Path*, 1969), *Üç Kağıtçı* (*The Crook*, 1969), *Kaçak* (*The Fugitive*, 1970), *Tersine Dünya* (*The World Inside Out*, 1986)

Drama *İspinozlar* (*The Finch*, 1965)

Memoirs *Nazım Hikmet'le Üç Buçuk Yıl* (*Three and a Half Years with Nazım Hikmet*, 1965)

Interview 'İstanbul'dan Çizgiler' ('Sketches from Istanbul', 1971)

Children's literature *Küçükler ve Büyükler* (*Children and Grown-ups*, 1971)

Studies *Senaryo Tekniği ve Senaryoculuğumuzla İlgili Notlar* (*Screenplay Techniques and Turkish Screenplay Writing*, 1963)

Works adapted for film *Suçlu* (*The Criminal*, 1960), *Devlet Kuşu* (*Windfall*, 1961, 1980), *Sokakların Çocuğu* (*A Child of the Streets*, 1962), *Murtaza* (1965 and again under the title *Bekçi* [*The Guard*], 1984), *El Kızı* (1966), *Sokaklardan Bir Kız* (*A Girl of the Streets*, 1974), *Bereketli Topraklar Üzerinde* (*On Fertile Lands*, 1979), *Kaçak* (*The Fugitive*, 1982), *72. Koğuş* (*The Seventy-Second Ward*, 1987), *Eskici ve Oğulları* (*The Ragman and His Sons*, 1990), *Tersine Dünya* (*The World Inside Out*, 1993)